VASILISA

A HEARTH AND BARD TALE

M. L. FARB

CONTENTS

For Jesse
You bring magic to my life

THE BARD

THE LINGERING scent of roasted goose mixed with the oak of the slowly burning yule log in the mayor's fire. Usually after the mid-winter feast, the mayor held a dance. But tonight he had a visitor he'd not seen since he was a child—a tale teller whose tapestry of words had filled his dreams for the next forty years. And now the bard was back with promises of new stories and a winter in which to tell them.

The mayor rubbed his hands with delight as he watched the servants clear the last of the tables and set the benches in a half-circle in front of the hearth.

A figure sat on the stone bench in front of the fire, leaning closer as if even the blaze was not enough warmth. A brown hooded cloak hid both face and features. Only an olive-toned hand showed, stroking a bob-tailed cat.

The mayor's wife, four children, and many grandchildren seated themselves on the front-most benches. His guests packed the other benches with children in laps and youth standing behind.

The mayor stepped to the side of the cloaked figure and bowed. "Honored Bard. We bid you welcome to our humble town. Your presence is more—"

The cloaked figure raised a hand to cut off his words, then threw *back the hood. Black curls tumbled around her face and down her back as she shook her head. Dark brown eyes crinkled with laughter, and a smile curved upward on a smooth, olive-toned face. Thick eyebrows lent a serious line to her otherwise mischievous features.*

Her audience gasped. The mayor did too, though he already knew that she looked like a forest spirit called forth by the druids of old.

She stood, sending the cat stalking away, and let the cloak drop from her shoulders to the stone hearth. A wool dress in deep forest green and embroidered with red holly berries covered her from neck to wrists and swept the floor with a rustle. The gown hugged her slender shape, then pooled at her feet.

"Gather in closer." She beckoned a wide-eyed child. "There's room for more on the hearth. And the night is chill."

"But you're a woman," protested a dandified man. He twisted a red felt hat. "He promised us a famous bard's tale tonight. Not some young woman's gossipy ramblings. The dance was canceled for this? A dark-haired, foreign-faced woman!"

She fingered a black curl, her eyes wide in mock surprise. "Why, so I am. Since my femininity so distresses you, here's a coin for your trouble, and you can go." She flicked a small coin, and it struck him across the bridge of his nose.

He bellowed and lunged.

Two of the mayor's servants grasped his arms and dragged him from the grand hall.

The woman's lips drew tight as she picked up her cloak.

The mayor bowed before her, his nose almost level with his knees. "Forgive us. No other will interrupt. And if they do, they'll spend a week in the stocks."

She stopped tying the strings of the cloak and let it slide again from her shoulders. "I'll allow that but once. Those who care not for tales that will live in your hearts and your dreams should leave now, and make room for those who want to breathe in magic."

The only shifting was of her audience leaning closer.

"I am the Bard. I've been Saoirse, Abrial, Lysandra, Amadi, Jiyuu, and many more. I was known as Palasha as I traveled Ruska, and it is there I'll take you tonight.

"Ruska is a cold land. The people are strong, for they yearly fight winter. Those who win live to see another summer. Those who do not, find a home in earth that is frozen half the year. Come and enter a land of wolves and ogres, tsars and wars, and forests vast enough to hold whole nations.

"A land where the servant will always be the servant—unless.

"Come see."

1

———

A DIRT CLOD shattered against the back of my neck between my two long braids.

"Forest born! Ogre child! You're nothing but a demon wild!" Their mocking voices rained from the summer oaks that lined the road from the fields to the manor house.

I broke into a jog, holding three snared pheasants against my chest and keeping my head down as another dirt clod hit my shoulder. *I'm not an ogre's child!*

A stone stung the crown of my head.

Heat rose in my chest. *I'm not an ogre's child, but I'm stronger than any of you!* I slung the pheasants over my shoulder, hiked up my work stained skirt, and clambered up the trunk of the nearest oak.

A boy yelped and dropped from his branch. Ten others dropped from nearby trees, like acorns in a storm.

The oak groaned and then shrieked in protest as I bent then broke a branch. I leaped down, waving the branch in circles over my head.

The bullies scattered, laughing.

I dashed after the largest of them—a boy who should have

5

acted like a man by his size. But they were all weak-minded and cruel. And slow. I caught him easier than a rabbit.

His laughter changed to yelps as I clobbered his back with the branch. "Help! She'll kill me!"

Kill? I wouldn't, but if I beat him beyond fieldwork use, they'd punish Mama. She'd been punished enough for me. I threw the branch aside and stalked off.

A boy's voice whispered, "Forest born, ogre child. You're nothing—"

I spun and glared.

The boys scattered over the fields, even the one I'd caught, though he hobbled like an old man.

I yelled after them. "Manor born, servant rotten. You're nothing but pig slop and ill begotten."

MAMA SCRUBBED the dirt from the back of my neck in the corner of the servants' sleeping shed. Other servants bundled their daytime clothes into pillows, the house servants huddled in gossip at one side, and the laundress burst into laughter with the cook. They ignored us in our corner.

Mama laid the coarse cloth aside and brushed out my hair. If mine were like hers—ripe wheat-colored—maybe the boys would stop teasing me. Mine burned with the bright red of a fox and a single lock as dark as a black bear's fur. Forest born, wild animal, no other girl looked like me. I was small like my mama, same narrow face, same slender hands. But my eyes were so dark blue they looked like the moonless night sky—black is what the polite called them, devil black if they were less polite.

Mama wove my hair back into two braids. "Vasilisa, you must ignore them. They can't hurt you."

"They do. They throw things at me. They call me names. It hurts here." I touched between my newly forming breasts.

"There will always be those who mock. You must be strong without falling to their viciousness. You must be careful. You have a gift of strength they will never have."

"I thought when I reached my fifteenth year, and started looking a woman, they'd be kinder."

Mama shook her head. "Those boys couldn't see beauty if it hit them between the eyes—which you've done before."

I laughed.

"But if you want the boys to like you, you may want to act more like the other girls."

"I'm not like the other girls. I don't look like them. And they don't act like me. They won't climb trees, run with the hounds, or swim in the river. I think I must be like my papa. Please tell me—who was he?"

"Not yet, my Vasilisa."

"Then at least tell me about him. I'm losing the memories I once had."

"What do you remember?"

"He had dark eyes—like mine."

She nodded.

"He was tall and strong. He carried me in one arm and you in the other, then set us in a tree to watch. Quiet, like the forest cat, he ran down the deer and, like the bear, he stilled it with one blow of his fist. We always had good meat to eat." I picked at the frayed edge of the blanket that lay over the pallet that mama and I shared. "He tossed me in the air, so high that I could see over the short trees, then caught me, swinging me around, then tossed me again. He loved me so much."

Mama wrapped her arms around my shaking shoulders.

"I remember that. More than anything. Though he never said it..." I paused, searching my ghosts of memories. He never spoke in any of them. Mama sang, scolded, and told stories. Papa protected, hunted, and played with me. Had he been a mute? No—one memory rang in my ears. *The night he died. Many creatures, covered in furs but standing on two legs—they'd been men!* I gripped Mama's arm. *Many men attacked our cave. Papa growled and howled as he protected us. The men died, and so did Papa. Mama buried him, then carried me away from the forest and into a life of servitude and mocking.* "He died to protect us."

Mama nodded.

"Why didn't we stay in the forest?"

"Because you were too little. Just a toddling thing. I could not provide for or protect us like he did. And," she tilted up my chin, "you will someday be a woman. The forest is not for you."

"I liked it better than here. I'm strong now. I can draw the bow of the archer, though it stands taller than me. Let's go back. I'll protect you, I'll provide for you."

She held me closer. "Vasilisa. I'm not made for the forest. Besides, what would Staver say?"

"There are songbirds in the forest to match his music. I won't miss him—much."

"He'll miss you."

"No, he won't. He only wants me around because I listen to him practice. He's a weakling, more so than all the other boys. No muscle in his arms. No adventure in his mind. Just music. Besides, he's the master's son. And I'm a scullery maid."

Mama lay down on the pallet. "We'd better sleep. Tomorrow's work will start before sunrise."

I snuggled closer to her and resolved as I did every night. *Someday I will be free.*

THE DEEP BLUES *of the moon-lit forest blurred past as I ran. The breeze raced behind me, tugging my skirts forward.*

Shouts shattered the stillness.

Hurry! I stretched my stride. I had to get there on time.

A roar overwhelmed the shouts.

The ground steepened into a cliff. I gripped a root and scrambled upward.

Grunts, roars, and shouts intermingled.

Halfway up the cliff, the roots disappeared. I sought fingerholds in the clay soil. I'd make it this time.

The clay crumbled, and I fell as the howling death cry echoed in my ears.

I shuddered awake beside Mama. She shifted, her breath soft in sleep and slow with weariness.

I'd not had that nightmare in years. But I made it further this time. I was stronger. I'd grow stronger yet. Next time I dreamed it, I'd reach the top of the cliff and stop them from killing Papa.

The forest called, and so did he.

2

———

I scrubbed at the ash-bottomed pot.

The cook rapped me on the top of my head. "Not too hard, girl! Slower and gentler. I don't want a hole in the pot before I've used it a year."

I lightened my touch, but scrubbed faster. As soon as I finished that pot, I'd start my one free half-day in seven, though the cook had kept me several hours into the afternoon.

The lilting notes of the balalaika floated through the open window, along with the afternoon breeze. Staver was getting better. When I'd first spied on him, when we were both little children, he'd sounded like rocks plopping into the water. I'd told him so. And instead of getting angry, he'd laughed.

I hung the finished pot from a hook on the ceiling and dashed out the door.

Staver sat on a stone bench. His sun-bright hair fell in thick locks about a face that was beginning to widen into a strong jaw. His triangle balalaika balanced on his legs and his fingers flew over the strings. But instead of the usual stately melodies, he played the twittering song of the marsh warbler.

I whistled in harmony. We sounded like two marsh warblers in their springtime courtship. I stopped whistling. He was just a silly boy who wasted his time playing that silly instrument.

He grinned, his pale blue eyes dancing. "Vasilisa, I'd hoped to test you on where I found my new song, but you guessed it before I asked. How about this one?" He played a slower and sadder tune.

"Nightingale."

He squished up one side of his mouth in thought, then the other. He played a third tune. One that made me want to dance.

"House wren."

He set down his balalaika. "You know all the bird songs. And I'll wager all the animal calls too. I wish I did."

"I can whistle more for you."

"Would you?" He patted the bench next to him.

I would not sit by my master's son. I'd got a whipping across my backside for the last time I did. Instead, I whistled a shrill song.

He plucked the strings, and within half a minute was mimicking the call. "I like that. It feels like what flight must be like for the birds—free and fierce against the wind. What is it?"

"A shrike. It is small, but savage as a hawk."

"It sounds like it. I would that I could see one."

"I can show you. There is a nest only a few hours' walk. If we ran, we could be there for its evening song."

Staver set his balalaika on the bench. "Which way?"

"North along the woodcutter's path, past the otters' den, through—"

He caught one of my motioning hands. "Just show me."

I gripped his hand, and with a laugh, ran towards the gate that led from the manor.

Chickens scattered with annoyed squawks, while a goose

hissed. The old coachman called out after us. "Young Master Staver, don't you go getting into trouble now."

Staver slowed, but didn't let go. "I'll be back by nightfall, and I'll be careful. Tell my mother not to worry."

His mother would worry. And I would get extra chores for it. Maybe I shouldn't show him. "Staver, we wouldn't be back by nightfall, unless we ran the whole way. I'll show you the otter den instead."

"I can run the whole way. Let's go!" He dragged me toward the manor gate.

Even if it was only for the afternoon, freedom in the forest was worth extra chores—especially since I had someone to share the freedom with. I stretched into a long loping run. The sun warmed my face, and wind cooled it. My braids bounced against my back to the rhythm of my stride.

Staver's hand grew sweaty and slick in mine. His breath came in pants.

I let go of his hand and slowed my stride to a jog. "Sorry."

"Don't be—I should—learn to—run—like that."

"You're faster than Gleb or Dmitri, even when I'm chasing them away from torturing some poor animal. They waddle like ducks."

He bent over in panting laughter, bracing his hands against his knees. When he straightened, he started into an easy jog.

The woodman's path split off from the road and passed into the cool greenness of the woods. Great pines swayed over white-barked aspens as a stream chuckled underneath. Trillium dotted the ground. The sharp tang of pine mixed with the rich moldering of last year's leaves.

A rabbit hopped onto the path.

Staver froze.

I stopped.

He slowly crouched down and extended his hand, holding a bit of grass.

The rabbit studied us with dark eyes, then hopped towards Staver but edged around me. It ate the grass from Staver's hand, then hopped off the path.

He watched a moment, then stood with a peaceful glow in his face.

I laid my hand on a pine bow. "I've never seen a wild animal come like that."

He shrugged. "I'm quieter than most. Don't tell the other boys that I feed rabbits. They think I'm a weakling as it is."

"Do you think you can charm the otters as you did the rabbit?"

"It's no magic. Just—"

"Do you?"

He scratched at the hair at the back of his neck. "Maybe. I can try."

I led him along the stream, stepping hunter-quiet. He matched my silence.

The chirps and squeals of otters chattered over the stream's chuckling.

I pulled Staver to crouch beside me. We slipped forward in a low almost-crawl, though only our feet touched the ground. I stopped behind a currant bush and pointed through its foliage.

The stream opened into a pond. Two otters slid down a muddy bank, while a third chased a fourth in a race through the water. One otter caught the tail of the other and they tumbled into a muddy wrestle.

Staver's gaze darted from otter to otter. I nudged his arm. Could he charm the otters or not?

He nudged me back and held a finger to his lips. I *was* being quiet!

He stood and walked from behind the bush with a peaceful ease, as if he belonged by the pond as much as the otters did.

The otters paused in their play and studied him with black eyes.

He bent by the pond edge, scooped up a handful of water, and drank. He didn't look at them, or even seem aware of them.

They watched him a moment longer, then took up their play on the far side of the pond.

He scooped another drink, then lay back in the grass and closed his eyes.

Gnats whined around me. What was he waiting for? I swatted a gnat on my neck.

Staver whispered a hush, then tilted his head toward the pond.

An otter swam toward him. It chattered, sniffed at Staver's feet, clambered over his legs, and settled on his chest.

Staver did have magic. I held in my breath and movement, letting the bugs dine. I'd not break the charm.

Another otter swam over and sniffed Staver, then wrestled the resting otter back into the water. The two swam off in a game of tag and dunk.

Staver scooped two river stones, set them in his pocket, then walked back to me. "Do we still have time to see the shrike nest?"

"Can you teach me how to charm the animals?"

He fumbled with the edge of his tunic. "I don't know. I'm just doing what I wish others would do for me—I give them space and let them come on their own terms."

I'd wager his father was pushing him to take up swordsmanship again.

He glanced back at the otters and then ahead along the path. The evening sun stretched shadows across it. "Do you think we can see the shrike nest?"

"Come on. We can still make it for their evening song if we run."

We dashed through the woods. I slowed when his panting grew louder than his footfall.

The forest thinned into a meadow. Westward trees cast their shadows across most of it. In the one band of light left along the meadow's eastern edge, a shrike's shrill song cut the air. Another shrike answered the evening call. The two battled their voices in an intricate weaving of notes. As darkness closed over the last band of ground, then climbed the shrikes' tree, they sang more fiercely. Perhaps they challenged nighttime's encroachment on their home. Then darkness pushed sunlight from their nest and they fell silent.

Staver touched the bark of the shrikes' tree. "Thank you."

A wind wove through the trees, chasing away the day's warmth. I pulled off my belted shawl and wrapped it around my shoulders. "We'd better get back."

He glanced up at the sky. "The stars will be out soon. But it was worth it, even for the words my mother will have with me."

And worth it to see him with the otters, even for the extra chores I'd be punished with.

We jogged steadily homeward. I let Staver set the pace, and I led the way through the dimness. The trees turned to black pillars, and the undergrowth grew in grey catchings for our feet. A blackness moved along our left—a large blackness that growled and lumbered into our path about five strides ahead.

An ogre! The laundress had whispered one had been roaming our woods. I froze. If we moved, the ogre would see us.

The shape shifted into the moonlight. It was just a bear. I let go of my held breath.

"Bear!" Staver pushed himself in front of me, then brought back his arm.

"Don't throw it," I hissed, grabbing his hand—and the stone gripped in it.

The bear huffed and stepped towards us.

Staver's hand tightened around the stone.

"Don't throw it!" I let go of his hand and held out my shawl like wings. It had worked before. It had to work this time too. I flicked the shawl, snapping it like a dusty rug.

The bear stepped back and huffed again.

"Yell like the house is on fire!"

Staver yelled, his voice cracking. I added my hawk cry.

The bear shook its head and growled.

Staver whipped his hand back and flung the stone. It struck the bear near its ear and bounced off.

"No!" I screamed.

The bear lunged forward, its movements angry.

He'll rip us apart. I broke off a branch and ran, yelling, at the bear, slapping him across the nose.

He bellowed, splattering me with spittle, then rose to his hind legs. I dodged back as he swiped where my head had been. Air from his paw whooshed across my face.

"Vasilisa!" Staver darted forward, flinging another stone. The bear turned.

No! He'll kill Staver! I dashed around the bear and slapped his ear. He swiveled, stepping clumsily on hind legs to follow me.

Around we danced. Staver flung stones. I darted, slapping the bear wherever I could, on his face as often as possible.

Finally, with a moan and a grumble, he fell to all fours and lumbered from the path. His crashing through the undergrowth died away.

Staver clutched my hand—our skin gripped clammy. "Let's get home."

We sprinted till we tumbled from the forest and entered the open farmland. The newly starred sky spread above us. Lanterns wove along the road and out in the fields. "Staver! Master Staver!" His name echoed from many voices.

"I'm here," he called back.

The lanterns converged on us.

A large man with frost-lined hair was first to reach us. He grabbed Staver by the shoulders. "Son, are you hurt?"

"No, Papa." Staver's voice trembled more than his father's.

His father turned to me and raised a leather-gloved hand. I braced myself for the blow. "How dare you take my son into the woods! How dare you—"

Staver shoved between me and his father. "Papa, stop! She—she saved my life."

He lowered his hand, and his voice dropped to a rumble. "You'll never lead him into the woods again."

"Never again, my lord." I attempted a curtsy.

He wasn't looking anymore. He wrapped his arm about Staver's shoulder. "Come. Your mother is ill with worry for you." The other lantern bearers—the stable master, the smith, and basically every manservant from the estate, including the old coachman—gathered around and lit the way back to the manor.

Darkness closed in as the lights drew away. I'd be paying for our jaunt into the woods for months.

I STOOD at the door of one of the manor rooms. Books lined the walls. A large desk dominated one corner. A fire crackled. Heavy drapes blocked out the night stars. Leather, polished oak, and the mistress's perfume tickled my nose. The mistress stood by a desk, a head taller than me, her square face stern, her broad shoulders tense under her brown-and-gold brocade gown. Dark blonde hair coiled in a thick braid on the top of her head, adding to her height.

A stoop-shouldered man sat at the desk writing on a sheet of parchment. He glanced at me as I entered. His eyes filled with pity—I think. It was only a moment, and then he kept his gaze downward. What punishment had the mistress planned for me this time? And why did her clerk need to be here? I should have been comforted that someone else was there, except his pitying glance gave little hope that he'd stand against her actions. The last time I'd been in this room, when I'd worn a hole in the mistress's dress trying to get a stain out, it had been just her, and she could leave bruises.

She motioned me forward. "Vasilisa. Today you almost killed my son."

"I didn't," I shot back. "It was just a bear. I kept him safe."

Her face reddened. "A bear could have easily killed him, despite your strength! What if it had been an ogre? Even the tsar's knight could do little against one!"

I should have kept quiet. Now my punishment would be much greater. I bowed my head. "I'm sorry, mistress. I'll work hard in recompense."

Her mouth hardened. "That's not enough. You should be whipped and cast off for your willful endangerment of him."

I shuddered. I'd seen the whip scars on the back of one of the field hands when he worked half-bare through the hot summer. They caught at his movements and hampered the swing of his scythe. Though if she cast me off I could return to the forest and I'd be free. The whipping would be worth it.

She continued. "But you are a strong girl and work hard. I'd be a fool to lose your labor. I have decided to fine you a thousand rubles. You are indentured to me. You will abide by my every order until your debt is repaid."

"A thousand rubles! I only get one a week. And there are only four weeks in a month, and twelve months in a year. It would take me..." I tried to add together the numbers.

Her mouth turned up in a cold smile. "Twenty years if you save every single ruble—though you will have to buy fabric for new clothes from time to time, and you'll not eat free with the other servants anymore."

My fingers closed in fists. She was always cold, but this was a new cruelty.

"Come here." She picked up the parchment the clerk had written on. Squiggles filled it. Words that I'd never learned and —as a servant—never would.

I kept to my spot by the wall.

She pursed her lips. "You'll only bring more punishment for your defiance. If you don't mark the indenture agreement, then I'll brand you instead, and that mark you'll bear even after you've repaid your debt."

Branding! Two servants on the Orlov estate bore a black eagle mark on their forearm. They were shunned even more than me. But I couldn't put my mark on something I couldn't read. I'd take the branding first.

I turned to the clerk. "Please, sir clerk. What does it say?"

He glanced between me and the mistress. Anger mixed with his pity, and then his jaw hardened. "Vasilisa, servant of the Orlov manor, is indentured to Lady Devora Orlov for the amount of two thousand rubles—a fine for endangering the life of Staver Orlov, Lady Devora's son and future master of the Orlov manor. While indentured Vasilisa will not leave to other employment and she will not marry. If she refuses to put her mark to the paper, she is to be branded with the eagle." He stopped and kept his eyes on the parchment. "That is the extent of it."

Anger flared up in the kindling of his words. I clutched my hands together to keep from striking the mistress. *Two thousand rubles! She lied! I'll never be able to repay it! Cruel trickster, Mistress!* A cooling thought flowed over the flames and my hands steadied. *I can be a trickster too. I'll leave. Not to a town or another manor, where she can hunt me down, but to the forest. She'll never find me there. Ruska's forests could hide whole villages, maybe even cities. I'll put my mark to the document. I'll work at every task the mistress gives. I'll never let her suspect. All the while I'll prepare to live in the forest. And I'll finally be free.*

I dipped my thumb in the inkwell and pressed it to the bottom of the parchment.

~

The deep shadows of forest twilight made every tree a fortress column, strong and protecting. No manor walls stood as sturdy. I walked between them, safe from the orders and spite of the mistress.

A low grumble warned me before a shadow detached from the trees. A bulky shape shuffled forward on four legs. Bear? But it wasn't quite. It reared to two legs and stepped from the shadows—a huge man with a craggy face stared at me.

Ogre!

My blood thudded like the blacksmith's hammer, pulsing iron-hot through my limbs.

His black-eyed gaze darted over my hair and face.

I wouldn't let him eat me. I grabbed a fallen branch and braced my legs to fend off his attack.

He followed my movement with his gaze, then growled in a rolling, bounding, rumble—something almost like laughter. His form thickened and covered with black fur, and he fell to four legs, a black bear.

I gripped my branch in white-knuckled fists as he shuffled forward and snuffed the ground near my feet. My breath came in shallow pants.

He looked into my face, and his eyes seemed bemused. He huffed then walked by me, his broad side brushing against me and almost knocking me over. His musky scent stung my nose.

I turned and watched the ogre lumber out of my dream. My arms shook with the branch that I still gripped. When I returned to the forest, I'd have to be better prepared than in my dreams. I had to be able to defend against animal and ogre.

But even with those dangers, the freedom was worth it.

3

———————

I SANDED the old paint from the pigsty. The paint and splinters of wood caught in my hair and dropped down the neck of my faded clay-brown dress. Soon I would paint it bright white, probably so the mistress could point out that it was dirty again and needed my cleaning.

The mistress sat weaving on the back porch of the manor house. She thumped the shuttle down on the loom. "When you have finished, you will empty the privies into the pull wagon and drag it to the field."

Staver came out on the porch and laid his hand on his mother's arm. "Please Matushka, she doesn't deserve this. She saved my life. She should be rewarded."

"Rewarded for taking you into the woods? Rewarded for keeping you out after dark? Rewarded for endangering my only son and delight of my heart!"

"I ask—ordered her to take me. It's my fault."

I frowned. It was his fault I was indentured. Though he'd not ordered me.

The mistress brushed the hair away from Staver's eyes. "You must use your authority more wisely."

"I'll learn to. Please stop punishing her for my mistake. If you could have only seen the otters or heard the shrike, you'd have found it hard to leave. It was more beautiful than the painting hanging over our mantel or the music that my teacher creates. Please."

He was pleading for me? It was too late for that. The damage was done. But—I paused in sanding for a moment to brush the paint flakes from my face—if I continued this level of labor I'd never have time to prepare to live in the forest.

Maybe she'd listen to him. I wouldn't say anything. I must show myself a submissive and obedient servant, so she didn't suspect. I sanded harder, so as not to let them know I was listening.

Her shoulders rose and then slumped. "Only if you promise me never to enter those woods again without a proper escort."

He wrapped her in a hug. "I promise."

She sat down at her loom and kept her face turned from me.

Staver glanced over and smiled an apologetic smile.

I didn't need his pity. I turned my head away from him.

Then he was at my side, picking up another sanding block.

"What are you doing?" I whispered.

He grinned at me, shook his head, and rubbed the sanding block across the wood. It skipped over the ridged and warped wood. Tiny flakes of paint fell on his tooled leather boots. He put his weight into the sanding block on the upward stroke. Paint flicked onto his face. Again and again he scraped the sanding block over the wood. Sweat darkened his white linen tunic and the embroidered flowers at the neckline.

"Staver." The mistress stepped down from the porch. "You will not do a servant's work."

He kept sanding.

"Staver. Stop."

"I will, when Vasilisa may stop. It was my fault. I'll bear the punishment too."

"She's a servant. It's not a punishment, but her duty."

"Then I'll endure the same duty."

Why was he doing this? I didn't like the work, but I could do it. He didn't know I was indentured—unless his mother had told him. I never would. He already gave me too much pity. I could make my own way against his mother's spite.

His slender fingers that often danced over the balalaika string were darkened with grime and red with splinters.

I pulled at the sanding block in his hand. "The mistress is right."

He tugged it back. "I'll work beside you until this is finished, and then I'll help empty the privies -" he wrinkled his nose "-and drag the wagon to the field."

The mistress laid her hand over Staver's, and her fingers brushed against mine, smooth fingers that only knew the work of thread. "You have your father's kindness. I'll release this girl back to her regular duties." She turned to me. "Get cleaned up and then help the cook prepare the midday meal."

My mouth fell open in surprise. Staver convinced her?

"Thank you, mistress." I glanced at Staver and mouthed the thanks I dared not say in front of his mother.

The servant bath was a shed built over a bit of stream than ran swift and cold even in the summer. I shivered through a scrub and rubbed out as much of the dirt as I could from my dress, then draped my shawl over my shoulders and wet dress and ran to the kitchens, which stood separate from the manor house.

I rushed through the door, and the cook rapped me on the head with a wooden spoon. "There you are, girl! Clean the breakfast dishes and then peel a sack of potatoes. I'm all sorts of behind today, and you'll work hard to make up for it."

The constantly busy ovens warmed and dried me as I

scrubbed dishes. My thoughts wandered.

Staver got me indentured by asking me to take him into the forest. But it was my fault, and the bear's, as much as his. It is his mother's fault most of all. She should bear the blame, not him.

I plunged my hands deeper into the hot water, soaking in the heat, and scrubbed the hardened egg from a plate.

He put himself between the bear and me. He lowered himself to scrape paint from a pigsty. Maybe that wasn't pity. Was it friendship? Did friendship turn his gentleness into bravery? He was brave, though I hadn't seen it under what I thought was weakness. But it wasn't weakness. He charmed the animals and gentled his mother. That was power. And because he used that power for me, I'm back to my regular duties and can pursue freedom.

I wiped the last dish dry and set it on the shelf, then sat on a low stool in front of an oven to peel potatoes.

I have to thank him. But how?

I peeled the potatoes and ran through ideas. *Wildflowers? No, silly, not for a boy. A cake baked just for him? I'd burn it.* The cook hadn't let me do more than peel, cut, and clean since the last time I'd filled the kitchen with smoke. *A painting?* Where would I get the paper or the paint, and even if I did, then what? I'd never drawn with more than a fire-blackened stick on rocks, and the pictures didn't look like much. *A flute?* Yes. I could hollow out a willow shoot and cut holes in it. He liked music and birdsong. He could create the one and mimic the other with the flute. It was perfect.

I set the basket of peeled potatoes on the worktable, and the cook snatched it up. "Wood for the fires."

The crickets chirped their night-time serenades when I crawled onto the pallet I shared with my mother. I'd made up for my missed hours of work in the morning with after-sundown chores.

Mama scooted over and gave me her warmed spot beneath

the blanket. "I'm sorry she's punishing you so harshly."

I grunted a reply. I'd not tell her of the indenturement either.

She wrapped her arms around me. "Master Staver is a good young man. I saw what he did at the pigsty."

"Hmm." I yawned and slipped toward sleep.

Her voice cut through the fog. "He'll make a fine master someday."

I stared at her indistinct form in the lightless servants' shed, then whispered so only she could hear, "Mama, even if he were my master, I'll not stay here past my sixteenth birthday. I'm returning to the forest as soon as I've learned the needed skills."

Silence stretched out. Mama's quiet voice trembled. "When you are sixteen, I will return to the woods with you, if that is still what you want."

She'd come! Ten months. I could endure that long. And I still had much to learn. I'd spend my free time watching the furrier tan hides, the smith smelt iron from ore, and all the other skills that I would need. We were going home.

Birds chittered and trilled in the afternoon. A thrush sang. I closed my eyes, letting the speckled light of midday sun and forest canopy fall on my eyelids, and opened my ears to hear more distantly. Warbler and wren added their tunes to the west. The extravagant song of the lark brightened the forest to the east. I spun, eyes shut, wrapping the music around me.

A new melody sounded behind me: the mournful call of the nightingale. The notes came in vibrating plucks. A voice added sweet notes on top.

Staver.

I wrapped the birdsong tighter around me, blocking his voice, and ran deeper into the forest.

4

———

"Vasilisa." Staver ran to catch up to me as I carried a damp bundle of laundry from the stream to the lines.

I quickened my pace. If he started talking to me, I'd have to listen, and then I'd be slower in my work and I'd not have time to work on the flute. I hardly ever had time. The mistress hadn't forgiven my trespass. I wasn't given more men's tasks, but I did more work than any of the women. Mama offered to take some of it, but she'd also been ordered to do more work, and I wouldn't add mine to hers.

I fit in working on the flute by the kitchen fire glow before the others woke or after they'd gone to bed. I was almost done. If he'd just let me alone, I could hang up these clothes, start my first half-day in two weeks, and finish the flute.

"Here, I'll help you with that." He took hold of the bundle. A tunic and hosen fell onto the dirt path.

"Bothersome! Clumsy! Can't you just let me do my work without adding to it!"

"I'm sorry." He stooped over to pick up the fallen clothes, now coated with dust, and started to lay them back on the bundle.

I stepped back. "Stop! You'll make me have to rewash all the clothes."

He backed away, holding the dirty clothes. "I'm sorry Lisa. I wish—."

"Just stop." Tears burned in the corners of my eyes. I pressed my face into the damp bundle and ran to the clotheslines.

A clean sheet lay on the ground. I dumped my bundle onto it, then snapped a red skirt free of wrinkles before pinning it to the line.

Staver came beside me, picked up woolen trousers and flicked them. The legs of the trousers wrapped around Staver's legs. He laughed, his voice undulating between a man's deepness and a boy's higher pitch.

The sound was so ridiculous that I laughed too, as I peeled the wool trousers off him and hung them.

He picked up one of the mistress's embroidered blouses and held the arms like a dancer. He set into a traditional Rylio, tap-step, tap-step, step-step-step-step, humming out the melody. The blouse flopped around to his movement. When he finished the tune, he bowed to the blouse, grinned sideways at me, and hung it up on the line.

We worked side by side until only one stocking was left in the pile. I grabbed the toe and he the top.

"I'll do it." He gently pulled it from my hand. "I'll talk to my mother. If she won't give you enough moments to even say hello once in two weeks, then she's working you too hard. Servant or no, you are my friend, and what she's doing is wrong."

"Friend?"

"Of course. How do you wash the clothes? Because I'll clean the ones I knocked to the ground."

"You'll get all wet."

"Good. It's a hot day."

I glanced towards the manor house. No face watched from the window.

He glanced back too. "She's asleep. We still have a little time before she'll wake."

"Does she ever scare you?" I clapped my hand over my mouth. I was speaking all sorts of impudence that day.

He nodded. "She is loving in her own way. And Papa is a gentling influence on her."

"That's where you got it from."

"What?"

"Your gentleness."

"Oh." His neck reddened. "I'm too gentle, even for him. I'm supposed to be strong and commanding—so I can manage the manor someday."

"Is that why he wants you to learn swordsmanship?"

He nodded. "And he wants me to be able to defend myself and my family if war comes."

"Do you think it will?"

Staver studied the ground, his face tightly intent. "It will come. Maybe not this year or in the next ten. But it will come. The Kahn of the Golden Horde is always pushing into the southern lands."

If war came, I'd be the better warrior. But I wouldn't be here. What would happen to him? I shrugged aside the thought. The Master had many men-at-arms. They wouldn't need Staver to fight, though he had other worthy skills. I grinned at him, trying to push away the gloom that had gathered in his brows. "Maybe you could charm the attackers as you do the animals?"

He scuffed his boots on the path. "A wolf wouldn't listen to my quiet. Sometimes people need to fight."

Should I fight his mother for what she forced me to? Or should I run? She was too powerful. I'd leave.

He jostled my elbow. "A tune for your thoughts."

"I'll learn to fletch arrows." I clapped my hand over my mouth. Where did that come from? He not only got me to speak impudence but also my secrets.

He laughed and cupped his hands around his mouth, then whispered, "No shame in taking up new skills. You'll do wonderful at it." Staver glanced up the hill to the manor. "I'd better go. But will you promise to at least nod when you see me? And on your next half-day, I'll teach you chess."

"Why?"

He called over his shoulder as he dashed up the hill, "Because you'll like it." He reached the door just as the mistress opened it.

After I washed the last of the clothes, I carved the final three holes in the flute. A mellow note floated upward as I blew through the wedged mouthpiece. It was ready. I'd give it to him on the next half-day, when he had promised to teach me chess.

I ran back to the stream and slid down to the bending willow. A grey stone nestled between the willow's roots. After a quick glance confirmed that no one watched, I brushed the dirt from the stone's edges. Then, with a grunting shove, I rolled the stone on its side to reveal a box made of broken tiles and pottery. Remnants of saddle leather, a broken horse's bit, frayed twine, and even a shard of red-and-yellow glazed china lined the bottom—treasures from the rubbish heap. I laid the flute on top, then reset the stone, brushing dirt back over the edges. Other servants kept their treasures tucked under their sleeping mats, but I planned on hiding away things that would get me horsewhipped if found—arrows, a bow, and a hunting knife.

Which should I work on first? I'd go to the fletcher. I'd brought him feathers from my snared birds before. He'd be open to teaching me. Then I could trade my arrows to the bowyer for lessons in making a bow. It would be better than stealing the weapons, and in the half-days I had before we left I'd have time to make everything I needed.

THE FLETCHER'S stall sat at the end of the smithy. The fletcher, a lean man with a perpetual scowl, sat cross-legged on a table surrounded by metal arrowheads, a pile of arrow shafts, and a box of feathers.

He picked up one of the arrow shafts and peered down the end.

"Master Fletcher."

He rotated the shaft, shook his head, and picked up a different shaft. "What do you want, wild child?"

"I have more feathers."

"Set them on the table. Come for your extra loaf tonight."

"I don't want bread. I want to learn how to fletch arrows."

He looked up. His scowl deepened. "Why?"

"Why not?"

"You're a girl."

"I only catch small birds with snares. I'd be able to get you turkey or goose feathers if I had a bow and arrows."

He tilted his head.

I hurried on. "I'll share my first turkey or goose with you."

"The first five."

"Two."

"Three, or you'll not get any learning from me."

"Two and all the wing feathers from the first five."

He grunted agreement and made a place for me to sit next to him.

I climbed up on the table and set down a sack of feathers from birds I'd snared before my hours of work increased.

I first peeled bark from coppiced saplings. They all looked

straight to me, but after several cuffs to my head for handing the fletcher bent shafts, I began to see the little variations, the insect damage, the twists and turns.

Next I chewed sinew until it became tacky. My throat tightened at the flavor. The last time I'd eaten venison was with Papa. I gulped to keep back the tears.

"Don't swallow it, girl!"

I spat out the sinew. "Now what?"

He measured feathers against each other and split three of them. I found three same sized feathers. "No! All right wing or left wing, otherwise it won't spin in flight."

"Spin?"

"Spin. Keeps it going straight. If you mix right and left wing, it will wobble all over the place."

When I'd split my feathers to his satisfaction, after ruining twelve and hearing a string of curses for my waste, I moistened the sinew again and wrapped it around the shaft and the base of the three feathers. It stuck to itself and the arrow.

After notching the back for the string and the front for the arrowhead, I dipped the point in pine resin and reached for a metal arrowhead.

He slapped my hand away. "You'll use bone chips." He pointed to a bowl of fragmented bones.

I swallowed my retort. I'd have to do without metal in the forest, so it would be best to start now. I wrapped a sharp piece of bone to the shaft with sinew and handed my finished arrow to him.

He held it up to the low sunlight of evening. A few grunts and scowls later, he handed it back.

"How is it?"

"It's a start."

"What's wrong with it?"

"The feathers aren't set equally around the shaft and one is higher than the rest. The bone is tilted in the tip. Make another."

I completed the second one in a third of the time it took me to do the first. The room grew dark enough that the fletcher lit the lanterns.

He studied my second attempt. "You'll come back tomorrow and make more."

"I can't. I have my duties."

"When your duties are done, you will come. You will fletch ten arrows for every one you keep."

"It will be dark."

"I'll see you tomorrow. And be careful in the forest. It's rumored that an ogre's been killing the sheep. He'd like nothing better than to feast on a young woman."

I laughed to shake off the chill. Ogres only roamed at night. At least that's what the laundress said. The servants gathered in the evenings to hear her stories. I didn't, but I couldn't block her words drifting over to my corner of the servant's sleeping shed. I hated her tales. Of men that changed into animals and tore the throats from their victims. Of the ogre witch, Baba-Yaga, who tricked young girls into becoming her dinner. Her tales that kept children from playing in the forest or servants from ever dreaming of escaping.

The forest was my safe place. I'd make a protected place for the night. I'd be safe, and I'd be free. No tale would change that.

I WALKED *along the top of a fallen tree in the slanting morning sun. Termites made tunnels in the dead wood around flat shelves of mushrooms. A squirrel raced down a pine, and a crow swooped at it. The squirrel chattered curses as it spiraled up the trunk into the safety of the boughs.*

Someone walked behind me. I knew who it was, but I wouldn't turn. This was my dream. Staver shouldn't be here. He didn't belong in the forest.

I skipped from one dead-fall to another that lay balanced across a stump. The dead-fall dipped, and I threw out my arms for balance. Slender fingers, stronger than they looked, caught my arm and steadied me.

5

———

THE MISTRESS REDUCED my workload almost to the level it was before our meeting with the bear. Staver must have spoken with her. Every day Staver practiced his balalaika outside the kitchen's open window, filling my work with his voice and plucked music. Whenever we crossed paths, he waved. I nodded back, as promised, and smiled if the mistress wasn't watching.

I split my evenings between fletching arrows and setting snares in the fields for grouse and quail. I cooked the fowls in the field so as not to draw attention, though Mama insisted we share the meat with the other servants. Why couldn't they just set their own snares?

On my next half-day, Staver found me as I finished shelling a bowl of peas. He popped a pea pod in his mouth then grinned a green smile.

I laughed.

He spat out the pod and grinned his white-toothed smile. "My mother lay down for her rest. What can I do to help?"

"I'm finished for the day." I reached under my three-legged stool and pulled out the flute. "Here, I made this. It's not much, but I wanted to do something to thank you."

He ran his fingers over the flute and blew a sweet note. "It's beautiful! But why are you thanking me?"

"You got me out of trouble with the mistress." At least, the trouble he knew about.

"I got you into trouble. You didn't have to do this. But—" he looked down at the flute, then back to me, "I love it. Thank you! Now it's my turn. I have something for you."

"What is it?" I tried to keep my voice calm.

"I'll show you after we play chess."

"Oh." My shoulders slumped. I'd hoped he'd share his new song. I wanted to learn the words to the one he'd been playing outside the kitchen window.

He touched my chin, bringing my face up. "You'll like it."

"Maybe. What is chess?"

"It's a war between stone pieces."

"War? And you like it?" I snorted as I followed him to a blanket set in the shade of a tree. On the blanket sat a square board, all checkered with red and yellow paint. Lines of little stone pieces sat in two rows on two sides of the board.

He sat on the white stone side. I picked up one of the black stones; a little man with a long beard stared back at me with stone eyes.

"That's a pawn," Staver said. "It's the foot soldier and can only go one space forward, at least most of the time." He picked up piece by piece and showed me how each could move. Then he picked up one of the tallest pieces. "This is the tsarina. She is the most powerful piece. She can move any direction, for as far as she wants."

I fingered my tsarina piece. Powerful. Could go wherever she wanted.

He picked up the tallest piece. A figure with a carved crown. "This is the tsar. He can move any direction, but only one space. If you lose him, you lose the game. Protect him, even if you lose every other piece. Capture my tsar, and you win."

I stumbled through the first game. He won quickly but filled me with tips on things to watch for. He won the second and third games.

On the fourth game, I started to look ahead to what moves each of us could make. I became the hunter. I tracked the possible paths and cut them off so he could only tread the path I wanted him to take. Move by move, I hemmed in his tsar until he couldn't move except into capture.

Staver tipped over his tsar. "I knew you'd be good at it. You should play Papa when you've had more practice. He'd enjoy the challenge. I'm too easy for him. You seem to think in a hundred directions at once."

"You think the master would play a servant girl?"

"He'd play the beggar from the highway, if he was good at chess."

I laughed at the mental picture of the master in his fine clothes sitting across from a patched and dirt-crusted beggar, battling each other with stone game pieces.

Staver gathered the pieces into two cloth bags. "Will you play again next week?"

"Yes!"

"Good, then here is my gift." He held out both stone tsarinas. "Choose one."

"But the set won't be complete without her."

"This is my set. And it will only be complete when I play chess with you."

My pulse quickened, throbbing along my arms to my hands and up to my face. "Why?"

He smiled gently and held the stone pieces closer, not touching my hands but close enough that the heat from his hands warmed mine. "Because you're my friend."

I bit the inside of my cheek against the hope that hopped like a fledgling sparrow. I couldn't give that hope flight. I was an indentured servant girl. He was the master's son. I was nothing here. I could never be anything more than a servant. Even our friendship would end when he married. But he was here now. He offered his friendship. Couldn't I enjoy it for the months remaining before I made my home in the forest?

He laid the stone pieces in my lap, his movements slow and easy, like when he'd sat by the otter pond. "Which tsarina do you want?"

They lay heavy in the folds of my skirt. I studied both tsarinas. The black tsarina had a girdle and a crown of roses, while lilies decorated the white tsarina's gown and brow. A gentle smile graced the white tsarina's face while the black tsarina looked into the distance with wisdom. An artist had carved them. I'd seen much poorer workmanship at the county fair sell for more than I made in a year. "I can't."

"Yes, you can. I'm giving her to you." His voice came as a gentle breeze, lifting at the hope fluttering within me.

I ached to hold and keep the white tsarina, and even more the black one. Both were beautiful in their own way. I took the black tsarina and tucked her into my apron pocket. I'd keep her safe until Mama and I left, then I'd return her to Staver. "Thank you," I whispered.

He placed his hand over my open palm and I bit my cheek harder to keep the sparrow hope from taking flight. But hope lifted and my world expanded with *what if?* I squeezed his hand and leaned toward him, my lips parted.

"Staver." A voice called across the yard. The mistress sat at her loom weaving.

I pulled back and jerked my hand away. How long had she watched us? Had she seen him give me the tsarina or our touch afterwards?

I bowed my head to him. "Thank you, for teaching a servant girl to play chess."

"Lisa?"

I gave a quick shake of my head and glanced back at his mother.

"I'll talk to my mother if she makes your life difficult again. When I'm master of the house, you won't be a servant."

He was only making this harder. I'd not be here when he was master. Even his friendship wasn't worth my freedom. And if I wasn't a servant, what would I be? A craftsman? The tsar's law didn't allow me to become anything higher. I had no future here. Not one that we could share. After today's touch, and almost kiss, the mistress wouldn't even allow me to talk to him. I shoved the sparrow hope into a cage where it couldn't hurt me, and followed Staver to the manor house, keeping two steps behind. He slowed for me to catch up and I slowed too.

The mistress watched us approach. "Staver. I am pleased to see you practice your chess skills, but wouldn't it be better with your father?"

"Papa said I should play against others, so I learn different styles. Vasilisa learned quickly, and she gives me a good challenge."

"I'll allow it, since it keeps you to the manor grounds. And Vasilisa, I see you have learned to show proper respect. Keep it so."

She'd allow it! She must not have seen him give me the tsarina or us touch. I held in a leap. Staver and I could still spend time together. I laughed silently at my excitement. I was indentured because of him, and now I wanted to spend time with him? Yet, I wanted that time. Why did I tremble with anticipation of more afternoons together? Maybe because I was safe with him. He'd never mock or hurt me. Maybe because he made me laugh and brought joy into my dull life of hard labor. Maybe because he delighted in the forest and in nature.

Maybe because—I stopped my rambling thoughts. I'd have to be careful. I'd never again let that hope out of the cage. Not my hope for him. I'd keep my distance to friendship, nothing more. If I didn't, I'd lose him completely, long before I left for the forest.

Instead, I'd focus on preparing. I'd learn to make arrows and bows, work leather and smelt iron. I'd keep myself so busy between my servant duties and preparation that I only thought about Staver when we were together.

Staver bowed to his mother. "I'll play some music while you weave," he said, and walked behind her to get his balalaika. He turned around as soon as he was behind her and mouthed, *next week*.

I tried to keep my face straight and dashed off before it could betray my delight to the mistress. Next week on my half-day.

Staver sat on a stool and started playing a tune in rhythm with his mother's loom shuttle.

I dashed to the bowyer as Staver's notes followed me, lilting and playful.

The bowyer had built his hut on the outskirts of the master's land, far from any of the other outbuildings. He'd given me archery lessons until a year ago when I picked up a longbow and shot the farthest target. The bowyer had snatched the bow, called me ogre strong, and told me to get out. He'd not spoken to me since that day. But maybe this day, with the bundle of arrows I carried, he'd listen.

He sat on his front step and smoked a cob pipe. Wood shavings peppered his beard and tunic. He scooted back as I loped into his yard.

"Master Bowyer. I brought these arrows to trade for lessons

in bow making. I'll make you as many as you need for the time you take in teaching."

He crossed himself. "Go away. Get you back to the forest you came from."

"Please. I will go back to the forest and you'll never see me again. But first I must learn to make a hunting bow so I can provide for my mama."

He ducked into his hut and returned with a sturdy hunting bow, about half my height. "Take this one and get you gone."

"No, Master Bowyer. If it breaks, I must know how to make a new one."

"Will you leave when it is finished?"

"I will leave when I reach my sixteenth birthday. My mama won't leave before then."

"How soon?"

"Less than a year. But you mustn't tell anyone or the mistress will stop me."

He crossed himself again. "I'll teach you to get you gone from these lands. But only in daylight. Come back tomorrow."

He'd teach me! But could I find time in daylight hours? "I have my duties."

"Then finish them before the sun sets."

He'd given me the chance. I'd made it work.

I SAT *in the mid branches of an oak above a forest pool. On the other side of the water, a yearling buck scanned the area then lowered his head to drink. The bow pressed against my palm. The string pulled tight against my fingers. An arrow sat lightly on the string, its fletching brushing my cheek, ready for flight.*

"Lisa." Staver entered the clearing next to the buck. He'd grown

tall in the dream. And his voice had deepened. He lay his hand on the shoulder of the deer and looked into my face. "Lisa. Come home."

"I am home," I cried fiercely, and the deer bounded off.

6
——————

THE LONG HOURS of summer filled from dawn-break past evening shadow with my duties, followed by lessons. I was always the outcast amongst the servants and field hands. But I didn't hear them much now because they were asleep when I rose and asleep when I retired.

I ventured into the forest thrice and shot two geese with a borrowed bow. Each time I stepped beneath the forest trees, they whispered, "Come home, come home."

"Soon," I whispered back.

The fletcher accepted all the meat and feathers for the cost of my apprenticeship. He even grunted a *thank you.*

Through the longest days of summer, I learned to carve and curve the bow, combining the wood's strength and flexibility. Those days I rushed through my duties to catch an hour of daylight to work beside the bowyer. He always sent me away as soon as the sun touched the horizon. Then, in the glow of the kitchen fires, I fletched arrows to pay him.

During the autumn hunting season, the tanner, who was a friend of my mother's, allowed me to assist him when the kills were brought back to be skinned and tanned. I gave him my

43

simple-made bow. In exchange he taught me and gave me many scraps of leather, calling them rubbish, though I'd watch him turn similar pieces into gloves.

Then as the weather grew cold, I joined the blacksmith in his forge. He valued my strength and let me stay long past sundown. For my apprenticeship, I gave him a leather apron I'd made from the tanner's scraps. It was a strange combination of animal skins, but he soon blackened it to a monotone greyish black.

Every week I lined up with the other servants and received one ruble from the steward. The clerk stood to the side and recorded the payments. When the rest of the servants left, I handed the clerk my ruble, and he marked the margin along the edge of the parchment with my thumbprint. Thirty-six marks, but eight of them were crossed out for eight months of food that no longer came free. He never looked in my face again after the night he'd read the indentureship agreement to me. I was just more numbers for him to record. Is that how he survived keeping track of the mistress's cruelties?

Staver was often gone during the week, but he always found me on Nedelja, the seventh day, helping me finish my half-day of work. He filled my ears with music, my mouth with laughter, and my mind with strategies and stories. We both grew in our skill at chess. He played his balalaika and sang, then told me the jokes and stories shared around his dinner table or sung by a minstrel around the evening fireside.

I held my heart and hope at a distance, never letting us touch again. And he respected it. Though sometimes his eyes filled with hurt when I pulled away from his proffered hand. It would have been easier if I used my half-day to work on my preparations. But each time Staver came to my side, I made an excuse to myself. *Next week. I'm tired. I need at least a few hours of rest.*

The days grew shorter, bursting into the flame of autumn, before being snuffed out by winter. Eight of my months had fled. Two more months would bring spring and my sixteenth birthday. Couldn't the days lengthen out again and the months stop?

A snowstorm dimmed the afternoon to an almost-night. I drew closer to the small fire in the separate kitchen, trying to warm myself as I scrubbed woolens in cold water. The main kitchen in the manor house would be warmer, but I wasn't a house servant. Even the servants' shed had a roaring fire in its clay fireplace that spanned one wall. And the servants' noisy gossip filled the air. I scrubbed harder. I'd rather be in the silence and semi-warmth, scrubbing woolens, than hear more jabs about the time I spent with the master's son. Couldn't they see I was nothing more than a friend to him, and let me have a small measure of happiness?

Staver entered the kitchen with a gust of wind and a swirl of snowflakes. He must have come from the manor house. What was he doing out in that storm? Even the short walk had covered his fur cap and coat with snow. He shed his coat, hat, and gloves, and laid them on a chair by the fire.

He'd grown taller and broader across the shoulders. His tousled hair had darkened to a rich honey. Three days earlier, he'd celebrated his seventeenth birthday to dancing and music. All the noble families had come. He was old enough to choose a betrothed from among his kind. He'd be expected to by his eighteenth birthday. I didn't want to be there when he chose. Our friendship would have to end. *Please don't choose before I leave. Let me have these last two months.*

"The storm is fierce and cold." His voice had broadened to a rich tenor.

"Cold enough to frost the fire's flames." I pulled the master's woolen underthings from the cool wash water. I shifted so the scrub basin stood between him and me, though it set me further from the fire.

He stepped around, brushing his arm against my shoulder. "How can I help?"

I flicked some water at him, and he backed up laughing, though it didn't reach his eyes.

I smiled apologetically. I didn't like pushing him away, but I had to. "Will you tell the rest of the story, the one you started last time, while I finish the wash?"

"I can help more than that." He stepped close again, but not touching me, his scent mingling with the lye soap.

I wanted to lean against him. To let him hold me. Instead, I flicked water again, splashing his front.

He held up his hands. "You win. A story." He backed up halfway across the kitchen where I couldn't splash him. "I'll tell you of the ogre that invited his guest to dinner, then changed into a wolf, and—"

"Stop!" I sent more water splashing his way. He knew I hated the ogre stories. Just as I hated being called ogre-child. He was just getting back at me.

He laughed. "Oh, you wanted the rest of the other story. Where was I last time?"

"The fool of the world had just asked the tsar for his daughter's hand in marriage."

Lightning pulsed the room bright for a moment. Thunder rolled outside, muffled by the snow. A second flash illuminated Staver's face as he settled on a barrel of apples, leaned forward with his elbows on his knees, and began. "The tsar wouldn't, he couldn't, marry his daughter to a peasant boy. But the boy had brought the flying ship. And that was the only requirement for her marriage. The tsar had to find some way around his promise. 'My good young man, my fine son-in-law, we must feast to celebrate.' Then the tsar spread a feast that would feed hundreds of men. 'You must honor me by finishing it all. If you don't, I'll banish you from my realm.' The fool—"

A flash far brighter than the previous lit the kitchen, followed by a deafening boom that shook the pots hanging from the ceiling.

I dropped a sodden skirt into the water and covered my ears with soapy hands.

More lightning and thunder overlapped each other. White spots swam between Staver and me.

He stood.

Lightning shot from the fireplace.

Pain flashed up my arms and over my body.

I flew backwards.

My head and shoulders hit the floor first.

My ears rang.

The room was dark.

"—sa, Lisa!" Arms wrapped around me, pulling me into a sitting position, my skin screamed each place he touched. "Are you hurt?"

"I, I—" I couldn't get my tongue to work.

"Come." He laid his coat over my shoulders, nestled his cap over my hair, and pulled me out of the kitchen. Snow drove sideways. Squares of light floated in the distance. Staver guided me towards them.

Lightning flashed, blinding out anything but the white driving against my face. Thunder rolled, crashing its sound against my back. I stumbled to my knees.

"It's not far. Come." Staver helped me to my feet and pulled me onward. The squares of light became the manor windows. Staver pushed the door open, and we tumbled through as more thunder crashed.

I huddled on the floor. My stomach churned, my head

pounded, and my face and arms felt like someone had scraped them with a sanding block then seared them.

"Staver!" The mistress's voice cut through my discomfort. "What are you doing out in that storm?"

"Vasilisa is hurt."

"Then she should go to the servant quarters and get one of them to nurse her."

"No, Matushka, she's staying here, and we need a physician."

I pushed myself to my knees. "I'm fine," I lied. At least my tongue worked again.

The mistress gasped.

"Get the physician, now," Staver commanded.

A maid standing in the corner of the room bowed. "I'll tell the coachman your order."

The mistress held up her hand to stop the maid. "Staver, I'll help her, and even send for the physician, if you promise me you'll—"

"I promise. If she gets well. I promise. Just help her."

She nodded to the maid. "Send for the physician as soon as the storm dies down."

"She needs help now!"

"I will help." She knelt next to me and touched my face. "What happened?"

I winced. Her touch burned.

"Lightning." Staver helped me to my feet and his mother took my arm on the other side.

I stumbled, supported between them, to a couch, and lay down.

"Get me cold water, bandages, and ointment." The mistress bustled about, putting a pillow below my feet and laying a blanket across me. She dabbed my burnt face and injured limbs with a damp cloth.

I bit my cheek to keep from screaming in agony.

By the time the physician arrived, the mistress had smeared an ointment over my burnt skin and bandaged me.

The physician shook his head. "My dear lady, you had no need to call for me. You've done as much as I could have."

"She's a valuable servant. I'll not have her crippled from service. Now tell me what ointments to use for burns and infection."

Staver smiled weakly at me.

What had he promised? Was it worth asking his mother to help me? She had helped me, more than I would ever have expected. "Thank you, Mistress."

She glared at me. "You'll thank me by resting and recovering so you can get back to your duties. Now sleep."

A timid tapping at the door woke me from a half-sleep of shattered pain.

Mama knelt at my side. "My child. Oh, my child." Her tears dripped onto my bandaged face. She turned and grasped the mistress's hand, placing her face against the back of the hand. "Thank you, Mistress, for tending to her. She heals quick. I'll take her back to the servants' quarters and tend to her there."

Staver coughed quietly.

The mistress glanced at him and then back to Mama. "She'll stay here until her burns heal so she doesn't take infection. You may visit when you are done with your duties."

Mama kissed the unburnt palm of my hand and left. The mistress left by a different door.

Only Staver remained. He came and sat by my side.

"What did you promise?"

He looked down at his hands. "I'll tell you later." And he sang.

> Fields of wheat, golden red.
> River flowing wild.

> Eagle soaring overhead.
> Sun from cloud unveiled.
>
> Fox and hound in lively race.
> Bear hunting honey.
> You and I shall find this place.
> Let us take this journey.

I slipped into sleep to his rich voice creating beautiful images.

7

———

I woke to pain, endured pain through a day of bandage changes and broths, and fled to sleep with pain holding to my skirttail. Pus-filled infections and fevers joined the legion of pain. The week passed in a blur.

Strong arms carried me under my back and knees. A clean, sharp scent of birch snapped in my nose. Who carried me? I tried to open my eyes, but they were glued as with pine pitch. A breath brushed against my blistered face. Where the breath touched, the pain eased. "Thank you," I murmured.

With my words, the pain pushed forward, shoving me out of the dream and back onto a straw cot. I lay in a small, mostly bare, room. A table tucked against the cot and jars of ointments covered it. Anna, an old house servant, dozed on a chair. It was her bed that I'd taken, yet she tended to me without a grudging remark.

Noon sun poured through the wax-paper window. The room was strangely silent. "Staver?" He'd been there when I woke earlier that morning. His voice was a balm on pains that couldn't be eased any other way.

Anna jerked her head up from sleep. "The young master is

tending to his studies. Your mother came to see you again. She left this." She handed me a cloth-wrapped object.

I unwrapped it. In the nest of cloth lay a bronze amulet, about the size of my palm. Etched into it, a wolf howled to the moon, every line of its body showing its plaintive note, till I could almost hear it tremble through the room.

Papa had worn it. He'd strung it on a cord and hung it about his neck. Where had Mama hidden it all these years?

I traced the etching. *Oh, Papa. Did you carry me in my sleep?*

The light caught it and cast a warm glow against my face. "Can I have a bit of string?"

Anna brought over a length of twine and strung the amulet for me. "That's a beauty of a picture, but wild enough to make my arms prickle."

I reached up to place it over my head, but my arms stopped halfway up. Curse the scarring. "Please put it over my head and place it under my dress." I wanted it against my skin.

She did.

As the amulet slid down and lay over my heart, a warmth pulsed through me. An openness pushed against everything around me until I felt that I was floating.

A woman's voice came from far away. "Girl? Girl!"

The amulet lifted off me, and I crashed back into the throbbing pain of my burns.

Anna leaned over me. "Girl, can you hear me?"

"Yes," I sobbed.

"Thank goodness. I thought you were dying. Your eyes rolled back, and you started shuddering like the quaking aspens."

"Please, give it back."

"No. It hurt you something awful."

"Please. It took away the hurt."

She looked at me then at the amulet hanging from her hand. "I know a little house magic, enough to tend small hurts and illnesses, but this is something stronger than I ever felt. It's not for a child."

"I won't wear it. Just let me have it. My mama gave it to me."

She frowned, studying the lines of the amulet, then tucked it into her pocket. "I'll give it back to your mother when she visits again."

I'd get it back from her when she was sleeping. I lay back and let her start the changing of my bandages.

She sucked in her breath as she unwrapped my right arm. "By all powers."

My arm was covered in peeling scabs and under the scabbing peeked red and raw new skin.

She pulled out the amulet and studied it again. Then she laid it in my hands. "This is a treasure to keep secret, or you'll lose it as sure as you lost your baby teeth."

"Thank you." I sniffed at a tear. "Will you please place it back over my heart?"

"Only for a moment. I fear too long will kill you."

The moment the amulet lay over my heart, the openness pushed me into a floating space. Warmth flowed through me. Tremors of energy radiated out from my heart to my fingertips and toes. Then the amulet left my skin, and my heart felt as if it ripped from my chest. I tumbled into blackness.

"Vasilisa."

I blinked.

A blur solidified into Staver. He leaned close with a pinched brow. Even his concerned lines were handsome.

"Hello, Staver." My voice came out a whisper, rasping against a dry throat.

"I'm glad to hear your voice again."

"Again? I saw you this morning."

"You've been asleep for three days. Old Anna said she gave you some herbs to help you heal. I didn't expect them to make you sleep like the dead. How are you feeling?"

"I don't hurt as much." I tugged at a bandage on my arm, unwrapping it the first inch. Pink skin showed underneath.

Staver touched my arm, his eyes wide and his mouth wider. "She worked a miracle. I'll get Anna and your mother." He ran from the room.

Anna had been right to only allow me to wear the amulet a short time. Three days! It could have killed me.

I tried to sit and fell back to lying. My skin was whole, but I was still weak. Why was I weak if I was healed? Maybe the amulet increased the speed that I could heal, but took just as much energy as if I'd healed naturally. Maybe. I hoped I'd get my strength back.

Staver came back with Anna, the mistress, and my mama. The small servant room barely held the four of them and the bed where I lay.

Mama and Anna unwrapped my bandages. I touched my face without grimacing and found smooth skin.

The mistress watched. "Thank you, Anna, for your care of her. I am impressed. You will now be our family healer."

Anna bowed her head. "I would not dare to treat your family with the same techniques. They are dangerous and could just as easily have killed her. I pray your family never has such need."

The mistress tapped the bedpost as she scanned me as though I was a problem she wished to be rid of, then turned to Staver. "She is healed. Now you must keep your promise."

"I will. Give me two weeks." He sat down on a stool beside me and took my hand.

"Staver." The mistress pointed out the door. "You've already neglected your studies too much in your care for this girl. She is healed. She will be back to her duties, and you must be to yours."

He squeezed my hand and lowered his voice, "I'll be back as soon as I can." He followed his mother out of the small room.

Once they were gone, Anna pulled the amulet from her apron pocket and handed it to Mama. "You should keep this safe again. It is too powerful a thing."

Mama tucked it into her own pocket. "Thank you Anna, for everything." She propped me up with pillows and spoon-fed me broth. "My little Vasilisa, can you walk?"

I tried to sit and fell back again. "I'm still too weak."

"I'll get some menservants to carry you to the servant's quarters. I dare not trespass on the mistress's hospitality longer."

I LAY in a bed of ferns. White clouds danced in a bright sky behind a lacing of aspen branches. An eagle hovered in the blue dome, sometimes disappearing behind a cloud. A gust of wind shook the aspen, and three leaves drifted down, dipping and sliding on the air like a child sledding. One leaf landed on my cheek.

A hand plucked it off.

I tried to turn my head, but I was too weak to do more than look upward at the sky.

Staver leaned over me. Longing made his face more handsome. But this was a dream. He didn't long for me. This was just what I wanted. I closed my eyes to shut away the lie.

He pressed his lips to my cheek where the leaf had landed.

I could not turn toward or away from him.

8

―――――――

"VASILISA, what are you doing out here?" Staver knelt by the straw pallet that Mama and I shared. He touched my cheek.

His touch sent tremors and tingles over my skin. I leaned into his hand, closing my eyes and melting into the warm softness.

"Vasilisa?" His question came pinched with worry.

I bit the inside of my cheek. I wasn't strong enough to keep the sparrow hope in its cage. I'd kept it locked for eight months. But Staver was too kind, too gentle. He held the key. If he opened it and hope flew free, it would fall like a bird turned to stone when I left for the forest. But if I didn't leave for the forest, I'd always be a servant, even forty years from now. I needed to make him leave me alone.

I rolled my head away from his hand and muttered into the blankets. "My skin is healed. The risk for infection is past. Please go. Your mother will be angry if you stay. I've already interrupted your studies enough."

"Lisa." He scooted closer to me and brushed my lock of black hair from my face, mingling it with all my red hair. "You still need someone to tend to you. You will sleep in the manor house tonight, and every night until you heal."

"Staver. I'm fine. I just need a few days' rest. I'll rest better out here with my mother to watch over me. Don't force me back where I'm not wanted."

His eyes grew stormy. "She shouldn't make you feel that way. You are wanted. But I'll not place you where you are uncomfortable."

"Thank you, Staver. Now please go."

The concern returned to his face. "You'll have music while you rest." He ran his thumb over my cheek.

I clenched my hands beneath the blanket. If I asked a question he didn't want to answer maybe he'd go. "What did you promise the mistress?"

He stiffened. "I'll tell you later."

Good, maybe he'd go. But he stayed beside me. I tried again. "Now, please. I have to stop worrying that you promised to tattoo the family crest on your face or travel to the far east in trade."

He laughed and leaned close. His breath brushed against my cheek.

I bit my lip. *Please don't. I don't want to feel like this for you.*

"I'll tell you, so you can stop worrying. I promised her I'd announce my chosen betrothed in two weeks."

Sparrow hope froze in its cage. "You've chosen?"

"I chose years ago."

I was only a friend. I'd never been more. By law, I could never be more. He'd chosen some nobleman's daughter—years ago. Why did I ever think his kindness was more than friendship?

I forced a smile. "I'm happy for you. I wish you all joy. I'm sure she's wonderful."

"She is. She's everything I could hope for in a friend and

future wife. I must finish some preparations then I'll ask her, though I'm sure she knows my feelings for her. She's—"

"I'm tired." I looked away so he wouldn't see my tears.

"I'm sorry, Lisa. I'll let you rest. But you should have something better than this." He toed the straw pallet. "I'll be right back, then I'll make music to help you rest."

"Not tonight. Just let me sleep." If I spoke another word, I'd shatter like an icicle falling from the eves.

He left and came back with a down pillow and quilt.

I feigned sleep as he lifted my head and placed it on the pillow, then spread the heavy quilt over me. When he left, I soaked the softness with my tears. I used to be Vasilisa the strong, the wild child from the forest. Why then was I so weak? I couldn't bear to hear him announce his betrothed. I'd gather my strength and leave before he announced her, even if I had to crawl. I'd find some cave and start my life there. I knew enough to survive. I'd come back for Mama when spring thawed the ground.

Wind whispered through snow-laden birch. "Vasilisa, Vasilisa."

"I'm coming. I have nothing left here. I'm coming."

The dream faded into the sniffling, coughing noises of my fellow sleeping servants. It had been three days since Staver visited. I ached with his absence.

I slipped away from Mama's warmth. She didn't even stir. She was exhausted from caring for me, as well as tending to her duties.

I donned every layer of clothing I had, from my summer dress to my winter wools, and wrapped my thin blanket over the top. I shook with the effort, but it was much better than when I couldn't even stand three days before.

The stone tsarina lay heavy in my apron pocket. I'd carried her with me everywhere. Now I must leave her behind. I rubbed my finger along her rose crown and wise face, then laid her under the down pillow. Staver would find her when he came back, or Mama would and give her to him.

It was good he'd been gone the previous three days. I couldn't have borne him talking about his chosen betrothed.

Servants shifted and moaned as I stepped around them. They were used to ignoring my early rising.

Then I slipped into the pre-dawn chill. Snow lay heavy on the ground and icicles taller than I clung to the roof.

I followed the slick path as far as I could before breaking through snow to my treasure box under the willow tree. I pried at the stone with my gloved fingers. It wouldn't budge from the icy earth. All my arrows, my bow, my tanned leather for shelter, everything was in there. I grabbed a wrist-thick branch and couldn't break it. I needed my strength, but it hadn't returned yet. I snapped off a narrower branch and wedged it under the rock.

Finally, it lifted.

I pulled my bow and arrows out and slung them across my back, slipped the hunting knife I'd forged into my sash, tucked a pouch of snares at my other hip, and laid my stitched patches of leather over my head and shoulders like a shell.

I was ready.

Then I rested against the willow tree. The sun rose before my shaking stopped enough that I could walk again.

I pushed back up the slope to the beaten path and headed out the manor gates and onto the road. The trees that lined the road reached their bare arms into the sky. Snow blanketed the master's fields, and smoke drifted from the chimneys of window-less field-worker huts. Windows let in too much cold for the winter. No one would watch me leave. No one would warn the mistress and stop me.

The sun stretched its beams sideways and inched higher above the horizon as I trudged along the road. I'd hoped to be in the forest before it rose, but I'd be lucky to reach the shelter of the trees by mid-morning at my slow pace.

Ahead, the door of a hut swung open and an ox shouldered young man ran out to the privy.

No. I lurched off the road and rolled into the stubble of the field.

He turned and glanced at where I'd been and tilted his head.

I silently cursed then pleaded. *No one's there. Look away. Go on with your morning business.*

He turned away and entered the privy.

I scrambled to my feet and trudged again along the road. I was more than halfway along the line of huts.

"Is that the Forest Child?" Gleb's familiar mocking voice came from behind me, "Hah! You look like a turtle today. Where are you stealing off to with a humped back?"

I trudged on. If I ran, he'd chase. Maybe he'd ignore me after he'd vented his words.

"Forest Child!" he sang. "You walk as slow as a turtle too. I wager I can catch you today."

He'd thrown dirt clods at me almost a year before and I'd beat him across the back with a branch for it. He'd not bothered me since then. But today, his footsteps thudded behind. I hurried my steps.

Another worker's door opened, and Dmitri stepped out with a bucket in one hand. He stared at me with a slack mouth. He'd grown taller in a year but his face still lacked intelligence.

"Hey Dmitri, you want some morning fun?" Gleb called.

Dmitri stood staring a moment longer, then dropped the bucket and picked up a wedge of firewood from his porch. "Yeh."

He stalked me from the right while Gleb's steps thudded closer behind.

I swerved to the left and broke into a jog.

Dmitri grinned and swung the firewood.

As the wood left his hand, I ducked, throwing off my balance. I smacked against the icy road with my arm and shoulder.

"Got her now!" Gleb or Dmitri? It didn't matter.

I scrambled to my feet as the first kick caught my thigh. I fell again and rolled away. My bow and quiver of arrows stopped me on my back.

Gleb and Dmitri stood over me with the same cruel delight that they'd shown over a broken-winged nightingale. I'd beaten them away then.

I drew my hunting knife.

Dmitri stepped back.

Gleb scowled. "You think I'm afraid of your little butter spreader. Put it away or you won't be able to walk when we're done with you."

I'd be lucky to be breathing. I held out the knife, keeping it pointed at Gleb's chest. My arm shook with the weight of it.

Gleb took a step forward. "You're just a weakling today. Something's taken away your devil strength."

Keep talking. I still have enough strength. I lurched to my feet, swiping the knife through the air.

Gleb jumped backwards as my knife snagged against his quilted vest and stopped. He grabbed my wrist and wrenched it.

Fire shot up my arm.

The knife dropped from my limp hand.

Gleb shoved me to the ground. "Come on Dmitri."

I rolled up, pulling my patched leather tightly around me, and covered my head with my arms.

They kicked me with ice-stiffened boots.

"Stop!" A rich voice of command.

Staver?

The kicks ceased.

"Well, if it ain't the master's sissy son." Gleb's voice dripped with scorn. "Where's your servants? Your girl-guard won't help you today."

"Get away from the lady."

Gleb laughed. "Lady, is she? Lady of dishwater and bedbugs."

"Step away from her."

"Or what?"

"I'll fight you."

"Oh, ho. Is that how it is?"

I peeked from my leather covering. Staver's tooled leather boots ran towards me. Would Gleb and Dmitri hurt him too? They were in rabid spirits and could do any numbers of cruelties without thinking of the cost to their freedoms or lives.

I lurched to my feet, ignoring the pain shooting down my sides and legs. Staver grabbed my arm before I fell again, and we stood facing Gleb, just a reach away.

He glared at us. Dmitri stood a short distance off, shuffling his feet and looking between Gleb and Staver. Gleb picked up my hunting knife. Staver pulled a knife from his belt. It was ornamental at best, nothing compared to the thick, solid blade I'd made and Gleb held.

I had to do something—even if they took me back for running away from my indenturement. I screamed, "Help! Villains are attacking the master's son!"

Doors burst open from multiple huts, and men and women piled out. Gleb growled and thrust the blade at me. Staver thrust out his own blade, and turned Gleb's. The hunting knife skipped along the ornamental one and pushed up Staver's furred coat sleeve.

A man stumbled drunkenly from his porch. "Stop, son!" Other men raced towards us.

Gleb looked at the blood beading up from Staver's arm and at the knife in his hand. He dropped it and ran. Two men tackled him to the ground before he took five steps.

Dmitri sat down on the ground and held his head in his hands. The others—? I swayed.

"Vasilisa?" Staver took hold of both my shoulders and looked into my face. "We need to get you home." He turned to the gathered field workers. "Get a wagon or something."

A work-lined woman stepped forward. "Young Master Staver, you are hurt. Let us tend to your wound first and then we'll take you back to the manor."

"Very well, but tend to Vasilisa first. I'm only scratched."

"No," I said. I tried not to lean on Staver, but I was uncertain if I could stand if I didn't. "Tend to the young master first."

After seating both of us on a table in one hut, the woman cleaned and wrapped his arm. "The scoundrel Gleb will go to the prison-work camps for this."

If Gleb damaged Staver's hand such that he couldn't play his balalaika, I'll—I balled up my fists.

Staver touched one of my fists. "Vasilisa, why did you leave?"

I looked into his face and crumpled. "Because you were soon to be betrothed and I could no longer be your friend."

His mouth opened. Surprise mingled with shock. He patted around in his coat and pulled out the black stone tsarina. "Vasilisa. I gave the tsarina to the one I desire for my own tsarina. I thought you understood. You are my friend and the one I want for my future wife."

My face must have matched his in open-mouthed shock, because he laughed.

The woman tending him thumped to sit on the dirt floor.

"But Staver," I finally said, "I can't... we can't. The tsar's laws won't allow a commoner to marry nobility."

His brow creased. "I know. I've been working on that. I think I have a solution. But you will never again be treated as a servant. I have at least that much figured out."

He wanted to marry me? I was the one he'd chosen years ago? "But why?"

He cupped my face with his good hand. "Because I love you. I have since you showed your elfin face over the wall and laughed at my first attempted songs on the balalaika."

"I'm just a servant girl."

"You are Vasilisa. Though you've served your whole life, I've never met someone as free as you. You were never a servant. You are the playfulness of the otter, the fierce joy of the shrike in flight, the honor of the hunting hound. Your quick-mindedness surpasses any of my tutors. You—"

"But why do *you* love me?"

He took my hands in his, though he winced as he moved the bandaged one. "Because you always treated me with kindness just as I was. You accepted me, when all else wanted me to change. Because you listened to me, talked to me, helped me see things in a new way. You are my Vasilisa. When I gave you my tsarina, I gave you my heart. I'm complete only with you."

Why, why, why? The question echoed in my head. I wanted to marry him. But I'd known for so long I never could that I'd hardened my heart against this joy. Could he find a way against the tsar's law? Did I trust him enough to hope? "I wish you'd told me earlier."

"I wanted to. But I couldn't in honor ask for your hand when I couldn't be sure to keep that promise. I promise you now that I will find a way and I will marry you." He paused searching my face. "If you will have me."

"Even with all my faults?"

"I know and love each of them. You already know all of mine."

"You have none."

"Then you have none, too. Will you?" His earnest face pinched.

"Yes, Staver!" I threw my arms around him. Each spot I'd been kicked cried out against the movement. I stifled a whimper.

Staver gently wrapped me in his arms. "Let's get you to your new home. I'll miss seeing you daily, but you need proper care."

"My new home?"

He held me close. "There is an elderly noble couple without children. I've convinced them to adopt you. By law they can't make you their heir, but in every other way you will be their daughter."

A noble family? I'd be treated like a daughter? How long had he been working on finding a way to marry me? A week? No! To convince a noble family to take me in was the careful work of months or years. And for his own parents not to know. What would they do when they found out? What would the mistress do? "Staver." I lifted my face and tears traced down it. "I can't go to the noble family. The mistress will find me and take me back. I have to go into the forest where I'll be safe. I'm indentured to her."

He gripped my shoulder with his good hand. "How much and how long ago?"

"Two thousand rubles. Last spring."

He clenched both hands. Blood bloomed along his bandaged cut. His gentle face folded into anger. "She did this after I went into the forest with you."

I nodded.

He turned to the peasant woman who still sat on the floor in a dazed heap. "Take care of her."

The woman trembled. "What if the mistress—"

His jaw stiffened. "Then hide her!"

She jumped to her feet and bowed, her whole body trembling.

He placed a hand on her shoulder. "I'll be back in an hour. Tell the other field hands that if they keep quiet about what happened this morning, then each person will get five rubles, even the littlest children."

Her eyes widened. "Yes, Master Staver. No one will say a word."

He turned back to me. "Vasilisa, you are safe. From now on, I'll always keep you safe." And he left.

I PACED the small room of the field-hand's cottage. My muscles pulled in complaint, but I couldn't stay still.

The woman who'd tended to Staver and me handed me a cup of hot barley tea. "Please rest. Master Staver will be back."

But what if the mistress came instead? What if she imprisoned me for running away from the indenturement? What could Staver do against her? He was still the son, not the master. And the master did everything the mistress said.

Staver promised I'd be safe. Could he keep that promise?

A hunting horn sounded, followed by the distant jangle of horse tack and indistinct voices.

I retreated against the far wall and looked for a weapon. The hut held a few pots and pans. A broom leaned against one corner. There. Under the table lay my bundle—bow, arrows, knife. I grabbed my bow and a handful of arrows. My legs wavered in weakness as I stood again.

The voices grew closer. A deep one called, "We'll catch that fox. She'll not escape today."

My arms trembled as I set an arrow in the bow. I wasn't strong yet, but I'd not go with the mistress willingly.

"Put that down! Come hide!" the woman whispered as she grabbed at the bow.

I jerked away, caught my balance, and stepped behind the table. It provided some shielding. The woman looked from me to the door and scurried behind the curtained sleeping area.

The voices drew close to the door. A hound bayed. "The dogs have scented her. She can't be far."

I braced my leg against the table and drew the bow, ready for the door to open.

Baying shook the air, and shouts mingled with whoops and galloping hooves. They thundered to—and then past the hut.

I stumbled to the door and opened it a crack. Five young noblemen, dressed in festive hunting tunics, galloped away from the huts and towards the forest. They were hunting a real fox. Not me. I slipped the door shut again, let my bow drop to the ground, and sat trembling against the wall.

STAVER RETURNED in an hour with a mule-drawn wagon. It wasn't one of the master's wagons but a hired one from the town. Mama rode in the back. She hopped out and ran to where I stood leaning against the hut door.

Staver reached me first and whispered in my ear. "You are no longer indentured. I've paid the fine. The clerk voided the agreement. You are free." He caught me under my arms as my legs wobbled.

I'm free. I shook my head, not quite understanding. I hadn't been free since Papa died and Mama took us from the forest. *Staver bought my freedom.* "Thank you."

He looked into my eyes and seemed to understand all the words I wanted to say within those two, then leaned closer and brushed his lips against mine—a gentle touch, full of promised joy to come.

My eyes overflowed at his touch, and I let hope leap from its cage.

9

———

IT TOOK a full day by wagon traveling south to reach my new home. I rested on a bed of mats and blankets so thick that I hardly felt the wagon jostle over the frozen ruts. Fire-warmed bricks lay wrapped by my feet and a thick fur cap protected my head from the chill. A bearskin lay heavily over me. Mama nestled next to me, stroking my face. Staver sat on the other side of me and sang songs of springtime. The wagoner added occasional rhythm as he clucked the horse along.

"Staver?"

He stopped singing and tilted his head.

"What place will my mama have there?"

"I've arranged for her to be your maidservant. She'll only have the work that you give to her." His voice took on a lilting note. "I imagine she'll rest for the first time in her life."

My eyes prickled and I squeezed Mama's hand. Staver had thought of everything.

Our road ran through a tall forest, over a bridge, between large fields lying fallow, and to a manor topped with a striped onion dome. I gaped.

Staver laughed as he motioned to the expansive grounds. "Welcome to your new home. Duke Nicholas and Duchess Manya eagerly await you."

"Duke and duchess? What did you tell them about me?"

"Only what is true. Your goodness, cleverness, sweetness."

"I think you are describing someone else. They'll throw me out as soon as they see me."

"They know you were a servant. They know of your recent injury from lightning. And I'll tell them of the attack today. They also know that you love the woods as they do, that you stood up to a bear, that you bore unjust punishment without complaint, that you spent every spare moment of your time learning new skills to care for your mother."

"I'm frightened." The words slipped out before I could stop them.

He clasped my hands. "What frightens you?"

I looked around—searching for the right words. "Nothing. I'm being foolish."

He dug his boot into the straw beside me. "Then I am as foolish. I was afraid you'd die when the lightning hurt you. I fear that you'll slip off into the forest and I'll never see you again."

My mouth dropped open. "I didn't know."

"I didn't want to worry you with my fears. But now that I've told you mine, please tell me yours."

"I—I'm frightened that I'm not good enough for you."

"Vasilisa." He gripped my hands tighter.

I pulled them away. "I'm frightened that you won't find a way for us to marry. I'm frightened to love you and then lose you."

Staver's shoulders trembled, and laughter followed. "We're both fools. We fear the same things. Though I already love you, so I only fear losing you."

"I do love you." The words came out before I could stop them.

"Then trust me."

The grand entrance door opened. Out stepped a silver-haired man with a long serious face. Beside him stood a woman, her wheat-yellow hair streaked with grey. She grasped his hand. "Nicholas, she's here."

Nicholas patted her hand and spoke to us. "Welcome, Staver, welcome, Nevena, and most of all, welcome, daughter Vasilisa."

He motioned with his hand and four serving men carried out a blanketed litter.

Staver put his arms around me to help me from the wagon onto it.

I pressed my face into his fur coat. "Staver, don't go." It was too much. I was falling. If he left, I'd be adrift in this dream world.

"I'll see you again as soon as I've spoken with Duke Nicholas."

I was being a baby. Where was Vasilisa the strong? I let go of Staver and lay on the litter. The servants bore me away from Staver, up the stairs and into an entrance rich with green marble. Then we went up more stairs and through a long hall, and into a cavernous room, before they laid me on a bed softer than duckling down. Mama kept at my side. She helped me into a tub of hot water that fit all of me, and not just up to my ankles. Scents of roses and lavender floated up from it. The water nestled all my aching parts until they almost didn't hurt.

A woman in a white smock entered after I'd soaked for long enough to prune my fingers. "If you are ready, I will tend to your injuries."

"Thank you, mistress—"

"Not mistress. I'm Irina, my lady's healer until she is well."

"Is the duchess ill?"

Irina smiled and shook her head. "She is well. You are my lady. I am your healer."

"I'm Vasilisa."

"My lady Vasilisa."

"Just Vasilisa."

She nodded and helped me stand from the bath. Then she hissed through her teeth. "You should not be standing." She motioned my mama over, and the two of them helped me lie down. "If I'd known it was this bad, I'd have had servants carry you to and from the bath, despite Master Staver saying you needed time alone." She muttered as she applied balms. "Deep bruising. Possibly, broken ribs. You look as though horses trampled you."

"Gleb and Dmitri kick as hard as horses." My laugh died halfway as my ribs protested the movement.

Irina's brow pinched. "They deserve to be on the receiving end of it." She wrapped my ribs and helped me into a flannel nightgown and into bed. "That's all I can do tonight. Drink this tea to help ease the pain, and I'll see you again tomorrow."

When she left, it was just Mama and me again. The tea turned the world into a foggy warmth.

THE YELLOW BIRCH leaves flickered like a dragon's golden trove. The howling song of a wolf echoed, unanswered by his pack. His plaintive notes hung in the air. My chest tightened. He called for me.

"I'm coming!" I ran through the birch trees, leaping from fallen tree to fallen tree. One log rolled, trapping my foot between it and another. "Wait for me. I'm coming."

"Vasilisa," Staver called behind me.

The wolf howled.

I tugged and twisted my foot, trying to slip it from between the two logs.

A hand touched my brow. An old man's voice invaded my dream. "She's not fevered. But something troubles her sleep."

I tried to push the voice away. I had to get unstuck and follow, but which one—Staver or the wolf?

"Vasilisa." Staver's voice was closer. A hand touched my shoulder and gently shook it. The woods shimmered and grew foggy. "Vasilisa, please wake. I must leave, and I would tell you why."

"Leave? Why?" I fought to pull out of the dream, but it held me as securely as the logs held my foot.

The old man's voice pushed in again, "I'm sorry. Irina gave her a tea to help with the pain. It must have had a more potent effect in her. I didn't expect her to sleep so long."

"Please take care of her," Staver's voice whispered. "I fear she'll not understand."

"Can you not delay your leaving by another day?"

"You know I can't. They could be here anytime. I must go while I still have an honorable option."

I tore at the rotten wood. Splinters slid under my nails.

"What should I tell her?" said the old voice.

Silence. Then Staver spoke. "Tell her I've found a way for us to marry, but I must be away for six months to do it. Tell her I love her and I'll write every day."

"Do you think she'll be satisfied with that half-truth?"

"Tell her the whole truth if necessary. But please wait until she's healed. She almost died when struck by the lightning, and to have this beating added to it... she needs time to heal before you can let her worry for me."

Where is he going? Please Staver, wait for me!

"The letters will be a comfort to her," said the old voice. "Does she read?"

"No. But you can teach her. She has the wit to rival the tsar's wise men."

"What if the war comes before then?"

"Keep her safe."

The wolf's plaintive note shuddered the air. I turned. A black wolf nosed my cheek. I wrapped my arms around his neck, and the voices from the cold outer world disappeared.

10

———————

*H*EAVY, *trapping weight lay over me. I lay sinking in a grasping bog. If I could roll from the bog onto firmer ground, I'd be free. I pushed against the weight and rolled.*

The bog released me off a cliff.

I struck hard ground.

My eyes flew open. A wood floor lay under my squished face. My ribs cried as I sucked in a breath.

"Irina, Nevena, help!" cried a woman's voice.

Several hands grabbed my arms and helped me back to the soft bed from which I had rolled. Mama, the healer woman, the duchess, and the duke surrounded me. Concern filled each face, except for Mama's. She chuckled. "That is one way to wake up. You'll have to learn how to get out of a bed, instead of roll off a sleeping mat."

The healer woman, Irina, clucked. "We'll get you a bed made up on the floor. I'm glad to see you awake, though sleep probably was the best thing for you to heal. How do you feel?"

My nose pulsed from flattening it against the floor. But my ribs hurt less than they had before I fell into the nightmared sleep. "I'd rather not drink your tea for pain again."

She nodded as she checked my temperature and pulse, then prodded my wrapped ribs.

I sucked in my breath. "They still hurt, if that's what you're asking with your fingers." I blushed as I realized my rudeness. "I'm sorry, Master and Mistress, for my complaints. I'm much better than I was. Thank you for caring for me."

The duchess grasped my hand. "Not mistress, but Baba, since I am old enough to be your grandmother. That is what we will be to you, your Baba and Dyeda."

Maybe, someday, I could call them that. But the most important person was missing. "Where's Staver? He promised to come see me."

Duke Nicholas pulled a chair closer to my bed and leaned forward. "You've been asleep for two days. He had to leave. I'm sorry. He'll be gone six months. But he'll write often."

Fragments of nightmares flitted behind my aching forehead. *Coming war. Staver in danger. Trapped and unable to help him.* "You're telling me only a part." I grimaced as I pushed to sit on the bed. "And you promised him to not tell me the whole until I healed. But I'll worry about him either way, so you should tell me."

Mama hissed, "Vasilisa, remember your place."

Duke Nicholas laid a hand on Mama's arm. "She is no longer a servant. She has every right to speak such." He turned to me. "I promised Staver, and I'll keep that promise. So I recommend you focus on healing so I can tell you the rest."

He wasn't what I expected of a nobleman. I sat straighter. "I heal quickly. Though I have other questions I hope you will answer. First, why did you take me in—an ignorant servant?"

His face darkened. "You should have never been a servant."

The duchess patted his arm. "Forgive his severe face. It's just, you look like our daughter. She had hair as red as yours, though without the black streak, and her eyes were a paler blue. She didn't live past her seventeenth year. The plague took her."

"Oh." Did my coming bring them pain? Would they expect me to be like her?

The duchess continued. "You are a balm on wounded memories. Staver visited us often this last year, despite our not having any young folk. He didn't mind listening to us ramble about past years. He didn't talk much, but when he did, he spoke of music and of a certain girl. I grew to love you as he did. When he spoke of his desire to marry you, and how he'd do anything to make that possible, I wanted it for him too. You shall be Lady Vasilisa."

I laughed, trying to shake loose the tightness in my chest. "I'm not a lady, nor shall I ever be one. You might as well try to crown a cat and call her the tsarina."

The duke's mouth twitched. "Lady or not, I promised Staver to watch over you. And I imagine your unguarded tongue will be refreshing after all the stiffness of proper ladies and gentlemen. This old heart of mine could use a surprise or two."

I laughed again, a little freer. "I'll try not to provide too many surprises."

11

———

THE BIRCH LEAVES BURST from buds, making a ceiling of sharp, new green. The black wolf walked beside me, his head reaching almost to my shoulder, nudging me northwestward. He leapt over a stream in a single bound. I followed, touching a foot on a stone in the middle before skipping to the other-side. Downs, pocketed with rabbit burrows, rose in front of us.

A loud crash caught me by my braids and jerked me backwards out of the dream. The covers tangled around me as I struggled to sit.

"Hush." Mama touched my hand. "It was only an icicle falling with spring melt."

A week of dreams, each night more vivid than the previous, tugged at me, making my rest far from restful. I'd always had vivid dreams. But these were so real that if I didn't wake, I'd not know I was dreaming. The wolf returned every night, taking me always toward the same place. But we never reached it. I shook my head to clear the double image of the forest and the dawn-brightening room. And still no letters from Staver. Where was he? When would the duke tell me?

Mama drew back the curtains. The eastern sun sparkled off dripping icicles longer than I was tall.

I stood and stretched before donning a fire-warmed robe, then watched the sky brighten into a full morning. My strength had returned, and my sharp pains softened to general aches and allowed space for worry. When would Staver write? He'd been gone a full week.

Heated voices echoed outside my room and drew closer.

"You will not disturb her." Irina's voice carried command.

"If the duke won't tell me where he is, then she will!"

I grabbed the window curtains as my legs threatened to crumple. It was my old mistress. What was she doing here? Would she drag me back to servitude? She couldn't. Staver cleared my debt.

The window rattled with my shaking arm.

"Please, Lady Devora." It was Duke Nicholas's deep voice. "Let us speak in the parlor. I'll tell you where your son is, may he forgive me. But do not trouble the young lady. She's not well."

"I don't care if she's not well," the mistress almost shrieked. "She stole my son."

My shaking flashed into anger. I strode across the room and flung open the door. "I did *not* steal your son!"

The mistress looked at me like I was a half-drowned cat, one she wished had stayed drowned instead of coming back to bother her, then tilted up her chin. "You bewitched my son. But you'll not stop me from finding him and bringing him home."

My harsh bark of a laugh echoed down the wood-paneled halls, "I have no magic. I did nothing to your son, other than treat him with kindness. I never sought his love. But I'll not give up that precious gift now that he's given it to me."

The mistress hissed through her teeth, "Trickster ogress."

She was the ogress, ready to eat away my life, one slow year at a time.

"That is enough, Devora," the duke boomed. "If you cannot keep a civil tongue, you will leave, without the knowledge you seek."

She glowered but silenced.

"Now," he continued in a calmer tone, "If you'll both sit quietly, I'll tell you where Staver is."

I swallowed a hysterical laugh. Finally!

We followed him to a sitting room filled with sunlight and cold air. A maid hurried in and stirred up the banked fire, setting in new wood.

The duke stood in front of the window. "It is against the law for a commoner to marry a nobleman. Every marriage of nobility must be approved and recorded in the tsar's registry."

The mistress nodded smugly. "True. He can never marry that common, dirty—"

He spoke over top of her. "So Staver forsook his inheritance and became a commoner."

The mistress shrieked. "He what? He can't do that. And even if he has, by the tsar's law, children must not marry against their parents' wishes."

I swallowed bile. I'd never heard that law. Staver had found me a safe place with the duke and duchess. He'd given up his inheritance and his title. But could we not marry without his parents' permission? "Is that a true law?"

Duke Nicholas nodded. "It is. And Staver prepared for that too. He joined the tsar's army. And by serving six months in the army, his commander would become as his father and could give him permission to marry."

The bile in my throat burned. He joined the army. What if war came? *Please let there be peace for the next six months.*

The mistress leapt from her seat. "You've sent my sweet, gentle son to slave in the army?"

He shook his head and softly spoke. "He didn't want to

choose that. He wanted your permission and to marry Vasilisa. You sent him there."

"Where is he? Novgorod? Smolensk? Murom? Sudak?"

"I don't know."

"Don't know? Or won't tell?" She strode to stand a short arm span from him. Her height equaled his, and her eyes flashed as she glared into his face.

He laid a hand on her shoulder. "I'm sorry Devora. I've lost a child too. Though you may get yours back if you can accept his decisions."

She batted his hand away. "I'll search every fort and encampment, just as I searched every noble's manor, until I find him. And I'll bring him home." She slammed the door on her way from the parlor.

My skirt bunched in my clenched hands. Staver gave up everything for me. He put himself in danger. *Please*, I pleaded to the heavens, *please keep him safe.*

Duke Nicholas sat next to me on the divan. He laid a cool, papery hand over my clenched hands. "Vasilisa, I wish you'd not heard her words. They are ones of an anguished mother, and the pain is the only truth in them. You are innocent. She brought this upon herself."

I didn't care what she'd said; it was wind through the trees. But what about Staver? I looked up. "Do you truly not know where he is?"

"No. He kept that information to himself so you wouldn't try to follow him."

I searched the duke's face and only found truth. If I could find Staver, I'd tell him I wasn't worth these sacrifices and he should go home. Would he go home? Probably not. He'd given everything for me. And if war came, he could give his life.

Fear and worry wrestled in my chest. I stood. "I need to think, alone. Please, may I have today to walk in the forest? I'll be back this evening. I'm healed enough. I'll be careful."

The duke glanced at Irina and Mama. Irina pinched her lips and shook her head, while Mama nodded. "The forest may be what she needs to heal the rest of the way. Whenever she was too burdened by the abuse of servitude, she fled there for an evening and came back strong again. She'll be safe."

"Thank you, Mama."

Duke Nicholas kissed my forehead. "Wait until Lady Devora's carriage passes through the gate, then go, with heaven's protection. And may you find peace."

I JOGGED BETWEEN THE PINES, the cold unable to seep through leather boots and wool socks. My wide-skirted wool dress allowed me freedom of stride. A water pouch bounced at my hip, along with a satchel packed with food, and flint and steel in my pocket. *Staver gave up his parents and his inheritance, for me. He joined the army, taking on the art of fighting, something against his gentle nature, for me. Can I be worthy of his sacrifices? What if he's hurt? What if I cause his death because a war starts and he has to fight? What if? What if?*

My feet led while my thoughts tumbled.

A shrill cry stopped me. A gnarled oak bent over the path and a goshawk peered at me from a branch, its black-and-white rippled plumage blending in with the black trees and snow.

It was *the oak*. The wolf always met me here, in my dreams. Tingles ran down my arms.

The goshawk cried again.

"Are you from my dreams too?" I called.

He swooped from the branch, his wings spreading almost as wide as my arms, and flew northwest. The way of the wolf path.

The breeze tickled a wisp of hair across my face, then blew my skirts forward.

I ran after, as the goshawk disappeared into the pines. My worried thoughts fell into the snow behind me. I'd pick them up when I returned. But for now—I breathed in the pine and frost.

I followed the breeze northwestward, through a meadow, curving around a frozen peat bog, twining my way between pines with trunks thicker than a field worker's hut was wide. The sun kept pace with me, following me westward.

Ahead, smaller tree trunks criss-crossed my path, pushed over by heavy winter snows. I leapt onto one and ran along it until I came to another and followed its narrow path. The third trunk shifted under my feet. I threw my arms wide to keep balance and skipped sideways to a new trunk. The trunk stopped rolling and settled against the others.

That was close. I blew out my held breath. If I got my foot stuck between the trunks I'd be trapped as well as a grouse in a snare.

The white bark of birch, striped with black, signaled a new part of the forest. I closed my eyes again to feel the way of the dreams, and a memory burst into color.

The white birch wore leaves as bright as fire. I flew upward, reaching out and grasping yellow leaves, then fell back into strong arms. Papa's laugh rumbled under my squeals. I pushed yellow leaves through his black hair then reached for more. He tossed me upward again. A lock of my hair snagged on a branch, yanking my head sideways as I fell. Papa caught me and I whimpered in his arms until he pointed up into the trees. Strands of red hair, hung like fiery spiderweb among the leaves. Papa pulled the hair down and braided it into a strand then tied it around his wolf pendant.

I sniffed back a tear as the memory faded. A slight minty scent came with the tear. Another memory pushed its way forward. *I sat cradled in Papa's arms. My head ached. I'd climbed into a tree and tumbled out, landing on my head. Mama stripped bark from a birch, then scraped the soft inner bark into a bowl. She mixed it with water and gave it to me to drink. It was minty and cooling.*

I pulled back a piece of bark, and the minty scent filled the air. I spun about, scanning the trees. Where were the rabbit downs?

A winter-thin deer broke from the trees. The forest began to darken. Winter days were too short. I should turn back. But I couldn't. I ran on. I swallowed the last of my water, aching cold washing over my teeth.

The land bunched into rounded folds, with snow lying deeper in the north-facing shadows. My foot slipped through the snow into a hole, and I lurched forward as a sharp pain shot up my leg. I pulled my foot from the hole and grimaced—*twisted ankle.* More holes dimpled the snow. Was this a rabbit down? I carefully limped onward.

The little hills merged into a single steep slope, almost a cliff. The goshawk sat in the snow, a white hare dripping red in its talons.

"So we meet again. I see you had good hunting. Where do I go from here?"

He tilted his head at me, then looked up the cliff.

I grabbed branches to help my climb upward. I was crawling as the land leveled out. A birch grove spread before me, and a rocky cliff backed it. I limped through the trees as memories snatched at me, pulling out laughter and tears. A large twisted pine sat in the corner of the birches.

Papa chased me around the twisted pine. I clambered into its branches. He climbed after me, the branches bending and groaning under his weight.

The east-facing cliff sat in shadow, but one shadow sat deeper than the rest.

Mama pushed aside a deerskin covering a split in the cliff. Smoke and rich roasted scents wafted from behind her. Papa lifted me to his shoulder, bent to enter the cave, and tossed me onto a pile of sweet grasses. He tore off a chunk of meat and handed it to me, blowing on it first. I tossed it from hand to hand. Grease dripped onto my bare legs.

I gathered moss from the north sides of the birch, tugged down winter-broken twigs and branches, and built a fire. The moss lit with the spark of my flint and steel, then the kindling caught, forming a damp smoking fire. The birch grove split into a hundred flickering shadows, and in the cliff face sat a narrow crack, black against the grey rocks.

I entered the crack with a flaming branch. Three red hand-prints sat one above the other along the inner wall. The largest was at the bottom, and the smallest, just a tiny child's print, at the top.

I laid my hand over Papa's, and it dwarfed mine. Then I laid it over Mama's, and we matched up, palm to fingertips.

The crack widened into a sand-floored room. Stained leather lay in one corner, all that was left of our beds. Animals would have eaten the dried grass we'd slept on. A few split wooden bowls and spoons sat on a shelf in the wall. Blackened stones formed a fire ring.

Where had Mama buried Papa? I searched outside along the cliff with my flickering light. The birch grove now sat in deeper shadow and the sky glowed with sunset colors. Then a last beam of sunlight touched the top of the single twisted pine and I remembered. I brushed snow from the stone. Two handprints clung to the grave marker, faded by rain and snow, but the red clung in the deep ripples of stone. Under it Mama had burnt in black words. I had to learn to read, to see what she'd dedicated to Papa.

I gathered pine boughs and set them about the grave. "Papa, I've missed you. I've found love. Or love has found me. His name is Staver. And I don't know why he's so good to me. He's a nobleman's son, but he gave that up and joined the army so we can marry. I'm worried for him. If you have any influence, please ask heaven to protect him."

I looked up to the starry sky. "Thank you for sending the wolf in my dreams to guide me here."

I'd return to the duke on the morrow. I needed the peace of my first home for a night. I gathered more wood, most of it damp from snow, and got a smoking fire going in my cave. I ate the last of the food I'd brought, then lay down and stared into the flames, blinking with the smoke and the light.

~

A BAYING JARRED ME AWAKE.

I sat up and then scooted backwards. A hound sat at my feet and bayed again, his voice echoing around the small cave.

"Oh, hush, won't you!"

He wouldn't.

I shoved him away, and he pushed back, lying down at my feet. Even after I struck him across the nose, he only moved a short distance and continued his echoing, head-aching baying. Finally, I grabbed a branch from the fire and limped out into the darkness of night. I'd get more sleep by Papa's grave.

The hound followed.

I set the torch in the ground, huddled by Papa's stone, and wrapped my arms around my head. The noise wasn't so bad in the open, but the night air was chill, even with my wool cloak wrapped around my shoulders.

He sat down next to me, his soft fur warm against my side, and bayed again.

Couldn't he be quiet? I wasn't a rabbit to be caught. Silly hound. If he was going to keep me awake, at least he could also keep me warm. I snuggled closer and drifted off again, despite his noise.

A FIRE SENT up a sweet smoke of oak and hickory. The black wolf sat beside me and stared into the flames. Overhead, birch branches made a black screen between us and the star-flooded sky. Around us, the trees faded into fire flickered shadows.

I leaned against the wolf. Pine and wild herbs scented his fur. I snuggled closer.

"Vasilisa?" Staver's voice called from the darkness.

A low growl rumbled in the wolf's chest and vibrated against my cheek.

"Stop," I ordered. Did I speak to the growling wolf or to stop Staver from getting hurt?

"Vasilisa." His voice was closer.

I turned and Staver stood at the edge of the firelight. He held out his hand. "Come back."

I stood and stepped toward him, reaching out. He was here.

The wolf's growling rumble turned to a whine.

I halted, torn between the wolf who brought me home and the man who promised me love.

"Please come back," Staver pleaded.

"I want to. But you aren't even there. You're in the army. What if you die?"

"Trust me. Come back."

I stepped away from the wolf and took Staver's hand.

"WE'VE FOUND HER! COME QUICKLY!"

Light pierced my closed eyelids. A hand touched my arm and then my neck.

"She's breathing but icy. Get a fire started."

A blanket wrapped around me. Someone rubbed its rough material against my shoulders and down my arms.

I shuddered as warmth scraped against numbness, and the shudder turned into uncontrollable shivers. I forced words between my chattering teeth. "There's a—a fire in the cave."

"You're awake. Can you understand us? Are you hurt anywhere? Can we move you?"

"I'm fine, just—just cold." I blinked my eyes open.

An ogre face leaned over me, dark shadows cast upward, long nose shading gaunt cheek, eyes sunken into darkness.

I shrank back. "Who are you?"

He raised a lamp from the ground, and the shadows shifted, changing his face to human, wrinkled with sun. "I'm the duke's hunter. We must get you warm."

My eyes adjusted. He was clad in hunters' leather embroidered with Dyeda's crest. Other men in servant clothing and hunter's leather stood about us. The hound that had driven me from the cave with his baying nudged me with his wet nose. Four other dogs sniffed at me before men drew them away.

I pulled the blanket closer around my shoulders. My shivering continued. "The cave." I pointed.

The hunter gently scooped me into his arms and carried me into the cave. A faint glow of coals was all that was left of my fire, but the cave held a remnant of warmth and cut out the chill breeze.

Men hauled in wood and built a new fire over the old one. Warmth and smoke reached me, biting against my skin and my lungs.

I coughed and shivered.

The hunter handed me a damp cloth. "Breathe through this.

If I may, I'll rub your hands and feet to get the blood flowing to them again."

I nodded.

He didn't add that frost could take off the ends of fingers and toes. I knew, and yet I'd been foolish enough to leave shelter in winter. The duke had sent out hunters and hounds to find me.

The damp cloth helped me breathe easier. The hunter rubbed my hands and arms, then unlaced my boots.

I muffled a cry as he touched my swollen ankle. It was worse than the evening before.

"You *are* hurt." He removed the boot and slowly rotated my foot.

I winced.

"Not broken, but sprained. Where else are you hurt?"

"Nowhere," I said through gritted teeth.

He turned to a man in hunter's leather. "Ride back and tell the duke we've found Lady Vasilisa. She's hurt her ankle and is chilled. We'll guard her through the night and bring her back when the day is warm enough for her to travel."

Shame added to my shivers. "I'm sorry. I'm so sorry to cause you—" coughs cut off my words.

"Hush. You are safe now." He turned to the other men. "Find dry wood. Something that won't smoke."

"Everything is damp," a man replied, his pressed servant clothes rumpled from a long ride.

"Then fan the smoke away." His voice took on an edge. Was he worried for me?

I was fine. Cold and coughing, but I'd lived through cold and smoke before.

The men took off their coats and fanned the smoky air from the cave, their own coughing ricocheting off the cave walls. One boiled up water and dropped herbs into it. It was bitter stuff, but it warmed me. My shivering stilled, and I lay my head on the blessedly quiet hound.

The hunter ruffled the hound's ears. "Good boy, Thunder; you led us to her. You'll get the best bones for a year."

I laughed. "Thunder is a good name. He's as loud as it."

The hunter smiled at the dog. "And he has the nose to follow even the faintest trail." He studied my face. "You led us on quite the chase, my lady."

"I didn't mean to. I found my father's grave."

"Did you plan to die beside it?"

"I wasn't out there for the first part of the night. But Thunder's baying echoed too much in this cave. I was fine. I'd—" smoke tickled my throat, and a cough rattled my words loose.

He shook his head. "I carried the duke's daughter to her coffin. I can't bear to be the one to carry back your body."

"I won't die."

He brought over two blankets he'd been warming by the fire and tucked them under and around me. "Good. Now sleep." He joined the other men in airing the cave.

"Sir Hunter?"

He turned. "What can I get you?"

"Your name."

"Adrik."

"Thank you, Adrik."

12

WHEN THE SUN lit the mouth of the cave, I'd not had any more dreams, but the one from before they found me still troubled me. Would Staver come back, or would war take him?

Adrik bent to pick me up, but I pushed him away. "I can walk."

"Not today. Our horses are a good distance away. We almost lost one horse to a broken leg in the rabbit downs."

"So you plan on carrying me down that steep hill and through the downs? You'll break your leg and drop me. I can limp along well enough. Just get me a solid stick to lean on."

Adrik looked to the other men. There were seven of them.

A hunter shrugged. "She speaks truth. It would be safer to lower her down the hill with a rope than carry her. Once we are down the hill, we could make a litter to drag her along."

Lowered by rope? Dragged along on a litter? I should have stayed quiet and let him carry me. But despite my arguments to let me climb down myself, they fashioned a harness of ropes and lowered me down. I kept my eyes tightly shut as Adrik climbed down beside me, holding me away from the branches and rocks as well as any firm support. If I was free to control my descent, I'd enjoy it, but this—I shivered, but not with cold.

When we reached the bottom, I turned to Adrik. "Just carry me, if you won't let me walk."

He half smiled then lifted me. Three other men picked out a path before us, seeking snow-hidden burrows. Adrik didn't drop me, and we finally reached the horses.

One of the tall beasts stood before me. I'd never ridden before, and it was much larger than a bear. "Please, just let me limp along."

Adrik ignored my words and handed me off to the other hunter. He mounted the horse then pulled me up to sit sideways in front of him.

I grabbed the horse's mane, and it neighed.

Adrik put a hand over my clenched hands. "I won't drop you, neither will the horse. Hold to my arm. You'll be safe."

I let go of the mane and gripped Adrik's arm as the horse lurched forward. We crossed the frozen brook, my heart leaping higher than the horse leapt, picked our way through the dead-fall, galloped between trees, and when I was sure I was as bruised from the horse as I'd ever been from a whipping, we emerged from the forest. The other servants rode ahead and behind us.

Mama ran fastest from the house to greet us. The duchess followed, and the duke stood at the gate of the gardens, leaning on the supporting arm of a servant.

I leaned over and caught Mama's outreaching hands. Adrik reined in the horse. "Please move. We should get the Lady Vasilisa inside." Mama nodded and let go of my hands.

Adrik rode the horse to the door of the palace then lifted me down into the arms of another servant. The situation echoed of a week before, when I first entered the palace. But this time I only had a sprained ankle.

I pushed against the servant's arms so he had to put me down. "I'll walk."

The servant looked from me to the duke and back. "If it pleases you, I'll carry you to your room."

"I'll lean on your arm while I walk to my room. I'm not an invalid."

The duchess caught up to us. "Let him carry you." Her smile wrinkles creased into a tight frown.

I let him carry me. Irina, the healer, waited for me in my room. Mama, the duchess and the duke trailed afterwards. The duke's face blanched as with illness. What had I done?

"I'm so sorry. I'm a selfish girl."

The duchess whispered, "Not selfish. But thoughtless." She turned to Irina. "Call me when you've finished tending to her."

The duke watched her go, then sat next to my bed. "Please forgive me for not sending help sooner. I wanted to give you space to heal. I should have sent servants at noon, as Baba wanted. Only when night was falling did I realize your danger, and we sent our men and hounds to find you. Will you forgive an old man?"

I shook my head. He was asking me to forgive him? But I'd been the one to leave and to cause him worry. "I'm sorry. I had a dream, and it led me to my papa's grave."

Mama grasped my hand. Sweat beaded on her forehead.

The duke bent his head forward. "Then you are she. I thought so."

"I'm who?"

"Come with me, and I'll show you."

WE WALKED down a hall wide enough to hold a banquet table. I leaned on a cane to help with my twisted ankle. The tapestries showed woodland scenes: a deer and her dappled fawn feeding in a meadow, a bear standing in the rapids and fish leaping upward against the current, two otters tussling.

I clutched Mama's arm. One tapestry showed an animal-skin-clad man standing next to a black wolf. His black eyes matched the wolf's, and his body tensed with the energy of a hunter.

The duke stopped and studied my face. "My daughter loved the woods, like you. She often spent whole days in them. The creatures never harmed her. One day she wandered into a new part of the forest. She heard a child's laughter and ran towards the sound, but a man stopped her. He stood taller than any she'd met before. Behind him she glimpsed a woman push a child into the bushes. She stepped to go around the man, but he matched her steps, keeping himself between her and the disappearing child. She finally turned and left that part of the forest, certain she'd just met three fair folk. She sketched out the images for the tapestry and used the wolf to help explain what the man's presence was like. Do you see the woman and child?"

I looked past the man and wolf to the foliage behind. The back of two heads showed through the leaves, one with wheat-gold hair, and the other with fox-red hair and a black streak down one side. "That's my papa, my mama, and me."

He nodded. "You are a fair folk child."

My breath caught in my throat. "Do you really think I'm one of the fair folk?"

"I'm certain of it."

"Others think I'm an ogre-child, not fair folk. They say I'm demon-wild and devil-strong."

He studied the tapestry as he spoke. "Is the shrike a demon because she is wild, or the elk a devil because he is strong? The fair folk are of the forest. They must be strong enough to live in the wildness of their home."

"Mama, is this true? Why didn't you tell me?"

She closed her eyes and mouthed what might have been a prayer. "I didn't tell you because your life was hard enough when people thought you were human."

The duke laid a hand on my shoulder. "You needn't worry about our knowing. My babushka four generations back was fair folk. Staver comes of the same line, though his father thinks this genealogy is a myth."

I was no ogre-child. All those years being told my father was a demon or a monster. All those years wondering if they were right. But I was fair folk. And worthy to marry Staver.

"Thank you Du…" I paused. He was family through our fair folk blood. "Thank you Dyeda."

I woke covered in sweat as images played before my open eyes.

Papa crouched growling in front of our cave. Ten men surrounded him with spears. One thrust, but Papa caught his spear and broke off the end. Three more thrust their spears, and Papa stopped two. The third buried in his calf. I struggled against Mama's hold and broke free. Papa grabbed me as I ran to his side and tossed me back into the cave. I tumbled in the sand, and when I'd cleared my eyes, more spears stuck from him. Papa pulled out one spear and swept it across the attackers. Mama held me tight while I howled against her. Screams and shouts drowned out my cries. Then silence. Papa lay moaning in a circle of unmoving forms. I broke free of Mama again and ran to him. He pulled me close and buried his face in my hair. He breathed in one long breath, like he did every time he held me. I breathed in his scent, mixed with blood. And he didn't breathe again.

For a moment his face changed to Staver's.

I cried into my pillow. Memories shouldn't be that vivid. Nor fears.

13

———

A MONTH PASSED. I learned to read haltingly. The wolf still hunted my dreams, but he slipped away with waking, and worries for Staver replaced him. I tried to ignore both, focusing my energies on reading, archery, penmanship, and even some ladylike activities of music, drawing, and embroidery. Mama seemed to enjoy the sewing and quiet conversations with Baba more than I did, though. Sewing only kept my hands busy and gave too much freedom for my thoughts. Drawing took more focus, and I grew competent in copying what I saw, be it animal, plant, or another's art.

Each time I escaped to the forest for an afternoon, it was harder to return. Only there could I shed my worried weight and the silence of letters.

The duke—no, he was Dyeda now, my grandfather—walked beside me as we strolled the garden path in the afternoon sun. Spring was in full bloom, and snow had vanished from even the deepest shaded spots. We stopped beside a cluster of purple bursting allium. Dyeda broke one off and tucked it into his buttonhole.

I bent over and sniffed it. "You smell like the turkey dressing my mama made last night."

He broke off another allium and handed it to me. "Yes, isn't it a lovely smell? And such a happy flower, too."

"If we're going to smell like turkey dressing, then I'll find some sage and thyme to add to our bouquets."

I searched the herb border until I found both, plus lavender with its spears of flowers.

He sat on a stone bench, beside the path. "Please, tell me about the ways of the fair folk."

"We lived in the forest, and the forest gave us our food and drink. Birds were my music and trees my playthings. Papa and Mama were my world."

He sighed. "It's a simpler way of life. I'd give up my dukedom for it, if my wife could be happy with it. But we are both too old now. And war—" He stopped.

"War?"

"It's nothing."

"What war?"

"It's the same rumors that have been passed amongst the nobility since before I was born. Nothing will come of it."

"But Staver, he could..." I shredded the lavender in my hand, letting my fingers voice what I couldn't in words. "Why doesn't he write?"

Dyeda wrapped his arms around my shoulders. "Vasilisa. I shouldn't have spoken of the rumors. War won't happen. Staver is fine. He'll write."

I threw the lavender to the bench and dashed into the forest.

I'D RUN hard for hours. The hound, Thunder, panted at my side, his tongue lolling in happy exhaustion. He'd found me within ten minutes of my flight, and stayed at my side through the rest of it, nudging me back towards the estate as evening fell. He bayed as we entered the garden, where lanterns pushed the dusk shadows from the gravel paths and lit the fading daffodils.

Adrik strode from the shadows of the porch and patted Thunder. "Welcome back, Lady Vasilisa." His overnight satchel hung heavy at his side. He'd been ready to go after me.

Anger and shame boiled. *I don't mean to cause them worry.*

Adrik held out his hand to take mine. "A letter from Lord Staver came for you."

"Where?" The burning in my chest lifted like smoke, leaving only warm hope.

"With Duke Nicholas in the library."

I dashed through the library doors that opened onto the garden and barely registered Dyeda's relieved face before snatching a folded paper from the desk beside him and breaking the wax seal.

Staver wrote in a large rounded hand, easier to read than Dyeda's spidery script.

"My Li-sa, I'm sour." I bunched my forehead trying to force the letters to tell me Staver's words.

Dyeda gently pulled me to sit next to him, laid a finger under the words, and read.

My Lisa,

I'm sure Duke Nicholas has told you where I am. I wish I could have told you in person. Army life is different but has its own joy, though it is short on paper. I had to wait till my first two-week pay to purchase the supplies to write you and to pay the messenger. Please forgive my tardiness. I'll send letters every week from now on with one of the tsar's messengers. You may send a reply with them. The tsar trusts them to carry army secrets, so I think we can trust them to carry ours.

I turned to Dyeda, "Is the messenger still here?"

"Yes, my child. He'll stay the night and take any letter you write tomorrow." His tender look reminded me of my earlier shame.

"I'm sorry, Dyeda, for being gone so long."

He patted my hand. "I'm sorry for voicing rumors."

I kissed his cheek. "Will you please read more?

The best part of my daily training is the hopak. It is a dance that tests endurance and agility. Sometimes we squat and kick out our legs, other times we cartwheel heels-over-head. I'm just learning to crouch with my legs crossed and alternately touch my knees sideways to the ground without touching any of the rest of my body. Can you imagine doing this and not falling? The older soldiers set me to shame, but I'm falling less often.

The worst part of the army is nighttime. If it isn't a chorus of snoring in our crowded tent, it's a horse protesting its flea-infested quarters. I understand the horse's complaints. I share my cot with a hundred jumping bedfellows. Though squishing them helps keep my thoughts occupied when I fall to melancholy for you.

My commander recognized my love for books and made me a clerk. I get to track all the comings and goings of men, animals, and supplies. He also assigned me to study strategy, history, trade, and politics for half of each day. I'd rather study poetry and music, but it is better than marching through muddy fields with boots still soaked from the previous day's march.

We had an interesting visitor the other day. The mystic Udinsky presented on the flow of power, the strength of the mind, and all things convoluted. But it was worth it for his sleights of hand. You'd enjoy his parlor tricks.

Did the duke teach you what these funny squiggles on the page mean yet? I can't remember a time when I couldn't read. It must look strange to you. I turned this page up-side-down and backward then looked at the image the lamp cast through the page. Maybe it is a little like that. Yet you read the world: the growing things, the animal tracks, the sounds of seasons groaning into place. Will you teach me to read the world when I return?

There are no tall trees to climb here, only watch towers. When you get this letter, climb a tree at noon and look northward, and I'll climb the tower and look southward. I'll play the song I've enclosed, and maybe the wind will carry it to you, even if it is just an echo.

I've kissed your name. Will you kiss it too? And then our lips will touch over the distance.

Staver

I took the page from Dyeda and pressed it to my face. Pines and wood smoke, sweat and Staver—each filled my nose. I kissed the page, remembering what he felt like, then unfolded a sheet of music.

Home

Timber grows tall.
Birds nest in its branches,
Squirrels in its trunk.
Rabbits burrow under its roots.
Home.

Timber falls to ax,
Sawn and shaped into
Walls and roof.
Live in its safety.
Home.

You are of the forest.
I am of the house.

Can we find a home together?

Your elfin face captured me.
Your laughter caught my soul.
Your thoughts—wild and wise.
Your courage. Your love.

My heart found a new place,
Not of house, not of forest.
And wherever we dwell,
I am your home and you are mine.

My Dearest Staver,

Dyeda is writing for me. Writing takes a long time. Even though his pen flies across the page, my words fly faster.

The duke and duchess are Dyeda and Baba to me, and though I've never known grandparents, I can't imagine kinder souls on earth or in heaven. Thank you for bringing me into their family and giving up yours for me. I don't know why you do this for me. I worry about you. I wish I could—

"Stop, Dyeda. Please start a new letter. I want to make him laugh, not feel sorry."

He dabbed his eyes as he set the unfinished letter aside and placed a clean sheet on the writing desk.

My dear poetic Staver,

Dyeda and Baba are wonderful. Life is beautiful. Except for the spider I almost drank. That wasn't beautiful. It probably didn't think I was beautiful either, as I almost swallowed it whole, but then it shouldn't have been sitting in my water cup.

I'm learning the finer skills of archery such as don't sneeze when releasing the arrow, if you try to hit the fly on the target it just becomes a smear, and ladies don't use longbows. Instead, they use a toy paraded as a bow. I grabbed Adrik's longbow when he wasn't looking and hit the farthest target. He's still wearing a stunned look. Adrik is my teacher in archery and horsemanship. He's a good teacher in both, though I'm a much better student in the first than the second.

I have something to confess. I'm terrified of horses. I love to climb and run and swim. But when I get on a beast that is ten times my size, I'm no longer in control. It can take me wherever it pleases. What if the horse decided that it was in the mood to swim, or, heaven forbid, climb a tree? I'd be clinging to its back, yelling at it to stop and let me do it myself.

I'm embroidering a coat for you to wear when winter comes again. I hope you like roses that look like a rabbit chewed on them.

Yours always,

Lisa

Are you laughing? I don't know how to make words sing like you do. But if I can make you laugh, then I've created music, and hopefully lifted your heart, as you have mine. When I think of you, I'm so happy, I think I'll split in half like a seed, and a new me will spring upward.

I looked over the letter Dyeda had written. There was still some room at the bottom, not enough to say all I wanted, but not even a book could hold that. "Please add this."

I just learned that I'm fair folk! I wish Mama had told me years ago. Dyeda told me, and said that you are part fair folk too. Is that why you are so good with the animals? I found my papa's grave and my first home. It is beautiful. I'll take you there when you return.

"Oh, and this."

Dyeda laughed. "Are you certain you don't want to start another letter without all the post-scripts?"

"Just this last one. Then we'll seal and send it."

He dipped the quill in the ink and wrote as I spoke.

If you find a spell to make the months fly faster, please send it to me.

I STOOD at the edge of Dyeda's garden looking into the evening forest lit with floating lights that flashed green, yellow, and red. One landed on my arm. It was a brownish beetle. It flickered green, then yellow, and joined the other flickering bugs. A breeze pushed away the summer's heat.

The black wolf stepped from the trees and watched me. I prepared to follow. I knew where we were going. I'd make it in this dream.

A strong hand took mine.

I looked up into Staver's face. "Will you come with me?"

His brow furrowed. "The wolf won't let me take that path. I'll be waiting for you. Come back."

I stood on my tiptoes and kissed him. "Make sure you come back, too."

The wolf howled, and his voice pulled me into the forest.

14

FOUR MORE MONTHS marched by like the army drills Staver wrote about in his letter, though the months were not as orderly. The riotous noise of spring birds gave way to the lazy heat of summer. Now the nights turned cool again and trees donned colors bright enough to shame the summer flowers.

The dreams continued to pull me toward the forest, but I fought their siren voices by reading Staver's letters each morning until I had them memorized. Then I filled each waking minute, till I didn't have a moment left to ache for the beckoning forest or Staver. In addition to reading, archery, and penmanship, I added chess and the hopak—the dance Staver mentioned in his first letter. I fell many times the first week, but now four months later I could outlast my teacher, the huntsman Adrik.

Only one more month and Staver could ask his commander permission to marry.

I released an arrow at the last target set on the stone wall at the end of the orchard. It struck the crabapple. I whooped. It was one thing to pierce the pear or even the plum. But the crabapple was only slightly larger than the head of the arrow.

I set the longbow aside, and Adrik took it. "Well done, Lady Vasilisa."

I wished he'd stop calling me *lady*. I wasn't one and wouldn't ever be. When Staver and I married, we'd become the caretakers of Dyeda's estate, but we wouldn't be nobility. When Dyeda died —hopefully not for many years to come—the tsar would place someone else there, and we'd either stay or find work elsewhere. But it didn't matter. We'd have each other.

Aching longing grew inside me with the thoughts. I shook my head. *Enough! Find something else to think about.* Dyeda liked to play chess in the afternoons.

I nodded thanks to Adrik for his archery lesson, then loped from the orchards, through the gardens, and into the library.

Dyeda sat, shoulders hunched at a table, reading a letter. His white brows knit.

I skidded to a halt. "Dyeda, what is it?"

He looked up and rubbed his right temple. "We must gather the women and children. You must leave."

"What has happened?"

"The Khan of the Golden Horde has raised an army again and is riding against Ruska."

The floor tilted. Since I'd learned to read, I'd favored the histories. Nations from the west had attacked Ruska many times over the years, and they never made it far. But the Scythians to the south were different. They lived a nomadic life on windswept steppes. They were as fierce and unyielding as their land. They swept through, killing indiscriminately. A child was no safer from their sabers than a soldier.

And they were coming.

I clutched the table. "When?"

He glanced at the letter again. "The tsar's army stationed two days south of us is preparing for the Khan's attack. The messenger rode as fast as his horse could handle to warn us, but it still took a full day. Depending on how long the army can hold them off, we may have three days. I must send messengers to continue the warnings north and prepare my own men to defend Ruska from them. The last time the Scythians attacked, they blazed a path without stopping, straight to the tsar's palace. We cannot let that happen again. We must slow them while the rest of the tsar's armies gather."

I bit the inside of my cheek. "Was the messenger the one that brings Staver's letters?"

He nodded.

That meant Staver was on the battlefront. I spun on my toes, ready to dash out. "Where is the messenger? He has to take me to Staver!"

"He's already gone northward to spread the warning."

"I'll find Staver anyway!"

"No." Dyeda's voice took on command. "Staver will be safer than most. Since he's a clerk, he'll not be fighting."

I caught hold of that hope, but my legs still ached to race southward. "I'm still going. He's given up everything for me. I'll fight beside him."

Dyeda took my clenched hand. "You don't know where he is, and we need you here. You know the forest. You will take the women and children and keep them safe from both wolf and ogre. Take them to your birth home on the cliff shelf."

"But many of them can't climb to it," I blurted, seeking any excuse.

He patted my hand. "The pulley my men built so I could visit your birth home last month is still there. Get the women and children to safety, then remove the pulley. Hide your presence. You will not come back until I send word that it is safe."

I growled my reply. "I'll take them to safety." Then added silently, *And when they are safe, I will find Staver.*

～

THE MANOR BECAME a flurry of war preparation. All the serfs gathered. Men brought out swords from the armory and tried the balance. Some looked comfortable with the weapons, but many did not. Others sat fletching arrows.

The long drive in front of the manor became practice grounds for swordsmanship. Some young men looked excited as they bumbled through the strokes. The experienced ones moved with grim efficiency. Dyeda strode from group to group, giving counsel, overseeing preparations. As he walked, he gripped his sheathed sword. The old leather sheath looked out of place next to his velvet clothes and silvered features.

For two days the women packed grain, bedding, tents, and medical supplies, some for the men when they marched against the Scythians, some for the women and children. And, too soon, it was time for us to go.

Grey dawn crept over the land as Baba threw her arms around Dyeda. "Keep safe," she whispered.

He embraced her, and I turned away as they kissed.

Dyeda's whispered words followed me. "I'll keep the hearth warm and the pillows plumped for you in heaven."

"Nicholas," Baba cried.

"Go, my love. Watch over our Vasilisa." He reached out to me. "Vasilisa, take Baba and go."

I hated Mama and Irina in their efficiency. They took charge, and in less time than it took for tears to dry, a cluster of women and children stepped into the shade of the trees, followed by mules carrying supplies. The soft floor and woody walls of the forest absorbed muffled crying. Most left behind a father, husband, or brother.

I carried one of Adrik's longbows and a quiver of steel-pointed arrows. I'd lead the others to safety deep in the forest then return. I had to find Staver. And I'd take out—I re-counted the arrows in my quiver—ten of the Khan's men while I was about it.

The women moved slowly, the children even slower, and the mules balked at every shadow. Horses would have been better, but the men needed them in battle. If the mules could have helped our men, then I'd gladly have left them behind too and had each person carry a load.

Baba stumbled at my side. I caught her arm as she fell to her knees. "Baba, I can carry you."

"No." Her knees creaked as she rose to her feet. She trudged on.

The day crossed over to evening. We settled down to camp next to a brook. Children pulled off their shoes and went splashing in the water. Squeals erupted as a little boy splashed his sister, and for a moment they forgot their tears and fears. A young woman buried her face in her mother's lap, her shoulders shaking. Women in peasant dress, servant's starched aprons, and finely tailored clothing worked side by side starting cook fires and setting out bedding.

I walked the periphery, then further out. I heard nothing but the sounds of camp. No army would follow a bunch of women into the woods. They'd be safe. I refilled my water pouch at the brook and grabbed a wedge of cheese.

Mama touched my arm as I tightened the lacing on my boots. "Take this." She handed me the wolf amulet. "You can help the wounded."

I strung the amulet over my neck and tucked it between my vest and blouse. "Thank you, Mama. If I'm not back by tomorrow, take them to Papa's grave. You know how to live in the forest as well as I. It will be safe."

She kissed my forehead. "I'll be waiting for you. Be careful."

I ran into the darkening of the forest, following the path flat-tened by our journey there. My feet beat in time to my thoughts. *Staver, stay safe. Dyeda, stay alive. I'm coming. Stay safe. Stay alive. I'm coming.*

15

———

THE HOURS FLEW by me in stripes of black trunks, bluish webbing of branches and leaves, and patches of velvet skies. A full moon lit enough path to keep me from tripping. I brushed by a twisted oak where Dyeda and I had sat a whole afternoon and watched deer feed. *I'm almost there. Hold on, Dyeda. Be safe, Staver. I'll find you.*

A voice sang out of the darkness, a weak tenor that gasped after each word. "... elfin face captured me. Your laughter..." he coughed.

"Staver!" I yelled then clamped my lips together. If the Khan's men were around, I would lead them to him. *Be quiet Staver, I'm coming!*

"Lisa?"

I stretched out my stride, leaping over the low underbrush.

A figure rose from a bush and stumbled towards me.

I dashed forward, the short distance between us lengthening into a day's run.

He fell to his knees and then his face.

Silence wove through the whispering wind and my thudding feet.

I crouched at his side and turned his face from the dirt. My hands brushed against thick hair, matted and sticky.

A groan answered my efforts.

"I'm going to help you." *Please stay alive!*

I felt around on his back, arms, and legs. No arrows and no more sticky wetness. I turned him over and felt his front.

A dent curved over his temple. Wetness from his matted hair trailed across his face, grainy with dirt and forge-scented with iron. Stickiness stuck a sleeve to his upper arm. No other wounds, at least that I could feel.

I pulled out the wolf amulet.

"Lisa?" His voice came, a hoarse whisper.

"I'm here. I'm going to use the wolf amulet. Don't you dare die."

"I can't. I promised to marry you."

A laugh broke from me, a hard bark of a sound. Was his promise stronger than death? I unlaced his shirt enough to bare his chest and laid the amulet against his skin. Then I laid one of my hands over his head wound.

His whole body shuddered. His head flopped from one side to the other while his wounded arm flinched.

The dent in his head smoothed.

I yanked the amulet from his skin and laid my ear against his chest. His heart beat steady and slow, so slow, as though in a deep sleep.

What now? Did I dare leave him asleep on the forest floor and go find Dyeda? A wild dog could be drawn by his blood and kill him. But what if Dyeda had survived and I could save him too? I gripped my braids. Why had Staver fought? He was a clerk, not a warrior. And now I had to choose between finding one or keeping watch over the other.

I wouldn't choose.

I bound my handkerchief around his still wounded arm. Did

the amulet heal the most vital first? I wouldn't chance it longer on Staver. I pulled him onto my back and dragged him to the twisted oak. His breath moistened the back of my neck. His boots dragged and caught at every root. The trunk split into two large branches at waist height. One curved upward in a shallow incline. I crawled along the branch until we were higher than a dog could jump, then laid Staver along the branch and secured him with my scarf.

I kissed his check and then his sleep-parted lips. He didn't respond. How long would he sleep? I'd slept for three days. "I'll be back, my love," I whispered against his cheek. I leapt down to retrieve my bow and quiver.

The bushes rustled along with heavy breathing. But not heavy enough for bear. I drew an arrow and set it on the string.

A skirted figure, blue-shaded in the moonlight, raced into the clearing. She held up her hands. "I'm here to help," she whispered, panting. "You led me on quite the run. I thought a peasant could out-endure any noble lady."

Relief washed over me like the feeling of falling in a stream. It was a serf woman, one of the stronger ones who'd helped in our flight. "I need your help. Sit up in this tree and watch over Staver while I go help the others."

She glanced up at the tree and gasped. "How did you get him up there?"

"I can't waste time. I'll boost you up if you don't think you can climb it."

She shook her head, whipping her waist-length braids around to her front. One braid caught on the hunting bow strapped to her back. "You stay. I'll go. I've someone I must find. Besides, I have a bow that I can actually use. The bow you carry looks scary, but no man will believe that you can draw it."

If it would get her to listen to me, then this bit of convincing was worth it. I reset my arrow on the string, bent my back against the bow and released, sending the arrow to a quivering stop in the ground a hundred yards down our path.

She stared, slack-jawed, then clicked her teeth together. "Then the rumors were true. I'm at your service, my lady warrior."

"What do they call you?"

"Agasha. The others call me Gasha. I've caught my breath. Let's go."

"You are staying with Staver."

"He's safe enough. I'm coming."

Dyeda could die in the time we took to argue. I sprinted off and Gasha followed.

I glanced back. "Whom did you leave behind?"

"The blacksmith."

"Your husband?"

"He will be, if— He will be. We'll be married at the end of harvest."

"We'll find him."

She nodded and picked up her pace. "He's too thick-headed and stubborn to die."

I fingered the amulet. She'd see me use it, and I needed her not to run off screaming or attack me. "Gasha, I have a fair-folk amulet. It helps heal those it touches. I—"

Gasha held up her hand. "Your mama told me before I left. Do what you must."

I retrieved my arrow.

The garden wall lay in a black band before us. The moon sat low in the western sky. The heavens grew a lighter blue in the east.

I set an arrow on a string.

Gasha edged the garden gate open. It stopped halfway.

A body blocked it. Not Dyeda's. Some man dressed in coarse

linens. Gasha bent down and touched his lips with her finger, then shook her head. "He's gone."

Memories of Papa's death rushed forward, his blood coating my hands, his hot body turning cold, his eyes unseeing. Bile burned the back of my throat and my bow rattled against my leg as I scanned the garden. Two more slumped forms lay across hedges. How many lay hidden from view?

The sun rose before we finished exploring the garden. We found eight dead and one still breathing. A pulsing iron stench mixed with his sweat.

I laid the wolf amulet on him.

He cried out, then went still. The wound in his middle only half healed, and his heart stopped.

"Why? It's supposed to heal you!" I yelled into my clenched hands to muffle my rage and fear. *What if that had happened to Staver?*

Gasha knelt next to me and closed the man's eyes. "He was too far gone. Not even magic could have healed that wound." She stood and walked with a ready bow around the side of the palace.

We still needed to find Dyeda.

If I could wash away the next two hours from my memory, I would. But it was a stain not even the strongest lye or stiffest metal brush could remove. The sun revealed hundreds of still forms strewn across the once green land between the palace and the road, both Ruskan and Scythian. Not all were still. Some cried out for water and help. None of the Khan's men emerged from the palace.

I bent over a man in the blue coat of the tzar's army, re-binding his leg. He winced as I tightened the cloth above a shallow gash running from his hip to his knee. He'd bound it earlier and stemmed the blood. It was the only reason he was still alive.

Gasha dippered water from a bucket into his mouth. "Thank you," he rasped.

Should I use the amulet on him? Maybe he could help us. He was the first to be aware enough to speak. "What happened?"

"The Khan's army pushed into our lands. We tried to stop them." Sweat beaded on his forehead. "Duke Nicholas and his men joined us in the fight. But the Khan's army cut through us and forced their way northward."

"Why didn't your commander leave men to help the fallen?" I clenched the wolf amulet. If they'd left someone to tend to the fallen then more men would be alive.

He closed his eyes. "He couldn't. He needed every man to continue to fight. We have to protect the tsar and Ruska."

At least that meant none of the Khan's men were here. Everyone, both Ruskan and Scythian, had marched northward. But at such cost. So many dead! I brushed my arm across my eyes and laid the amulet on the soldier. He shuddered, his leg wound closed, and he fell into the deep sleep. He'd survive.

Where was Dyeda?

We approached the road where the fallen were thickest. Some of the men lying there wore the plain browns of serfs, some the green of Dyeda's household staff, some in the Scythian furs, and others the blue of the tsar's army. The tattered remnants of a flag with Dyeda's family crest hung from a tree. A foul image marred it.

A strangled scream came from the road. Gasha knelt next to a huge man in a blacksmith's apron. He was missing an arm. Gasha's broad shoulders shook as she washed the blood and dirt from his face.

I pulled at the smith's shirt to set the amulet on him.

Gasha pushed my hand aside. "No. He's gone. Leave me."

I spun around, looking and not wanting to look. What was that? A spot of yellow? Yellow embroidered velvet stuck out from under another fallen man. I gasped as I recognized the top form. It was Adrik. He grasped a broken bow. Several arrows sprouted from his chest.

Beneath him lay Dyeda.

I pulled Adrik's stiffened form off Dyeda, splashing Adrik's whitened skin with tears.

Dyeda coughed.

"Stay alive, stay alive, stay alive," I muttered as I fumbled to unbutton his waistcoat and pull at the neck of his shirt. Hoof-prints marked his clothing and bruised the skin beneath.

His breathing caught in his chest as though there wasn't enough room for it.

I laid the wolf amulet on his cold skin.

He shuddered.

I pulled it off, and he coughed again.

Again and again, half a moment at a time, I laid the amulet and removed it.

His breathing grew easier and his skin warmer.

I brushed his silver hair from his face. "I'm here, Dyeda. We'll take you someplace safe." But how? We'd saved twelve men, but they'd be asleep for days. Gasha and I couldn't drag twelve men back to the forest, and what if others still lived in this mass of bodies? Had the Khan left men behind? The estate seemed deserted, but what if they discovered us?

I ran from man to man, feeling for breath and moving on when there was none. I no longer watched with a bow. Four more lived and fell into a deep, amulet-induced sleep.

Gasha joined me. She wiped her face on her sleeve, leaving a dirt smear across her right cheek. "There is a wagon and mule stabled by my hut. The mule is strong."

"The Khan would have stolen him."

She shook her head and sniffed. "He's a stubborn beast. He only listened to Deniska and me. I know, I should have brought him with the women to help carry supplies, but—I wanted Deniska to have a way to flee. He didn't."

She was gone half an hour while I dragged together all the Ruskan men who lived. Sixteen had survived among hundreds. A Scythian cried out as I passed. I bit my cheek as I opened his double-layered tunic and lay the amulet on his chest. He shuddered and fell into the sleep. That was all I could do. Even if we had room, if I tried to take him and the other Scythians back to the camp, the women who'd lost husbands and fathers would kill them. The wounded enemies would last longer sleeping on the battlefield. Gasha wouldn't have liked my doing even that much. But I couldn't bear to hear their cries any longer.

The rumble of the cart first announced Gasha's coming, then the dust on the road, and finally the spotted mule pulling a woven-sided wagon.

And still the palace lay silent.

Gasha and I propped the unconscious men in the cart, six seated along one side with their legs stretched out, their heads lolling with the movement. We bound a rope around their chests and through the wicker siding to keep them from falling over. We placed six more on the other side sitting on top of the legs of the first six. Then laid three crosswise over the legs of the others. The bottom ones' legs might be damaged with all the weight, but at least they could all breathe.

I saved Dyeda for last. Gasha and I nestled him lying with his head on the opposite side of those below him. One more space lay ready for Staver beside Dyeda.

Gasha dragged over the smith. "I'm bringing him too."

I placed my hand on her shoulder. "He's already dead."

"I'll not have him ravaged by dogs or a scavenging ogre. I'll carry him back if you won't allow him in my cart that I'm letting you use."

I bowed my head. I'd do the same for Staver. I helped her settle the smith beside Dyeda. She clicked her tongue, and the mule lunged against the weighted cart. The wheels creaked, and the cart groaned forward.

I walked beside the wagon, scanning the land, my eyes flitting over the death between us and the forest, then glancing back to the palace. Something moved at a lower window. A watching face.

I fitted an arrow.

The face disappeared. It must have been a thief. He'd ignored the cries of the men, but he'd also let us tend to them. I could sing praises to his cowardice in letting us be.

I watched the windows with a ready arrow as the wagon slowly pulled past the dead and into the woods. Only when the palace disappeared behind trees did I turn and run to the twisted oak.

Staver lay on the branch. One arm hung limply down.

I climbed up and felt for his breath. It came slow and quiet. I laid my head on his chest and emptied my tears onto him.

"My lady warrior," Gasha called up, "whether he be alive or dead, bring him down, for we should go."

"He's alive, and he'll stay that way."

Daylight showed the damage that night had hidden. Blood and dirt coated Staver's face. A muddy hoof print marked a cheek. Evidence of hooves spotted his blue military uniform. He'd been trampled like Dyeda. I stroked his face.

Gasha called up again, "My lady."

I unbound Staver. Gasha took his legs as I lowered him from the branch. Then we nestled him between Dyeda and the smith. I double-checked that all were still breathing and bit my lip as I ran my fingers over the smith's mouth. All but him.

16

MAMA RAN at the front of the group of women as we rumbled into camp late that night. They hadn't moved onto my forest home, and it was good they hadn't. We couldn't have taken the wagon that route.

"You brought Staver and Dyeda," Mama said, grasping my hand.

Baba rushed forward. "Nicholas!" She looked into the wagon and swooned. Mama caught her.

I should have stopped Baba. The men looked like a stack of corpses.

Irina pushed her way to the wagon's edge and touched Dyeda's face. "How many are still alive?"

"All." I swallowed and didn't look at Gasha. "All but one."

She turned to the women milling about. "You, get mats laid out for them. You..." She sent each off with an order and we fell to our assigned task.

Soon the men were laid on bedding near fires. The women whose menfolk hadn't been brought back separated into two groups. One moaned and rocked, pulling children close and dampening each other's shoulders. The other group helped tend the wounded. They washed the men and bound up their wounds. I didn't dare use the wolf amulet enough to fully heal them.

One woman cried out as she washed the blood from skin after removing a gashed sleeve. "My Fyodor has but a scratch, yet he's covered in blood. And why is he asleep as though he's under a spell?"

I looked up from bathing Staver's face. What could I tell her and not have her think me a witch?

Gasha answered. "You got your son back. Don't question the blessing. He'll wake when he's healed enough."

Thank you, Gasha.

My arms grew heavy as I dabbed dirt from the cut on Staver's arm. I'd not slept since the morning before. My head nodded, and I jerked it back up.

Mama wrapped a blanket around my shoulders. "I'll finish tending to Staver, and Irina is tending to Dyeda. Sleep."

I curled up next to Staver and for a moment glowed with our closeness before darkness stole me away.

THE NEXT DAY WAS A WEARY, heart-rending journey. Two more men died in the night. Two more families clung to each other in grief. We buried them, and Gasha's smith, then spoke in prayer the names of all the men lost.

The rest of the wounded slept, not even breathing more deeply as we strapped them to litters and carried them farther into the forest.

Staver's legs and shoulders bore bruising and a cut crossed his upper arm, but his head felt solid.

I walked at the back of the group, scanning the forest and keeping my bow ready. But often my eyes stole back to where

Staver lay, carried between Gasha and another tall woman. And then to Dyeda. What if they didn't wake? They had to. They'd lived this long. Their wounds were healing.

We trudged on. Even the children walked in solemn silence. The ones I loved were alive; still grief pressed against my chest like a millstone. How did the others bear the weight?

Finally, we reached the rabbit downs. The pulley was still there from the time I'd brought Dyeda and Baba to see my home. A toddler squealed and clapped in his mother's lap as he rode the bench to the top.

When the last people made it to the top, along with all the supplies, we set the mules free. They'd head home. We couldn't haul them up, and we couldn't have them drawing attention. Gasha's mule looked back at her and gave a parting, puzzled *neigh-hee-haw*, then, at her slap across its rump, it trotted off after the others. I led the mules across the rabbit downs.

One last thing.

I gathered the strongest women. "We must dismantle the pulley."

"How will we get down?" one protested.

"We have enough food to last us several weeks. By then the tsar's armies will have driven the Khan from our lands. And if they need a little more time, I'll hunt us meat. A clear spring falls from the cliffside behind you. And the hill is only steep, not a cliff. I'm sure many of you can climb it as well as I with a few practices. We'll be safe here."

One woman's face grew redder with each of my words. "So we are just going to hide!"

"Hush, Lara." The woman next to her placed a hand on the angry woman's shoulder. "She saved our men."

"She didn't save my brother or father. And the others seem to be under a witch's spell. I'm done listening to this fox-haired girl. I'm going back and killing every Scythian I can find."

"Don't, Lara." Her companion took hold of her arm.

"I will." She shook off the woman's hold, marched back to the pile of supplies, and grabbed a bow and quiver.

I stepped in front of her as she headed for the hill. "You are free to go. But not to come back."

She glared and shoved at me.

I didn't move.

She clenched her hands. "I have nothing to come back to. Papa and Levka were all my family."

"I'm sorry," I whispered and stepped aside.

She skidded down the steep hill and stalked from sight.

We unbound the rope on the pulley and brought it piece by piece back to the birch grove. Now we were less visible, though we'd need to keep a constant watch. I organized the women who knew how to use a bow into watches of three.

Then I followed the string that had pulled at me through the whole day and found Staver. He lay so still on a mat near a fire. Dyeda lay on the other side of the fire, his face drawn but not as pale as it had been when I found him on the battlefield. Baba cradled his head in her lap, murmuring words for his ears only.

Irina stood from Dyeda's side and laid a hand on my forehead. "You should rest."

I smiled at her concerned gesture. She'd first known me as a patient. "I'm not feverish, just hot with exertion. And I don't need rest. I need to be with Staver."

I sat next to Staver and cradled his head in my lap. "Staver, I heard you sing. It was more beautiful in your voice than I could have imagined. We will find our home together."

I sang in my quavery alto.

> My heart found new place,
> Not of house, not of forest.
> And wherever we dwell,

I am your home and—

Staver's lips parted, and he whispered "you are mine."

STAVER SLIPPED in and out of sleep for two more days. He never woke for longer than a few minutes, long enough to spoon some broth into his mouth and sometimes even a whispered word. Then he'd go limp again into sleep, though this one a troubled, whimpering one.

My world narrowed to him. Food appeared at my side, the fire was rebuilt, and others moved like shadows at the edge of my awareness. The weeping from another funeral tore at my ears, but I did not leave his side.

Dyeda woke, bringing cries of joy from Baba, and like Staver, fell asleep again.

I became a watching statue. Only my heart changed in movement, jumping each time he twitched or moaned.

On the morning of the third day since we set camp in the birch grove, Staver woke again and his eyes cleared of the confused fog. He reached up and brushed his fingers along my cheek. "I dreamed of you, and you are here."

I longed to kiss him but instead reached for some broth. If he was only awake for moments, he needed the nourishment.

He touched my wrist. "Not yet. I think it has something to make me sleep."

I dropped the spoon back into the bowl with a splash. Irina! Yes, he needed to heal, and I'd give him the broth, after we had time to talk.

He chuckled then touched my furrowed forehead. "You are beautiful, in all your emotions. But I prefer your smiles and laughs." He pulled me closer.

When we parted, he traced his forefinger along my lips. "And your kisses. Five months between a kiss is too long."

"You were gone for those five months, and I sent you plenty through letters!"

"You did. And I loved every one, and the laughter and joy. I treasure each word. But it was too long. Blast this war!"

"You remember?"

He winced. "All too much. I—"

"If it hurts, don't tell me."

"I want to."

I stroked his hair from his face, then traced along his red bristled jaw. The red beard was a surprise in contrast with his wheat colored hair, and it lay over pallid skin.

I'd stop him talking if he became worked up. Staver closed his eyes. "The Khan's army swept around our fortifications and rode northward. Our arrows felled some of them, but it didn't slow the main body. They didn't seem to care about securing the border, and our general feared that they'd sweep across Ruska and take the tsar's palace. We harried them from the back and sides as they rode northward. But we were only a thousand men against their ten thousand. Our general forced us to travel quickly. The cavalry rode ahead, and the footmen marched until they fell in weary heaps at the end of each day. The general left the wounded strewn behind us. We didn't have time. We had to stop the Khan. As a clerk, I was one of the few lucky enough to have a horse. I kept the numbers of supplies, numbers of men, numbers of dead. I'd like to forget the last."

I lay my hand on his cheek and kissed his brow. I also wished to forget the images burned into my dreams.

He leaned into my touch. "As we neared the duke's estate, I circled past the Khan's armies and found the duke. He told me you were safe. That was enough for me. I'd fight beside him to protect you. The Khan's army came. We fought. I fell."

I stroked his sweat-beaded forehead. "Staver. We're safe. You don't have to tell me more. Rest. I'll get you the broth now."

He took my other hand in his. "I need to talk out the nightmare and the miracle. When I woke, my head pulsed with a pain so strong that I could hardly breathe. I crawled until I made it into the forest. There my strength abandoned me, and all I could do was sing my nightingale's lament for losing you. Then you called out for me. You held me. And you took away the pain."

"Not all." I touched the bandage over his wounded arm.

He glanced sideways at it and half smiled. "That hurts, but I'll heal. I wouldn't have from the other. I could feel my life seeping away with each flaming pulse in my head." Then he frowned. "I shouldn't have lived when everyone else died."

"They didn't all die. Look, Dyeda is healing, and others too."

I helped Staver lift his head to look over at the still form of Dyeda. Baba smiled weakly at him. Her eyes bagged with sleepless worry.

He sighed and went limp in my arms. The sleep had stolen him again, even without the help of the broth. But maybe his dreams would be less troubled now that he knew he wasn't the only one alive.

17

———

MY WORLD EXPANDED BEYOND STAVER. I still didn't leave his side, but I watched the goings-on around me. The day filled with more joyful awakenings. Some men even took short walks amongst the birch trees while supported by a wife, sister, or child, often several of them. Laughter rang out, and murmured conversations filled the corners of our camp.

Dyeda still didn't wake except for that one short moment days before, though his heart continued slow and strong. Had the wolf amulet put him into a spelled sleep? How long could he go without food and water? The healer, Irina, resorted to dosing Baba with the same sleeping potion she'd used on Staver and the other severely wounded. Baba slept through the rest of the day beside Dyeda.

Evening shadows reached me as I checked the fletching on arrows and packed a satchel with snares.

"You're not planning on running off, are you?" Staver's voice sent a comforting delight up my back.

I plopped to my knees beside him. "No, I'm not running off."

"Good," he chuckled, "because I'd follow you, and I'm not feeling up to that yet."

"But I do need to start helping around the camp. I've ignored everyone for days. I promised Dyeda that I'd take care of and protect these women and children. So I'd better start doing it."

Staver pushed up on his elbows and glanced around at the tents spread between the trees, then fell back to his bedding. "It looks as though they are doing just fine."

"Yes, but they've used up all the deadfall wood, and I won't let them cut my birch trees, so we'll have to gather wood from the lower forest. And you could use some fresh meat to supplement the grain; we all could, so I'll set snares in the rabbit downs and hunt for some deer. And—"

Staver's chuckle turned into a full laugh. "Dyeda left this army under a good commander."

"That I did," whispered a hoarse, papery voice. Dyeda turned his head and looked at us.

I jumped up and squealed. "Dyeda, you're awake! I wish Baba was too. You have to stay awake long enough for her. Please. She's so worried about you."

He closed his eyes. "I'll try. This sleep is heavy on me."

The healer, Irina, came running and bustled about spooning broth into Dyeda's mouth and mixing up fresh tea for him. "Just rest. Don't talk. We'll get you well again, my lord."

Staver reached up and twined his fingers through mine. "You didn't shout like that when I woke."

"I kissed you instead."

He grinned. "I'll take the kiss over the shout."

"How about a dance for joy?" I moved a little way from Staver, giving myself a wide circle of clear ground, then crouched into the dance position that he'd described from the army and which Adrik had taught me. I swallowed a lump at the thought of Adrik, arrow pierced and pale, then shook the shadow away. I would be bright and joyful for Staver. I jumped and kicked and leaped, all the while keeping the careful line of balance that was the difference between only my feet hitting the ground and the rest of me smacking into it.

Staver clapped his hands in rhythm to my movements. "You never wrote you'd learned this, only that you tried and fell on your backside."

"I was keeping it a surprise. I thought we could dance together." Leaves crushed under my feet as I spun about and came to a stop by his side.

He laughed again. "I know some other dances that I very much want to dance with you. But ones that are much slower and much closer."

Heat rose up my neck and cheeks.

"And I have many nights worth of songs to sing for you, and stories to tell."

"When you are strong enough again."

"Stories don't take more than the tongue's strength."

I settled next to him and stroked his hair. "I'd love a story."

He closed his eyes and sighed at my touch, then began.

Once there was a young woman, Annika, who had seven older brothers as handsome as the days of the week. When her mother died, her father married again. The new mother wanted the admiration and more from her stepsons. When they each refused her, she turned them into swans.

Annika pled with the witch to change them back. The witch sneered and drew out from her dress a roll of parchment. "They can only be changed back by wearing shirts woven from stinging nettle gathered at midnight in the grand duke's graveyard. You may never speak before your task is complete. If you speak or fail to create the shirts, you and they will be my slaves for a thousand years."

Annika nodded solemnly, already resolved to be silent as the witch wrote in red ink on the parchment. Then she pricked her finger and pressed her beading blood to the agreement.

The witch and the parchment dissolved with the morning sun. Her seven brothers trumpeted and took flight, leading her over many weeks of weary journey to the grand duke's land. She made a home in a hollow tree an hour's walk from the graveyard. Her brothers brought her food each day, and every night in the midnight hour she harvested nettle, then spent her waking hours separating the fibers, twisting them into thread and weaving them into cloth. She never cried at the burning itch that covered her hands and lower arms.

I rested my head on Staver's chest and listened to his voice reverberate in melody over the beat of his heart. He wrapped his arms around me and continued.

One day two years later, the grand duke's son was out hunting and found Annika weaving in front of her tree. She'd grown from a young woman into a beauty that shone like the morning star. The duke's son had always taken what he wanted, never thinking it mattered what another thought. And when he saw her, he wanted her. He carried her back to the palace and married her. She never said a word against it, but only clung to her small loom and two nettle shirts.

Every night she sneaked from the palace and gathered the nettle, and every day she wove until the duke's son claimed her attention. In time she gave birth to a boy. But her joy was cut short when Zariyah, her husband's mother, entered the room. Zariyah had always made Annika shiver, but that evening as Annika clutched her newborn, Zariyah looked at her such that Annika almost broke her vow and screamed for help.

Zariyah leaned over and brushed her long knobby fingers over the infant's head. "A delicious child. I haven't tasted one in years. He will be perfectly plump in a month's time. And you, as a mute and a simpleton, can never tell your husband what happened."

I pushed away from Staver. "Don't tell me an ogre story!"

He clasped my hand and kissed it. "This will be the only one I ever tell. But let me finish. It ends well."

"Then be quick about it. Or I'll be sick." My stomach knotted up and threatened to make my words true.

He nodded and kissed me again. "I'll make it short."

Zariyah was an ogress. Her son didn't know, nor her husband. She'd not had man flesh in years, but she longed for it. Annika took her infant son to the forest and left him with a woodsman and his wife, then she redoubled her efforts to make the nettle shirts. Zariyah was furious and claimed that Annika had killed and eaten her own child. Annika could do nothing but shake her head to deny it, and her husband believed her.

Four more years passed, and she had almost completed the nettle shirts, when she bore another child, a girl. Annika didn't wait for Zariyah to come, but took her child to the woodsman the day after she was born. This time when Zariyah claimed that Annika had killed her own child, her husband believed and set a date for her execution. Annika wove and sewed all that night, and only lacked the sleeve of the last shirt when they carted her to be burned. Her seven brothers flew to the cart, and she threw the shirts over them. Each turned back into a man, save the youngest still had a swan's wing where his shirt lacked a sleeve.

Annika then spoke the truth, and Zariyah, the ogress, was imprisoned. Annika gathered her children. And her brothers never left her. Her husband learned to listen now that he had a wife who spoke gently but unabashedly. In time they grew to love each other and spent many happy years together.

My brows pinched. "Why did you tell me that story?"

He caressed my fingers. "I know my mother has acted much like the ogress in the story. I never want to be like the duke's son who was too blind to see and almost lost his wife and children. Please promise to tell me if ever someone mistreats you. Let me share in the pains you bear. Let me keep you safe. Tell me if I'm ever acting blind and stupid."

His earnestness cast off the chill of the story. "You are nothing like that duke's son." I leaned over to kiss him.

"Promise me. Please. I should have done more to protect you from my mother."

I rested my cheek against his. "I promise."

I WALKED *hand in hand with Staver through my birch-grove home. The sunlight dappled his hair and face. He leaned close to me, and his eyes danced with mirth. I tilted up my face for a kiss, but he placed his hands under my arms and lifted me, spinning me in a circle.*

I squealed then laughed, flinging my head back and opening my eyes to a spinning world of greens and blues.

Staver stopped spinning and pulled me close. The world slowed to a heartbeat.

A roar tore the air.

A giant of a woman, with matted brown hair down to her waist and a shaggy bearskin covering, pulled herself up onto my birch grove shelf. An ogress! She ripped a branch from one of my trees and flung it at us.

Staver pushed me to the ground as the branch swished by.

The ogress charged and grabbed Staver by his arm, lifting him into the air. I screamed.

"Vasilisa!" Staver shook me awake. "It's all right. I'm here."

I shuddered in his embrace. "Don't you ever, ever tell me another ogre story."

He buried his face in my hair. "I promise."

~

I THREW the empty snare across the rabbit downs. Empty, empty, and empty again! No fresh meat that day. We'd camped here three weeks, and that was a week too long for the rabbit supply.

"You're worried." Staver's voice startled me.

I whipped around. "How did you get down here?"

He held up dirt-coated hands and shrugged. The knees of his pants and shoes were coated in the same dirt. "I climbed down after you."

"You shouldn't. You're not—"

"I've healed. And I'll help."

"You can help with plenty of things without climbing down that hill."

He placed a hand behind my back and pulled me close, then whispered against my cheek. "I followed you so we could have a moment without everyone looking, and where we could talk without you worrying that others would overhear your fears. Now tell me what is worrying you and let me help."

I nestled into him and breathed deeply—birch, soil, soap, campfire, and under it a rich tangy sweetness and a lingering scent of herbs and illness. He wasn't healed yet. "Sit down and I'll talk."

We settled onto the grassy down, Staver's arm around my shoulder and holding me close against his side.

I blew out through my nose to clear his scent and my thoughts. "The rabbits have disappeared into our cooking pots or migrated to new homes. Our supply of grain is dwindling. The latrines are stinking up the whole camp and the flies are a plague. Papa's home was only meant for a small family, not for over a hundred. We'll have to spread to new parts of the forest."

"We could travel north and join the other refugees."

I shook my head. "Who knows where the battles are. I won't lead us into the middle of this war."

"Then we'll just spread to new parts of the forest until the war is over."

I bit my lip.

Staver tilted my chin up and studied me with his clear blue eyes. "What else? Something worries you even more than this."

I blinked back tears. "Did you know that Dyeda has a bad heart? I didn't! Irina finally told me, when I pressed her about why Dyeda was growing worse instead of better. He needs an herb she used to give to him daily, but it is back at the palace, or growing on a river bank many weeks to the north. She's used other herbs that grow in the forest to help him, but it isn't enough, not with how broken he is from the battle. He shouldn't have been in that battle! He shouldn't have been made to guard the border of Ruska!"

Staver stroked my arm and listened.

I took several breaths. "I'm going back to the palace to get the herb."

He stilled, his touch turning rigid.

"I have to. Dyeda will die if I don't."

"Then I'm coming with you. I carry three jewels we can use to bribe anyone in the palace to let us past."

"You don't have any jewels. I've washed every stitch of your clothing." I blushed. "But Irina was the one to take your garments off you, I didn't see—I mean there wasn't anything in your pockets. The Scythians or battle-followers robbed you."

He pulled one of his feet into his lap and tapped against his boot. "They are in here."

"Your boots were empty too."

He pulled a small knife from his belt and wedged it into the heel of the boot, then wiggled it back and forth until a section of leather separated from the rest of the heel. He pushed his fingers into the hole and pulled out a pouch. From the pouch he poured into my hand two gems as red as fox fur, and a third as small as a drop of water and as bright as a star. "The rubies were for your wedding earrings and the diamond for your ring."

The gems glittered in the forest sunlight, fire and snow side by side. They sat cool in my hand. Staver had chosen these for me. He must have saved every coin of his military pay to buy them. He'd wanted me to wear them. I closed my eyes to imprint their image in my mind, then poured the gems back into the pouch. "They are beautiful. If need be, they will buy my way into the palace to get Dyeda's herbs."

He half smiled. "I'm sorry. I'll find other jewels just as precious for you." Then he frowned and took the pouch from me. "I'm coming with you. If you sneak off without me, I will follow."

He would. Could I ask the other men to bind him to keep him at the camp? It would be better for him to struggle against ropes than run after me. I didn't need the gems. I'd sneak into the palace, find the herbs, and sneak out again.

Staver kissed my cheek. "What else is worrying you?"

"You."

He laughed. "Then we are even. We'll start for the palace as soon as we've gathered some supplies. But before we return up that hill I want to steal five minutes of time to just be us with no worries."

"Are you a thief then?"

He pulled me to my feet and led me off the downs to the firm ground at the base of the hill. He placed my left hand on his shoulder, held my right in his left, and placed his right hand on the small of my back. A breath of space vibrated between us.

I tilted my face up for a kiss.

Instead, he hummed a slow, swaying melody and moved in floating steps. I stumbled against his smooth motions, but he kept me from falling, and I began to understand his hand on my back guiding me and the sure steps of his legs. I merged into his movements and we became one, separated by a breath and bound by a heartbeat.

His hummed melody died away in a long sweet note, leaving the twittering of birds to serenade us. He bent and kissed me, and not even a breath separated us.

I couldn't leave him again. But I had to. I'd be back by the next day. Then I'd never leave him again.

Staver kissed me once more, a quick brush of lips. "May I have your next dance, when we return?"

I took a shaky breath. "We should hurry."

We scrambled up the hill. At the top I looked around the birch grove. "I'll ask Irina exactly where the herb is."

Staver nodded, his breath labored. "I'll pack some food." He wouldn't be able to walk the distance between our camp and Dyeda's palace, let alone run it. Why did Staver think he could come?

I found Irina crushing herbs near Baba and Dyeda. Dyeda's face had grown ghostly pale. "I'll get the heart herb from the palace. And I need a quick sleeping drought for Staver, or he'll try to follow me."

Irina lifted her eyebrows and opened her mouth, then closed it. Finally she put down the bowl and pestle. "Vasilisa, I don't like drugging Staver, and I don't like your going back there, but..." Her lips thinned. "I don't know any better way." She explained where to find the herb, plus what other useful herbs to bring, all the while mixing a tea for Staver. Then she took it over to him. "Something to give you strength before you go."

He drank it then continued to pack supplies. I moved over to help.

His movements grew clumsy. He fell forward. I caught his shoulders and rolled him over, cradling his head in my lap.

He stared into my face with a mix of betrayal and sorrow. "Don't go without me."

"I'm sorry Staver. I love you. I'll be back by tomorrow."

His eyes closed.

Several others in the camp came running. "Is Master Staver hurt?" Gasha asked.

Irina leaned over him and checked his heartbeat. "I believe he overexerted himself climbing the hill. He will be fine when he wakes." Then she muttered just loudly enough for me to catch, "He'll have a headache and a worse heartache. Don't keep him waiting long, or nothing I do will keep him here. I don't dare give him a second dose of the sleeping drought."

I nodded, belted on my water pouch, slung my food satchel over my shoulder, and added my quiver and bow. Staver stretched out on his sleeping mat near Dyeda. Mama knelt next to him, her face tight with worry. Irina must have told her, or she'd guessed. I ran back and gave her a quick hug and handed her the wolf amulet. "Keep this safe, and use it if you need to. I'll be back soon. Watch over him for me."

She squeezed me tightly. "Be careful."

I slipped down the hill.

18

BROWN TENTS, shaped like upside-down bowls, filled the grounds around the palace. Cooking fires flickered in the twilight. Had the tsar driven the Khan back here? If so, then the war was almost over. But Dyeda couldn't wait even another week. I still had to enter the palace.

Four men sat drinking around the cooking fire closest to me. One belched and pounded his chest over his padded jacket. He spoke in a slurred and heavily accented voice. "You Ruskans know your spirits. Arkhi is nothing compared to this—what d'you call it?"

Another man, wearing the simple linens of a Ruskan field worker, responded, "Vodka."

"Ah yes, vodka. We'll drink this every day when our Khan rules this land."

The Ruskan downed his drink. "That'll be soon enough. The *Little Father*," the man cackled, "cares more for his weakling son than all the rest of Ruska."

The Little Father? That was an affectionate nickname for our tsar, not that this man held any affection for him. What had they done to his son?

A third man, wearing a conical hat, stood and yelled at the others in harsh and guttural words with lots of *chr* and *shc* sounds. Almost as though someone had combined a growling dog with a snake.

The others around the fire laughed and waved him away. The man shook a clenched hand at them and stomped toward the forest, and me.

I nocked an arrow in my bow, then lowered it.

He was unaware. This wasn't a battle. Could I kill him? He'd been part of the army that killed Adrik and almost all the other men. If it weren't for them, Dyeda wouldn't be ghost-white and dying.

I raised the bow again.

He thwacked a tree branch as he walked past it, then settled under a pine.

If I killed him, I could steal his clothes and enter the army more easily.

The man pulled out a small knife and a partially carved piece of wood.

I bent my weight against the bow.

He began to hum and carve.

I squinted.

He was carving a doll.

For whom? A little girl? His daughter?

My fingers trembled against the weight of the draw. I relaxed my arm and placed the arrow back in the quiver.

If I shot him, I'd tear and blood-stain the clothes. That would make it harder to go undetected.

I picked up a thick deadfall branch and crept forward. When I was a stride away from him, a twig snapped under my feet.

He looked up as I swung the branch, then fell with a grunt. The doll and knife slipped from his fingers to the ground.

I picked up the doll. The last of the evening sun showed wide-set eyes crinkled with an open-mouthed smile.

I stripped the man of his outer clothes: a long padded tunic that crossed in the front, wide-legged pants, curled-toed boots, and a conical hat.

Then I laid him against the tree and nestled the doll in his hands. "May you return safely to her and never see war again."

The clothes were baggy over my frame, but they were not too long. This Scythian was a short man, with powerful thick shoulders, probably from years of archery.

I donned the clothes and shoes, then tucked my braid into the conical hat, wetting down the stray wisps and pushing them under too. The man had black hair. My red hair would stand out like fire on a moonless night.

I set my bow high in the boughs of a pine and picked up his smaller bow and tested it. The draw was heavy for so small a bow, and the curve doubled back on itself. It felt strange, but my longbow would set me apart from the others even more than my red hair. As long as I kept to the shadows, my face shouldn't give me away.

I unpacked the last of my food from the satchel and set it beside my bow. I'd eat the food on my return trip, but I needed the satchel empty for Irina's herbs.

Too much thinking. I needed to move. I walked back into the tent-filled garden.

The men at the fire motioned me over and the Ruskan laughed. "See, he's cooled off. Come join us."

I shook a clenched hand and stomped past them.

They just laughed more.

The men around other fires ignored me as I moved past. Their noise level climbed with raucous laughter and off-key singing as more and more men downed vodka.

The library doors opened onto the end of the garden. Light

poured through the large windows. Irina's study sat in a room above it. Those windows were dark.

All I had to do was enter Irina's study, find the herbs, and leave. It would be simple. Let the tsar drive the Scythians out.

A thick grapevine clung to the wall and wound its way to a balcony. An easy climb. But window light and fire illuminated it, and four men stood guard at the library doors, their mouths stiff lines, their eyes scanning the growing revelry of the surrounding camp.

A soldier drunkenly stumbled from one of the campfires toward the library door. One guard drew his bow and grunted at the man, who laughed and continued forward.

The guard released the arrow.

The man fell with a strangled scream.

I swallowed at the acid rising in my throat. *No. Not that way.*

I slipped around to the south of the palace. An orchard sat along that wall, but the closest tree was twenty feet from me. I moved in the shadows of the trees, past a wheelbarrow and three wooden crates. Those I could stack.

I grabbed a crate in each hand, but then the rising moon revealed something better.

A ladder leaned against an apple tree.

I dropped the crates, swung the ladder over one shoulder, and slipped to the palace walls.

Fewer tents and campfires sat along this side, but still at least ten fires glimmered and cast the shadows of drunken dancing and wrestling warriors. *They won't notice me. There aren't any guards. I'll be fine.*

My pulse throbbed in my hands against the ladder.

One window sat open. Whoever opened it was probably also sleeping in it. But maybe he was also drunk.

The ladder only reached halfway up the wall to the open window fronted by a daisy-filled flower box. I stood on the top rung, stretched out my fingers, and grasped the window ledge. My feet scrambled against the plastered walls as I pulled upward.

Once my elbows were up level with the ledge, I hooked my arms over the small lip that lay in front of the flower box, then swung one leg and then the other up into the daisies, and curled upward. The crushed flowers competed with the scent of fear.

None sounded an alarm.

I slipped into the room and pressed against the wall.

Clothing lay draped across a rumpled bed.

Nothing moved.

I drew my bow—the Scythian's bow—and approached the bed.

It was empty.

I brushed dirt from my pants with trembling fingers, double-checked my cap, then opened the door to the hall. A glow from a stairway at the end added enough light to reveal a long line of closed doors. Irina's study would be along the west wing.

Music poured down the hall. Twangy instruments and thumping drums mixed with singing that was fiercer than the drunken singing outdoors. Deep, guttural, undulating, and sometimes rising to shrill cries, it was more animal than music.

I walked towards the light and the noise, trying to keep my stride silent but purposeful. *I belong here. I am a servant, an invisible part of keeping food, clothing, and comfort before those in control.* I'd spent most of my life in that role. It should be easy. I wiped sweat on the padded tunic. The area under my arms grew damp.

The hall turned at the top of a lighted stairway, one which led to the great hall. Men leapt about on the floor, their long tunics swishing around their legs.

I clung to the wall as I turned the corner at the top of the stairs. Irina's study sat along this new hall. The music followed me. Her study would be at least three, maybe four doors down.

I cracked open the third door to an unlit room. It only had a four-poster bed, an armoire, and a mirrored desk. I opened the next door. Jar-filled shelves and books stacked in tall wooden cases filled three of the four walls; windows filled the fourth. In the middle sat a table topped with bowls, pestles, and knives. The items were scattered, as though someone had left in a hurry, but nothing was broken. The enemy hadn't entered the room, or if they had, they'd not found it worth their time to rummage through it.

I shut the door quietly behind me, then lit a small lamp and searched for a large green glass jar. One sat on a shelf a little above my eye level.

I held the lamp up. Irina's writing was more cramped than Dyeda's or Mama's.

It wasn't the herb.

Another green jar sat on the table. *Dragon Slipper* was scrawled across the white label. *Found it!*

I searched and found three of the other four herbs that Irina asked for, but the last one, *lacewing root,* hid amongst the many small clay jars that made up a majority of the containers. I looked more carefully through a shelf, shifting the jars, and looking at the labels.

The offkey singing and boisterous laughter had died away outside the window, and the wildness inside had changed to a mournful sound that could have been a ballad. It was almost beautiful. How late was the night?

I tucked the jars I'd gathered into my satchel. *Lace* showed on a clay jar between two others. I shifted the jars to find *Spider's Lace.* Why did she have so many herbs? And why didn't she order them by the beginning letter of their name? Did Dyeda need lacewing root? Or could I leave without it? Irina had said *Dragon Slipper* was the most important, and—

The door swung open and a bright lamplight filled the room, my shadow becoming a dark shape against the shelves.

I spun about, whipping my bow off my shoulder and placing an arrow onto the string. I squinted at two blurred forms.

A quavery voice, matching a quavering light, cried in perfect Ruskan, "Don't hurt me!"

The forms solidified into two men. A mousy man held a lamp and a piece of parchment. The other wasn't any taller, but his broad shoulders were twice the width of the first man's, and he wore the Scythian cross-chest tunic. He held a curved sword in one hand. He grunted something in Scythian, glared at me, then spoke in broken Ruskan. "Put bow down."

"No." I held my bow bent and ready to release.

"Please!" The mousy man stepped back, so he was halfway into the hall. If he ran for help, I'd never get out of here.

"Stop." My voice combined with the Scythian's.

The man froze.

I stepped towards them. "I only came for herbs to help the injured. If you let me go, you'll both live. But otherwise, at least one of you will die, and I haven't decided which one yet."

The Scythian's brows pinched in confusion, then rose at the word "die". He wore a finely tooled leather tunic and boots. He must have been one of the higher officers.

The parchment crackled and shook in the mousy man's hands. "I'm a healer, too. Take the herbs and go. We won't harm you."

The Scythian shook his head. "Not man. Woman voice and face. Take prisoner." He lunged forward.

I released the arrow.

It struck the Scythian in the chest. He stumbled to one knee, then rose with a roar, swinging his sword.

I turned and leapt onto the window seat, thrusting my shoulder against the glass. The window shattered, and I fell outward, onto the grape arbor. Shouts came from behind and below me.

They couldn't take me. I had to get the medicine back to Dyeda. Ignoring the sting of glass shards, I rolled to my feet on one of the arbor cross pieces then leapt to the ground.

Someone tackled me.

"Get off!" I yelled as I threw him from my back.

More strong hands grabbed. Guttural shouting surrounded me.

I swung my fists and elbows and kicked. At each crushing contact, a hand loosened, but another took its place.

Then a point pressed against my neck, and a tickle of blood pooled around the sting.

"Be still, beast."

I took a shallow breath and stared down at a long spear held by one guard—the one who'd shot down a man earlier that night for approaching the doors. Two other guards held my arms. Why hadn't they killed me?

The man with the spear had blood running from his nose.

A deep voice called in Scythian from the window. He sounded too strong for having been shot in the chest.

One guard ripped off my helmet. Shattered glass rained over my shoulders, and my braid tumbled down my back.

The mousy voice gasped from above. "It *is* a woman. The Khan will find this interesting—especially if we can find where she gets her strength."

With the pressure of two spears at my back, I walked down the stairs and to the cellar door. The inside corners of my eyes stung, and I sniffed. I'd been so close to obtaining the herbs and getting away. At least they'd left the pouch of herbs with me. *Hold on, Dyeda. I'm going to get free and help you.*

A guard unlocked the door, and at the insistence of the

spears, I walked into the cool, dark room. The door clanged shut behind me.

"I see they've sent me a companion." The voice was quiet, melodious, and sounded too much like Staver, except the man had the slight burr of northern Ruskans.

"Who are you?" I felt out in the dark and found empty grooved shelving where bottles once sat. Had the army emptied the whole cellar with their drinking?

"I'm Askold, son of Rurik."

"Rurik? The li—" I stopped feeling my way along the shelving.

His voice dropped to a whisper. "The Little Father. The tsar."

19

———————

I KNELT beside the prince of Ruska, heir to the throne, and wished for a lamp or a window. He was a voice in the darkness, radiating warmth in the cool room—close, invisible, and injured.

I fingered the bump on his head and the puffy skin around one eye.

Askold's jaw tightened as I touched torn skin at the base of his ear.

"I'm sorry to hurt you."

"You are gentler than they were. All they did was pour vodka on my wounds and throw me in here."

"How are you here?"

He laughed darkly. "I was a fool and trusted a man who promised us an easy victory."

I poured some water from my pouch over the torn skin.

He continued. "Two days ago—maybe three. It is hard to tell in a room with no light. A man entered our army encampment with a stolen message from the Khan to one of his generals. That is what the man claimed. My father, in more wisdom than I'll ever possess, turned the man away. I followed the man out of my father's tent and ordered him to show me the message. It detailed a time and a place that the Khan would meet with a general."

His voice caught. "I'd never seen death before this month. And in these weeks I've seen enough to fill each place in every ball and banquet from my earliest memory. The land stinks with it, and this man promised a way to end it."

I took off my padded Scythian tunic and laid it under his head. Then I tore off a strip of fabric from the lower edge of my riding dress and bound it over his bump and the torn ear. "So you followed him?"

He shook his head, loosening the knots I was trying to tie. "I'd have never made it past my guards in daylight. I waited until the night when the moon set and slipped away. The sentries almost caught me, but they were looking for men approaching, not leaving. When I'd walked a mile or two down the road, the man who'd brought the message met me. Together we'd kill the Khan and the war would end. I never suspected otherwise. He was Ruskan with simple peasant speech and a strong work-bearing back, one of our loving and devoted subjects. I am a fool!" He struck the floor, and it echoed dully.

"What happened?"

"He led me to the Khan and his army. They gave me gifts of a beating and a swift ride south. If I'd not left, our army would have driven the Khan's army from the last part of our nation, just as we'd driven them thus far. But now I am a pawn that they'll use to take the tsar."

A pawn, the tsar. It was a game. One the Khan had the upper hand in. But we could turn it around. We had to.

Askold touched my hand. "Why are you here?"

The weight of the reason fell heavy on my shoulders. I'd managed not to think about it while he told his story. "My dyeda is dying and needs herbs that were stored in this palace. I was caught trying to take them." I touched the satchel with the herbs. The guards hadn't taken it from me, though they took my bow—the Scythian's bow and helmet. If I could get free, would I take them back to Dyeda? Or would I help the prince escape?

"I'm sorry, my lady."

"What I don't understand is how the Scythian didn't die when I shot him."

"Who?"

"The Scythian officer in the healer's room. I shot him in the chest. He fell, then rose again, and almost cut me down."

He chuckled sadly. "The officers wear a stiffened leather tunic backed by chainmail that stops many of our warriors' arrows. A lady's bow would hurt no more than a child throwing a block."

So that was it. Even with the Scythian bow's heavy draw, it didn't penetrate his tunic.

"You should sleep," I said. "It was late night when they caught me. A few hours of sleep will help when we escape."

He took a sighing breath. "You are right. It would be better for me to die trying to escape, than be used against my father. Rest in heaven's watch until we reach its glorious realms." He added in a whisper. "I didn't expect to see it so soon."

I took off my wide-legged Scythian pants and laid them over him, humming one of Staver's songs, the one about the eagle and the bear. I was now back to my short riding dress and leggings.

We wouldn't die. We'd escape.

I BLINKED awake to a bright lamp light and rough hands grabbing my shoulders. I stifled a scream as a face resolved to my sleep-blurred eyes. It was my childhood tormentor—the one who'd almost killed me and injured Staver when I tried to leave the manor. "Gleb!"

He sneered, and an overpowering stink of vodka came from his open mouth. "The ogre spawn came to rescue the tsar's fool of a son? Did you grow tired of the attention of the simple nobleman?"

My fist hit his temple.

He crumpled on top of me.

"Heaven preserve us." Askold's voice came muffled through Gleb's heavy, reeking body.

Holding my breath against Gleb's breathing near my face, I rolled him off.

Three spear points greeted me. One pressed against my now thinly protected chest, only a cotton vest and riding dress between the point and my skin. The other two wavered inches from me. The bearers of the spears looked at me with fear. Some of my own fear evaporated.

I pushed at one spear, so its tip slipped sideways over my shoulder. "Don't point that at me."

A voice came from behind them. It was the mousy man, though this time his voice didn't tremble. "The Khan will see both of you now. Don't fight, or the prince will be in worse shape when his father sees him, and that would be a pity. I really hoped to bring him whole."

I glanced behind me to the prince. Askold looked nothing like Staver, though his voice was similar. Under my green linen bandage, his dark brown hair hung in sweaty tangled waves to his shoulders, and his heavy black brows sat over mournful brown eyes. His face was thin with sharp cheekbones, one I'd sooner expect to see on a winter-starved peasant than a well-fed noble. Though he stood tall, he had narrow shoulders. He was no warrior.

Even if I could fight my way free, Askold couldn't. I let them bind my hands behind me.

One guard held up a dipper of water. I sipped it. It was tainted with something sweet and slightly salty. I spat it out at his feet.

It was a chess game, and we were the pieces. I had to watch and see the Khan's moves, and figure out my own. Gleb was a frightening piece, but not one with much thought. I could disregard him. Was the mousy man the tsarina of the game? Who was he? He'd claimed to be a healer. "Master Healer?"

The mousy man inclined his head.

"The prince is injured. If you want him whole to show to the tsar, don't you want to tend to those hurts first?"

He shrugged. "You seemed to have already tended to them. And if his father won't listen, then the prince won't have to suffer much longer from them." He took a step towards me and touched my face. His fingers came away with flaked blood. "You, I want to keep alive. We should have cleaned the glass cuts yesterday, but I was still too shocked to think well." He pulled out a flask and poured some on a pressed handkerchief, then dabbed it to my face and neck.

It stung, especially on my neck, where the guard had pressed the spear the night before. I thrust my head down and sideways, pinching his fingers between my chin and shoulder blade.

He squeaked and jerked against my pinch. "Let go!"

"Why should I?"

"I'll speak in your favor."

"No, you'll let me speak in my favor for as long as I want." I squeezed his fingers tighter between my chin and collarbone, though not too hard, yet. I didn't want to break them if I didn't need to.

"Yes, yes, you can speak. Just let me go!"

"You swear."

"On the tsar himself."

How would I keep him to his promise? "Means nothing. You betrayed him." I pinched my chin tighter, and his knuckles creaked.

He cried, "I swear by the Khan whom I serve. And these men are my witnesses."

I kept my chin tight against his fingers. "Do you men understand and witness his oath?"

The three guards sniggered, until one elbowed his companion and their faces drew back to semi-seriousness. "We hear. We'll hold him to it."

It'd have to be enough. I released the mousy man.

He backed away from me, rubbing his pinched fingers with his other hand.

I stared into the man's wide shifting eyes. "Who are you?"

"You'll find out soon enough. Let's go."

THE PRINCE and I followed guards, and more guards followed us, up the cellar stairs. The pouch with Dyeda's herbs still hung at my side. I'd not taken it off, even to sleep. If only I could break free. The prince stumbled behind me and groaned as a guard cuffed him.

No, I couldn't escape yet, not without him. We were marched through the kitchens and dining hall, ending in the great hall. At the far end sat a dais made of the dining hall tables, pushed together, and on top of the dais sat a man in Dyeda's favorite chair, a stuffed green velvet with a matching footstool.

As we approached, his features resolved from a round face with a long black mustache—a feature most of the Scythians seemed to favor—to a man with high straight eyebrows, dark eyes that watched me with an intensity that sent a shiver down my back, and a firm emotionless mouth.

The spear at my back jabbed me. "On your knees," hissed the guard.

Askold tumbled to his knees beside me.

I turned and kicked the spear out of the guard's hands.

Six other spears pressed against me.

"Hold." The Khan's voice was deep, guttural, and calm.

The pressure of the other spears reduced.

I clenched my teeth to keep them from chattering. Hopefully that meant they wanted me alive. Could I show my strength, as long as I didn't threaten the Khan's life or try to escape? Let it be so. I wouldn't bow before him. I'd remain strong. I'd win the Khan's respect. And in that strength and respect, I'd move my pieces into play.

I turned back and stared into the Khan's face.

He inclined his head. "Come, sit." He motioned to the velvet footstool.

The mousy man ran forward. "She's dangerous, my lord."

"Yes. A beautiful wolf." He spoke in unstuttering Ruskan, despite his guttural voicing of all the hard sounds.

I leaped onto the waist-high dais. Because of my bound arms, I landed slightly unbalanced, wavering.

The Khan stood and grabbed my arm with a firm grip. "Sit."

I sat on the footstool.

He fingered my hair, tracing my black lock, then rubbing my red locks between his fingers and thumb. "Did you dye this?"

I held myself rigid to keep from pulling away. I would win his trust and his respect. "I was born this way."

"Not wolf then, but fox. Where did you get your strength?"

"I was born with it."

He grabbed my chin and turned my face to one side then the

other. "You hide your strength in a frail form. Thin bones, slender muscles. What magic do you use?"

I locked eyes with him. "None, but what I inherited from my father. It cannot be given nor taken."

"Ah!" He smiled, and I shivered. "Then it can be given to my children. I've not taken a new wife in more than a year."

I leapt backward off the stool. "Never! You'll die first."

"Then, I'll just have to weaken you until you are safe enough to take to wife." He turned his gaze from me. "Take her back to the cell. No food for a week, but give her plenty of water and keep her wounds clean." He then said something lengthy in Scythian.

The room burst into laughter.

What piece did I have left to play in this game? Why had I told him the source of my strength? I should have lied and told him it was from a potion that required ingredients gathered in the harvest moon, and winter's shortest day, and spring time's first flooding. I'd be less a prisoner in a cell waiting to gather the ingredients than in his harem. I could have escaped a cell.

And what about the prince? Askold needed help. All of Ruska needed help. I had a week before I'd be called to the Khan. How long did the prince have before he'd be used to force his father's hand?

The mousy man barked out orders. "Get her back to the cell. Don't make the Khan wait."

The two guards leapt onto the dais and pressed their spears against me to make me step away from the Khan.

"Wait!" I glared at the guards, and they fell back a step, then turned to the Khan. "That man swore an oath on your name that I could speak as long as I wanted. And three of the guards witnessed it."

The Khan held up his hand. "Is that true, Yakov Udinsky? Then speak, foxling. I honor his oath."

Udinsky? Hadn't Staver mentioned him in his letters? A mystic who claimed one could be strong just through thought. Was this mousy man the same person? He trembled under the Khan's gaze. He lacked power of body and mind.

I snorted. "Not a healer, but mystic Udinsky. Purveyor of cheap parlor tricks. What did you promise the Khan? Eternal life? Strength beyond that of a man? All of Ruska?"

Yakov twitched on the last one.

"And what part of Ruska did you give him? You are camped on the southern border, driven like sheep from the wheat field."

Yakov lifted his chin. "I got him the prince, and the tsar will give up Ruska for him."

"You didn't get him the prince. Some strong-backed peasant did. And you are not a strong-backed peasant. Maybe a peasant, but there is nothing strong about you."

The Khan laughed. "Well said, foxling."

Yakov stuttered. "My K-Khan, my oath leader. It was m-my plan that brought him." His stuttering smoothed into slick words. "And it is my plan that will give you Ruska, despite our losses. If you'd followed my advice and sent assassins to the duke's palace before the army approached, we would have taken them by surprise. But even now I offer you Ruska. The tsar loves his son. He will do anything, especially when his son pleads for his life."

"I won't." Askold knelt with head high. "You may threaten to kill me in front of my father, but I will never ask him to trade our motherland for me."

Yakov smirked. "I have my magics to make you plead and cry like a girl-child, and you'll never remember it."

I elbowed the satchel of herbs that I still carried. Could Yakov also be an herbalist? Irina taught me a little of herbs and what they could do, including one that could do what Yakov threatened. Was that why Yakov had entered Irina's study—to use her herbs?

I turned to the Khan. "If he can use his magics against the prince and the tsar, how long will it be before he uses them against you? Do you think he'll be content to serve you, when he could become Khan of both Scythia and Ruska? He is an oath breaker, even if you are not."

The Khan lowered his brows. "Do Ruskans break oaths that easily?"

"Any who have joined your armies are oath breakers. For each child from their first year of speech swears an oath to love, honor, and protect the tsar—not once but on each name day. Yakov must have sworn it fifty times in his life."

Yakov touched his lined face and scowled. "What do you know of oaths?"

"I love a man, whom I would marry, but for my oath to obey the tsar's laws that a commoner not marry a noble. And for that oath I was willing to leave and live alone in the forest."

The Khan settled back into the chair. "Foxling, I find you interesting. Tell me of this man and this oath. And then I'll decide what to do about the oath breakers in my ranks, especially the one who seeks my power."

Yakov paled. The Khan's once powerful piece tottered. Or did Yakov think himself the tsar of this game? Not now, with guards that once surrounded me closing in around him.

I'd almost removed the Khan's trusted tsarina and many of his pawns. I had a week to find my own freedom. I'd worry about that later. For now, I must win the Khan's trust with a tale —and not break in the telling.

"There was a young nobleman who was a friend to a servant girl. But the law forbade more than friendship, and I didn't allow myself to hope. When I learned he would announce his betrothed, I ran off to the forest, though I was injured by lightning and weaker than I'd ever been. Two field hands, one who now serves you, beat me and would have killed me, but the nobleman came to my rescue. He told me he'd found a noble family to take me in and he promised he would find a way so by law we could marry. Only later did I learn that he also gave up his inheritance and joined the army, so he could marry me within the bounds of the tsar's law."

I rolled back my shoulders. "Our love is stronger than any desire for power. And our oaths to the tsar are stronger than love. I do not swear lightly."

The Khan clapped slowly. "You will provide much evening entertainment with your tales. I would hear the story from your young nobleman and see if it matches. Does he still live?"

I swallowed, as memories pushed forward—of his injuries, and long days of sleep. "He lives, but he was injured in the first battle, as were many others. I came here for herbs to tend to them."

"I see. The pouch you carry wasn't for your strength but for them. I'll have it delivered and bring them back here."

"You can't!" Why did I reveal that? I spoke too much again. Had the small bit of tainted water made my tongue like a wagging gossip's? If I was to be a gossip, then I could lie and send him the wrong direction. "They are hidden too well in the eastern," my voice quavered on the word and stuck in my throat. I forced it out, "eastern forest. You'll never find them."

The Khan grabbed my chin and jerked my head to face Yakov. "My *oath breaker* used his magic to make you tell the truth. When you lie it shows in your voice and face like mud on a white horse. Don't try again."

So it was the water. But I'd not swallowed. How could so little do that? Or was it in the liquid he dabbed on my wounds?

The Khan released my chin and leaned back in his chair. "I'll find them. One of my other Ruskan *oath breakers* saw two women carry the wounded into the *western* forest shortly after the battle."

The room spun. I'd not removed Yakov from the Khan's use and now I'd placed all whom I loved in danger.

The Khan clapped his hands twice. "If you don't have more stories to entertain me, or pleas for your beloved nobleman, I have preparations to make for the tsar."

"When will he be here?" I threw out the question. I'd not speak in anything but questions until the spell or potion wore off.

"He is here."

I tilted my head to listen. There were no battle sounds.

The Khan laughed. "He won't attack while we have his son. And tomorrow he will have him again, when I am ready."

"What will you do to the prince?"

"That depends on the tsar."

"And Yakov?"

The Khan's lips thinned into a cold smile. "He'll join you in your cell. I'll even have you unbound. And if he's not alive tomorrow, then it is one less prisoner to feed. Now go. I have no more time for your questions."

I stumbled to the edge of the dais as two guards pressed me with their spears. I'd betrayed Staver. I had to warn him. I had to warn them all. But how?

20

Yakov Udinsky's rapid breaths echoed around the empty cellar. He kept to a corner far from me, and except for his breathing, he made no noise.

Askold curled up in a different corner and fell asleep. I checked his breathing and his head. One was steady, and the other was no more swollen than before, though he was too warm. My wolf amulet would have helped him, but I'd left it with Mama.

I settled into a spot away from the other two, rubbing my arms and wrists where the ropes had burned them. I'd strained against the ropes when speaking with the Khan, and my skin bore many small slivers. The burns and slivers were distractions from the pain inside and the bubbling anger. I reached for the pouch that held Dyeda's herbs, then stopped. The Khan had taken it.

If the prince hadn't been stupid enough to leave the tsar's camp, he wouldn't have been captured, and the Scythians would not all be camped in Dyeda's palace, and I'd have gotten the herbs and gone back. He was a fool! But an innocent one.

Yakov was the traitor. He'd convinced the Khan to attack.

Thousands were dead because of him. Staver had almost died and he could be captured because of Yakov. No! That last part was my fault. I'd betrayed Staver by telling the Khan where he was.

I thumped my fists against my legs.

I needed to think, not feel. I closed my eyes, though it was already black in the cell, and pictured my father hunting a rat that had once bitten me. He didn't kill the animal. He stalked it. Quiet, sly, watchful. Until he found its nest. Then he killed them all.

Yakov was a rat. Could I use him against the other rats? Could he help me escape and warn Staver? He was a trembling animal. Could I lie yet? I couldn't kill him, but I needed him to think I would. Then I could force him to my will.

"Traitor Yakov."

He yelped.

"I give you a choice. Die now or help me."

He shifted in his corner. "I should have given you the herb to make you docile. What beast are you?"

"I'm fair folk."

He barked a laugh. "They don't exist."

"Then who do you say I am?"

"A product of a powerful mystic. A monster created to win wars. I've read the books on such attempts. But none have succeeded. Did you kill your creator?"

I took a step in his direction. "I am fair folk. I've not killed any man, yet." I took another step, thumping my Scythian boot against the floor.

He scrambled. "I'll help you. I have men loyal to me, both Ruskan and Scythian. They'll free us."

"How do you know this?"

"One of the guards who pushed us into this room is mine. I

signaled him with hand signs. He'll gather the others, and at the appointed time they'll free me—us."

"And that time is?"

"In the fifth hour from sunset."

I bowed my head, clenched my hands, and then released them. A shiver ran over my skin, and the tightness in my chest loosened a breath. I'd be free. I'd race to Staver and the others and warn them. The trackers wouldn't find them today. They couldn't.

Yacov could be lying and just trying to stay alive, but it made sense that he'd have men loyal to him and a plan of escape if he fell out of favor with the Khan. I'd be free tonight.

I wrapped that hope around my shoulders and pulled it tight, muffling my fear.

The hours passed in darkness. Yakov fell to a soft-breathing sleep, a relief from his panting fear. Askold shifted but didn't wake. The guards changed twice, their heavy tread thumping down the stone stairs and then other tread fading upward and away from me.

I ripped another couple strips of fabric from my riding dress. My dress now only fell to my hips over my soft leather pants, instead of just above my knees.

Yakov jerked awake as I bound his arms behind him. He muttered, "Monster... beast... insulting wench... I'll—"

I pulled the bonds tighter.

He groaned. "Please, loosen them."

I loosened them slightly, then paced along the opposite wall. It would be time soon.

Soon took longer than winter.

Staver, stay safe. I paced. *May the trackers get lost and wander in circles. May they break their horses' legs in rabbit holes.* I turned at the wall. *May the women archers be watching and stop them. May the men be healed enough to draw a bow. May... may... may. Please.*

The guards changed.

I shook Askold awake. "We'll escape soon. Be ready to run."

"Thank you, my lady. I will try. But do not wait for me."

Soon, soon, soon.

The guards changed again.

A rooster crowed outside.

My hope unraveled. No one was coming.

THE DOOR OPENED. Three guards stepped through: two with spears and one with a lantern and a bucket of water. They were all Scythian.

I leapt to my feet. "What time is it?"

The two with spears thrust them towards, but not touching, me.

The water bearer studied me, then shook his head and spoke in Scythian. The Khan sent those who didn't speak Ruskan. I couldn't even have the comfort of asking my questions. *Did they find Staver? Is he here? Will I get to see him again?*

The water bearer set down the bucket then pulled a jar from a pouch. He opened it and held it out to me. A salve to help my cuts? Water and healing, but no food. The Khan kept his word.

And I would keep mine. I'd escape and free Staver. I needed to keep infection away. I took the salve.

He bent over Askold and changed the bandage around his head. This Scythian had more compassion. Would he help?

He turned his mild gaze to Yakov and motioned to him.

Yakov lay, bound and white faced, in the corner, his pale eyes pinched under his sandy eyebrows.

"He's not hurt," I said.

Perhaps the Scythian understood, because he shrugged and turned to leave the room.

"Wait!"

He turned back.

"Please let me free." I put my hands together in a pleading motion. Surely he understood that.

He did. He raised a hand in a motion of shooing a cat, and left my cell, taking the light with him. The door clanged shut.

I should have grabbed a spear and fought my way free. "Next time," I muttered.

I drank a dipper full of clear water then gave some to Askold until he turned away.

"Thank you, my lady," he whispered, his voice weaker. "I'll fight, too, when they come."

"How did you know I'd fight?"

"You are warrior-hearted, like my father. He'd not sit in a cell, waiting. I'm not like him, though I try."

"But you are injured."

"I'll not exchange Ruska for my life."

"Then you are like the Little Father." I rubbed his wounds with the salve the Scythian gave me. He burned with a fever. He needed more than water and a bandage.

Yakov stood and stumbled in the darkness.

I grabbed a dipper of water and walked to him.

He gulped as I poured water into his mouth, then asked, "Why?"

"Maybe I'm not the beast you think I am."

"Or maybe now that you can lie, you hide it better."

"Maybe." I untied his bonds. "You will still help me. When the guards come you will attack one spear bearer, while I attack the other."

"I'm a man of books, not the sword," he sputtered.

"You're not a man at all. But even a rat can bite. Knock him over the head with the bucket, or throw the water in his face, if that is all you can manage."

~

A HORN CALL pierced the air.

Askold sighed in the darkness. "Ruska is safe. My father attacks. I am thankful. I will fight when they come to kill me, and perhaps you can still escape."

I knelt at his side. "Maybe they won't kill you."

"The Khan is a man of his oath. He promised I'd die in the hour that my father attacked. Please. Help me stand."

I pulled one of his arms over my shoulder.

His hands were icy while his head burned. He stumbled to his feet.

I yelled over my shoulder. "Yakov, if you have a barley kernel of honor, get over here and help."

Yakov shifted in his corner. "What do you want me to do?" His voice was a full whine.

"Do you want to live through this day?"

"You'll not kill me. And the Khan will need me again, when he sees the mess he's made. I could have convinced the tsar, but the Khan can't. I'm not helping you."

"Very well." I lowered Askold to the ground, unwrapped from my waist the strips I'd once bound Yakov with, and yanked Yakov to his feet.

He struggled against my grasp.

I bound him hand, foot, and mouth, then left him standing like a spider-wrapped fly and returned to Askold's side.

A thump let me know Yakov had sat or fallen. I didn't care which.

Askold had struggled to his knees and braced himself against the empty cellar shelving.

Shelving! I had a room full of weapons!

"Prince Askold. I have a plan. You must lie out of the way of the fighting." I yanked the shelving away from the far wall. It groaned in protest and moved. Then I helped him over to the bare wall and placed the shelving in front of him.

Boots thumped down the stairs.

I ripped off the cross bracing for a shelf—a solid club of wood.

Swords clanged outside my door.

Swords? Who was fighting our guards?

A man bellowed in pain.

I grabbed the wooden bucket, hefted my club, and stood by the door.

Another cry cut through the clanging. And a groan.

A twang.

Bows. Swords and bows. Has the tsar sent in a rescue? If only I could get to the other side of the door and help them.

The fighting continued.

Tears dripped down my clenched jaw for each cry of pain in the other room.

Then silence.

Who had won?

A guttural war cry answered me. The Scythians. I swiped tears away to clear my blurred eyes as a grim calm settled over my shattered hope. The Scythians had won, but they'd pay dearly for our lives.

The lock rattled.

I pressed myself against the wall by the door and raised my club.

The door swung open. A man in a conical cap stepped in, his outline dark against the torchlight of the other room. He crumpled under my blow to his head.

Beyond him lay still forms in both Ruskan and Scythian uniforms. Too many lives lost.

I had to get the prince out of there, or those men would have given their lives for naught. I tipped over the shelving and pulled Askold up so he leaned with one arm on my shoulders.

He stumbled forward with me.

We pushed a path through the fallen. I grabbed a bow and three arrows, looking away from the man who'd held them. We ascended the stairs. Halfway up, Askold sagged and slipped from my support.

I grabbed his hand and hefted him again to standing.

"Go," he whispered.

No! I couldn't leave him. He was the tsar's son. My oath to honor and protect the tsar extended to him. But how to take him?

The door at the stair top opened, and a man in rich robes and long mustache stood with drawn sword. The Khan had come to make sure the prince was killed.

The tsar piece moved into check-mate.

I let Askold slip to the floor, drew my bow, and shot the Khan.

He stumbled back. Shock and anger mixed on his face. Then he rushed down the stairs, swinging his sword.

Curse those stiffened armor tunics! I shot again. The arrow grazed his cheek. Blood flowed from the scored line.

His sword arced at me.

I blocked it with my bow and swiped a leg at his.

His sword slid down the hardened bow, and he tumbled past me. He roared a guttural cry of anger, which rose in pitch as I shoved his back. He tumbled down the stairs, just missing Askold, and landed on still forms at the bottom.

I jumped down swinging my bow like a staff. He twisted, catching my foot. I kicked him under the chin with my free foot, then whacked him over his temple with the bow. His grip on my ankle loosened, and his eyes rolled back.

The bow rattled against my leg. I dropped it and clenched

my hands to stop their shaking, but my whole body took up the tremor.

This wasn't the time to fall to weakness. Others could still come. Which man to move first? I needed to protect Askold, but the Khan could wake up at any moment, and I needed him as a prisoner to buy our freedom.

Stop thinking and start moving!

I grabbed the Khan under his arms and dragged him into the cellar.

The lamplight from the other room showed Yakov's round eyes.

I snorted at his surprised fear. But my trembling doubled as I tore off more strips from my riding dress to bind the Khan. Rope would be better, or chains. Once I'd trussed him like a spring calf for branding, I ran back to Askold. He'd slid to the bottom of the stairs.

I threw his arm over my shoulder and half-dragged him back to the relative safety of the cellar. Even though I could fight my way to freedom, I couldn't bring Prince Askold with me.

He slumped down in a corner. "Thank you, my lady warrior."

"We'll get out of here," I promised. "We have the Khan; we'll get out."

He only nodded and held his head.

Others had to come soon. They would. And they'd help.

I tumbled the man who lay half in the door out of the way, then shoved the metal point of an arrow into the cellar lock. I broke the arrow shaft so the head was lodged in the keyhole, hopefully preventing someone from locking us into the cellar again.

The door only had a lock on the outside. I'd have to find some other way to stop the enemy from entering.

A lantern cast a ghastly light over the slain. I grabbed it, a bow and arrows, and a knife, then retreated into the cellar and barricaded the door with several empty shelves, shoving wedges of wood under the door to hold it shut. It was the best I could do to keep others out. Still, it would slow them down enough that we could talk. If they spoke Ruskan.

My throat tightened as I re-imprisoned us.

I ripped Yakov's coat into strips. It was a solid woven material that didn't rip easily even with the knife, but neither would it snap easily. I bound the Khan with a second layer of bonds.

He groaned and blinked. Then he roared. He writhed and rolled about the floor, banging against shelving and walls. He crashed into Yakov once.

I kicked him when he came near Askold.

The Khan stopped thrashing and glared at me. "I'll skin you for your pelt, foxling."

"It's *your* pelt that you should worry about." I held out the long knife.

He turned a yellow grey. "What do you want?"

"Freedom and you to leave our lands."

The corner of his eye twitched. "You are still as much a prisoner as I."

He was afraid.

Whoever came next, be it the Khan's men or the tsar's, they would help us. I had the tsar piece. The game was over.

21

———

MY SHAKING INTENSIFIED as I sat between Askold with his searing fever and the Khan, who struggled against his bonds. When would someone arrive? Surely someone had noticed the Khan missing. Would my plan work?

Then boots thundered down the steps. A voice yelled in guttural exclamations, but the only word I understood was *Khan.*

I turned to the Khan and drew my knife. "You will tell them you are a prisoner and I will kill you if they try to enter the room."

He bellowed a command, and the voices stilled on the other side. His eyes flicked between my face and the knife.

I drew closer to him. "Tell them they must bring the tsar's men here to remove the prince. When the prince is safely away, he'll tell the tsar a special signal to play on his battle horn so I know he's safe."

The Khan nodded with lowered brows but a touch of a smile.

Had I won a measure of respect? It would make this easier.

I raced on. "Then you and I will leave this room together.

We'll meet the tsar's commanders in a neutral space and discuss your imprisonment or release."

"Or death," he added.

"Or death. But I think not. In chess, the tsar is only captured, because he is more useful alive and off the board than with a new tsar taking his place."

His brows lifted. "I know chess and I know war. How do you know either?"

"Your men await your instructions."

He grunted and bellowed out more orders.

I whispered in Askold's ear. "Have the tsar play *Wind over the Marsh*, the first seven notes. Do you understand?"

"Yes." His voice came out weaker than my whisper.

A long wait later, the clank of armor filled the room on the other side of the door. "Knyaz Askold!"

"He's here," I called back, "but injured."

"We've brought a healer."

I pulled back the barricade from the door, then yanked the Khan to his feet and held the knife against his throat, and placing myself in front of Askold. These men could be some of the Khan's who spoke Ruskan. "You may enter now."

Men entered, wearing rows of overlapping metal armor draped over their long tunics.

The front one fell to his knees and removed his pointed helmet. "Knyaz Askold."

I kept between them and the prince. I called over my shoulder. "Do you know him?"

Askold shifted behind me. "Yes. He is my father's healer."

A loaded wagon's weight fell from my shoulders. These were loyal Ruskans.

One of the backmost soldiers pushed his way forward. He cried out, "Vasilisa!" Only one man had that voice.

I stood rooted to my spot. The soldier pulled off his helmet, his honey-wheat hair falling about his strong square face. Staver glanced at the knife that I still gripped, then pulled me into an embrace. "Vasilisa, you left without me."

I stood stonelike in his arms. Questions, shock, and relief warred within me. "How are you here? In the tsar's armor?"

"I'll tell you later. We should leave."

"But, I can't. I have to make sure the Khan remains a prisoner while the prince is safely removed."

Staver stroked my hair. "Someone else can do that. Come with me."

"I can't. I have to make sure the war ends. I can't just leave the Khan. What if someone here is a traitor and lets him go?"

"Vasilisa. It's all right."

"It's not. Everything's been wrong since this war started." I trembled in his arms, and tears I'd held back for him poured out.

The soldier who had bowed to the prince—the healer— stood. "I've tended to the prince as much as I dare here. We'll take him and the Khan. We can carry the lady if need be."

I laughed, the sound biting in my throat. "I'll not be carried. But that traitor should be." I pointed to Yakov.

Staver looked over my shoulder and started. "The mystic? What is he doing here?"

"I'll tell you later. We should leave."

Staver smiled at my echoed words, took the knife from my hands, tucked it into his belt, and lifted me like a child in his arms. "I agree."

I leaned my head against his shoulder and breathed in his sweet, musky scent—joy and fear. I snuggled deeper into his embrace, then pushed against him. "You'll not carry me either. You're still healing."

The Khan's voice startled me. "So this is your nobleman."

Staver turned to place himself between the Khan and me. "Yes. I am hers. And you'll not speak to her again."

I leaned on Staver's shoulder a moment longer, safe and home, even in this place of death. "You really should put me down."

He set me down and kept his arm about my shoulders.

Ruskan soldiers slipped metal armor and helmets onto Askold and me, then lifted the prince onto a blanket-softened litter. They were less gentle as they shackled the Khan and the mystic. We exited the cellar surrounded by thirty Ruskan soldiers, each armed with sword and bow. If the Scythians attacked us, the Ruskan soldiers would kill the Khan. I hoped that knowledge would grant us safe passage to a neutral area between the two armies.

We ascended the stairs and went through the kitchen and out a side door. The bright light stung after so long in the darkness. I squinted between the shoulders of the Ruskan soldiers surrounding us. Blurred forms took the shape of Scythians pressed around the base of the kitchen porch and spread by the thousands across the manor grounds. A thundering growl of voices rolled. The anger and outrage of the closest men echoed on further away faces, until they were but blurs of color under fur caps.

A common Scythian soldier raised his sword and barreled through the Scythians in front of him. He made it three steps before an arrow sprouted in his chest. An image of the spear stuck in my papa's chest flashed before my eyes and I stumbled. Staver steadied me with one hand, drawing his sword with his other.

Why am I weak now? I've seen plenty of death. Bile rose in my throat as the pierced man stumbled to his knees.

A Ruskan soldier drew another arrow and set it on his string while a Ruskan officer pressed his sword against the Khan's neck. "Remind your men that if they attack, we'll kill you."

The Khan yelled a gutteral order, and it was repeated by a Scythian officer who stood at the base of the steps.

The mass of the Scythian army parted, leaving a path the width of a wagon, though the clamor of their voices continued to press upon us. I tensed as we stepped down between them. Even with thirty Ruskan soldiers guarding us, my fingers twitched for a weapon. A bow would settle my trembling.

The Khan and the mystic marched at the front, their feet kept to the short strides of their shackles. A soldier pressed a spear to the Khan's back, and another kept his sword close to the Khan's chest. Behind them two soldiers carried the litter with the prince. Most of our guards kept tight ranks around him. Staver and I came last with the remainder of the soldiers.

Time stretched in the path between the manor and the endless shouting men. My head ached with the noise and my body shuddered with lack of food. I stumbled as I stepped on a broken spear shaft.

Staver caught my arm. "Let's run away deeper into the forest next time and not to war."

"Agreed."

When I thought we'd never reach the end, the Scythian army thinned into an open battlefield.

A hundred mounted Scythians joined us in a menacing guard as we stepped beyond the main army. They were probably there to make sure we only took the Khan as far as a neutral place between the armies.

Fifty horsemen in Ruskan armor galloped out to meet us. Eight circled the prince. One lifted him from the litter, and the healer mounted behind another horseman. The fifty galloped away, leaving us again with the thirty tsar's soldiers, who'd first come, pressed even closer around the Khan. The hundred

Scythians who also guarded us grunted out oaths and kept their hands on their swords.

I gripped Staver's hand and marched across the killing grounds between Dyeda's palace and the road. I wanted to run, dash away from the Scythians like a rabbit fleeing the hound.

Staver whispered behind my ear. "Soon. We'll be safe soon."

Another fifty Ruskan horsemen galloped south down the road and circled us and the Scythian guard. A horseman with a red-and-yellow embroidered bird over his chest stabbed a fire-bird pendant into the ground. "I, Duke Zhar-ptitsa, in the name of our beloved tsar, take into custody the Khan of the Scythians."

A Scythian with gold-embroidered cuffs on his tunic rode forward to meet Duke Zhar-ptitsa. "He stays here, between our two armies. If you try to take him back to the tsar, we kill him and all who guard him."

The duke thumped his hand over his chest. "I swear." He nodded to another mounted soldier, and the soldier blew three ascending notes on a horn.

A hundred more Ruskan horsemen galloped from the road, bringing with them a wagon. They set up a village of tents, in two groups, with one open-walled pavilion set between them. A Ruskan soldier shoved the Khan into a chair in the middle of the pavilion, which started a yelling match between the Ruskans and Scythians. A swordpoint to the Khan's throat stopped it.

Duke Zhar-ptitsa's voice carried over the silence. "The Khan is now a prisoner of the tsar. Ten Scythian soldiers are allowed to stand under the pavilion beside our guard of fifty. But if any others step under the pavilion, they will be shot."

I stepped towards the Khan, forcing the movement before my resolve failed me.

"What are you doing?" Staver whispered.

"I hope never to see the Khan again after this, and I have words to say before we leave."

"You don't have to."

"But I will." I took another step toward the pavilion. Staver stayed pressed against my side and slightly in front of me.

"Khan," I called out as I came within a leap of the pavilion.

He looked up and gave me a thin-lipped nod.

I clenched my hands. What would I say? That he'd never have me to wife. That he was the dung stuck to the fence of the pigsty. Not those. "If you live to return to your lands, remember a woman captured you. Ruska is full of men and women with more valor than mine. We won't be so merciful next time. Never, ever return to Ruska!"

He stared at me with the intensity of a starved dog sniffing a fresh kill, but barred from tasting it.

I shook off the chill and gave him a mocking bow. As I straightened, the world tilted and lights flashed in long streamers.

I woke in a cot with Staver sitting near, holding my hand. A brown tent stretched over me. "Where am I?"

He smiled and kissed each of my cheeks and then my lips.

"That's not an answer."

He grinned. "You're with me."

"Then, where are *we*?"

"In the center of the tsar's army, and as safe as the tsar himself."

"How did I get here?"

Staver's skin creased between his eyes. "You fainted. We carried you back to the tsar's camp. Irina checked you for injuries and found none except for your scratched face and neck, and they were uninfected. She said you were exhausted from whatever had happened. So we let you sleep, but maybe for too long." He smiled sheepishly. "I'm sure you're hungry."

I groaned as I realized the source of my aching complaints. It was the sides of my stomach rubbing together. "Yes, please. I haven't eaten since the day I left to get the herbs for Dyeda."

Staver cursed: a word I'd heard plenty from my fellow servants, but never from him. He dashed through the door of the tent and spoke with someone then returned to my side. "Food will be here soon. Four days is too long."

"Four days? I've slept that long?"

"Just half a day, but you left me four days ago."

I tilted my head. The days had merged in the cellar without light. "How are you here?"

He scooted onto the cot next to me. "If you'll rest quietly, I'll tell you the story."

I laid my head in his lap. Shivers ran down my arms as he stroked my hair.

"I slept through the day you left," he started.

I blushed. I was the reason he slept through it.

"It was late at night when I woke, and Irina convinced me you'd be back in the morning. I think I wore an ankle-deep path in your birch grove as I paced the hours away. I'll show it to you when we return. We can pave it with river stones and walk it together."

The corners of my eyes stung.

"Morning came, but you didn't. I gathered the men well enough to go with me, plus several of the women, and we set off."

My throat tightened. Did the Khan's men find the rest of them unprotected? I jumped from the bed. "Staver! The Khan sent men to find our camp because I—I told him I was taking herbs to Dyeda. We have to go help them."

He caught my hand. "They are all safe."

"How do you know?" With my free hand, I grabbed one boot from the floor by the cot.

"Because they are all here."

"Oh." I dropped the boot. "How is Dyeda?"

Staver squeezed my hand. "He's weak, but the tsar's healer had the herbs that Irina needed, so he will heal. Now lie down, or I won't tell the rest of the story."

I sat down next to him on the cot and turned so I could watch his face.

He kissed the tip of my nose. "That's not lying down, so you'll only get a short story."

"Staver!"

He shrugged. "After we left, we came across a mounted group of the tsar's soldiers. They'd circled through the woods to find a way to rescue the prince. One of them had spied it out and found that the prince was still alive and that a woman with red hair had been captured. I knew it was you."

He traced his fingers along mine. "They'd left half their numbers in the forest near the back of Dyeda's estate, but they didn't dare storm in for fear that the Khan would kill the prince. The rest were returning to report and form a plan. They helped gather all from our camp and headed back to the tsar's camp. I didn't go with them. I had to find you, to rescue you. I tried that night. I made it no farther than the first campfire before someone spoke to me, and when I responded, he called me a *sneaking nobleman scum*. And I fled like a sneaking nobleman scum."

I ducked my head down so I could look into his lowered eyes. "I'm grateful your way of speaking gave you away. They'd have killed you at the palace doors if you'd gotten that far, and if you'd died—"

"Will you forgive me for not rescuing you?"

"You did rescue me." I stroked my finger along his chin. "Can you forgive me for not trusting you enough, and for putting a sleeping herb in your tea?"

"My sweet, Vasilisa, in this war we've both done things that I hope we'll never do again. I love you. And I trust you. I just don't know if I'm strong enough. You need someone who can protect you, as you protect others."

"You do protect me! You protected me from your mother's wrath when you scrubbed the pigsty beside me. You protected me when the lightning struck me, and you made sure I was cared for. You protected me from a life of servitude when you took me to the duke. You protected me with each of your loving, hopeful letters. You—"

He stopped my words with a kiss.

I pulled away after a melting minute. "I love you. I need you. And I always will."

A scraping of a boot on soil sounded from behind me. I spun around, my cheeks aflame.

A boy, maybe twelve years of age, stood with a platter of food. His gaze was fixed on the floor and his face cherry-red.

Staver coughed, then spoke with a husky voice. "You can leave it on the cot."

The boy did and fled the tent.

Laughter bubbled up from my stomach and escaped in bursts of giggles. "I don't think he's seen that before."

Staver nodded solemnly, though his eyes twinkled. "He'll have plenty to boast to his friends about."

We sat on the cot. I bit into an oven-hot roll and forgot about kisses or apologies.

Staver ate a bite or two, but most of the food disappeared into me. As I ate he asked, "Do you want to know the rest of the story?"

"Yes."

"I rode with one of the tsar's soldiers to help the tsar form a plan of rescue. I found Dyeda and the others well taken care of in his camp, and the tsar grey with grief and indecision. The Khan had said the tsar had until the sun set to either give up half his kingdom or watch his son torn limb from limb by horses. We talked, and I told him of your strength and that you'd protect his son if you were imprisoned together. He grasped that slight hope and chose to attack the Khan in the early afternoon. His men, hidden in the back of the estate, knew that if the battle horn rang, they were to fight their way to where the prince was imprisoned and try to free him."

Images rose unbidden—dead piled outside the cellar. "None survived."

He nodded. "But you protected the prince and captured the Khan. They didn't die in vain."

"They protected the prince. The Khan only came after the battle had killed almost every man. I couldn't have done that."

He fell silent.

I wound my fingers through his. "What happened next?"

"The tsar pushed his army against the Khan's. I pushed my way to the front of the battle, determined to reach you. It seemed some unseen hand kept me from the blows that felled all around me." He looked at his hands again and his eyes clouded.

"But the battle soon stopped."

"Yes." He looked up. "A glorious white flag waved over the Scythian ranks. A messenger rode forward to say that the Khan had been captured and asked the tsar to send soldiers to retrieve the prince in order to preserve the Khan's life. I begged leave to join the group to get the prince. And found you."

I snuggled into his warm embrace. "A sad and beautiful tale. Better for books than living through. But you lived; we both did."

"We did, and we will never live that tale again."

"Amen," I whispered.

~

THE WAR WASN'T OVER, only stalled. It should have been over. But one of the Khan's generals decided he didn't need the Khan, and the Scythian army reformed in defensive ranks. It had to be the man who'd threatened to kill the Khan and everyone else if the Khan was taken into the tsar's camp.

I strode to the tsar's tent. He'd sent the invitation for me to attend his war council that morning, probably to hear the story that I'd already told Staver.

Two guards blocked the entrance. I held out my left hand and showed them the red mark that the messenger had stamped there hours before.

The guards stepped aside, and one lifted the tent flap. "You may enter, my lady."

I didn't look like a lady. An army didn't carry a lady's dresses, and the women only had the clothes they'd fled with a month before. So I wore my leggings with a soldier's blue tunic over top, because my own riding dress was improperly shortened.

A tall man stood at the head of a table. He had the same lean face as the prince, but his hair and beard were grey. "Welcome, Lady Vasilisa." He motioned to a stool to his right.

All the others around the table stood. Each man bore the crest of his land and family. Dukes and princes, all of them.

Staver stood to the right of the stool the tsar had motioned to. He smiled and nodded towards the chair.

It wasn't right to sit in the tsar's presence. I bowed to him, then stood by my stool.

The tsar continued to stand and motioned to the stool again. "Please sit."

I sat, and the Little Father of Ruska sat next to me. The scraping of stools shifting over ground filled the next moments, long enough for Staver to reach under the table and squeeze my hand.

The tsar bowed his grey head to me. "Thank you for saving my son. He has told me a small part of what you did, in the moments he's been out of his fevered state. I don't know how much is the fever and how much happened."

I briefly told him my tale.

The tsar nodded. "Then it was not a fevered tale. You are wise as well as strong for one so young. I beg your wisdom in our next step of this war."

"Your Majesty, I have no more wisdom in war than what I know from chess. And already I've guessed wrong in much. If you want to end this war, speak to a man who knows peace." I motioned to Staver.

Staver's eyes widened.

The tsar turned his intense grey eyes on him. "What do you suggest?"

Staver paled.

I nudged him. "Staver, you've sought peace and honor for our marriage, at the cost of your inheritance and six months of us being apart. You know the cost of peace."

Staver bowed his head. "Father of my mother Ruska, what does the Scythian general demand?"

"He demands the lower forests of Ruska, plus all the people that dwell there, or he'll continue this war until he's won all of Ruska. He swears that he cares not for Scythian blood nor Ruskan."

"Do you believe him?"

"Yes. My spies tell me he has a bloodlust that makes the Khan look like a kitten next to a Siberian tiger."

Staver squeezed my hand under the table. His own trembled. "Yet, though he says this, he must know that he'll eventually lose. But he expects you to give in to preserve thousands of lives."

The tsar nodded. "Yes. I would do almost anything to preserve my people from further death, except sell them into slavery to the Scythians. We've driven back the Khan's army almost to our borders, but the new leader vows to call together all Scythia to fight against us. It will be a drawn-out war."

Staver fingers shifted in mine, forming chords against my palm. He paused, his brow furrowed, and then he started fingering different chords.

Listening silence thickened the air.

Staver stopped fingering chords and leaned towards the tsar. "The Khan is the less dangerous leader. If we release him to lead his people again, he'll remove the general."

"But he'll continue to fight," said a prince with a bear emblazoned across his coat. "We'll have traded one war for another."

"Not if we offer him something he desires."

The tsar shook his head. "I'll not enslave even one of my people to him."

"I'm not speaking of our people," Staver said. "But of the other riches of Ruska. Scythia lacks our forests, our rich farms, and our gold mines. If we opened trade with Scythia, free of a tariff, the Khan would grow rich. They have plentiful mines of iron, zinc, and even coal with which we could warm our homes in the long winters."

When had Staver learned all this? He wasn't just a musician anymore.

A portly nobleman with a dimpled chin and a white swan on his tunic scoffed. "He'll demand a tariff for any goods we trade to him. He'll grow rich and we'll grow poor. Let us just send the portion of our serfs and servants to the Khan and be done with it. They breed fast enough, and we'll not be stuck with trading with those barbarian Scythians or suffer a robbing tariff."

Staver brought a fist down on the table. "The southern families have borne the burden to keep the rest of Ruska safe. And yet you complain of a tax on goods that would sit unused in your storehouses if they weren't traded to the Scythians? Have you lost family in this war, or does the Swan family live so far north that you think you are safe?"

The nobleman's neck bulged. "I'm here. I've seen my share of blood. How about you? You only showed up a few days ago. Where were you hiding?"

The tsar stood. "Peace!"

The nobleman and Staver fell silent.

The tsar cast his gaze over each of us. "My generals will ask the Khan if he accepts the terms that Staver has suggested. If so, we will sign an agreement of peace and trade, and release him back to his people, with a guard to protect him until he can remove the other Scythian general. Thank you. You may all go."

I stood to go, but the tsar placed a lean hand on my shoulder. "Please stay a moment."

"Please Sire, may Staver stay too?"

"Yes."

Staver and I stood side by side as the rest of the tent emptied. I held my head high as many cast curious or less friendly looks at us. Staver had saved us from a drawn-out war but earned enemies. Why did they have to be so selfish?

I dug the toe of my boot into the trampled grass. What did the tsar want with me?

Finally, it was just the tsar, his guards, and Staver. The tsar lowered himself into his chair with a gingerness that hinted at injury.

"Are you well?" I asked.

"I am well. My son is back."

I wanted to comfort him as I would Dyeda. "He's a good man. He'll be a good and merciful tsar."

"He will. And it is because you saved his life. He is yet unmarried, and I offer you the place of future tsarina by his side."

The room spun, and my words poured out before I could temper them. "No. I can't marry him." I covered my ill-speaking mouth. "I'm sorry for my bluntness. I've already found my tsar."

A slow, sad smile graced the tsar's face as he looked from Staver to me. "I understand. What can I give you to show my thanks?"

Sparrow-hope hopped so vigorously in my chest that I could hardly form the words. "Please change the law so that a commoner can marry a nobleman."

The tsar chuckled. "That is all you ask? If only all my petitioners were so humble. I will change the law, and," his smile broadened, "grant you such titles that none will ever remember your common birth."

"Thank you!" I bowed, then turned and threw my arms around Staver.

He leaned over and whispered. "My lovely Lisa, when would you like to marry?"

"Today!"

22

MAMA CLUCKED her tongue as she rearranged the yellow autumn leaves in my hair.

I wore her dress, the one she wore when we escaped to the forest before the battle. It was a simple grey linen gown, threadbare at the knees from kneeling in forest ground. She'd scrubbed it clean and now stood behind me in a soldier's tunic, as there wasn't other clothing in the army camp. To enter Dyeda's estate could break our tentative peace.

Mama circled me, adjusted another autumn leaf, then held up a polished shield so I could see myself. Half of my red hair sat in a braided crown, my one black lock weaving through it and for once looking as though it belonged. The rest flowed down my back and over my shoulders in waves of red. Yellow birch leaves nestled like coins. Papa's wolf amulet lay, a comforting warmth, between the layers of my under- and over-dresses.

My ruby earrings flashed as the evening sun slanted through the tent door. An army blacksmith had fashioned the earrings from the gems Staver had purchased before the war and hidden in his boot. They hung heavy and unfamiliar on my tender ears. It was a painful beauty I'd choose each day, because Staver had selected them for me, along with the ring that he'd soon place on my finger. Irina had assured me, when she'd driven a needle through my skin, that they'd not hurt long and soon I'd not even notice them. Yet, I wanted their reminder. I wanted to always remember what Staver sacrificed for me.

Mama set down the shield, placed another birch leaf in my crown and stepped back. Then she reached for my hair again.

I caught her hand. "Mama, he'll come looking for me if you don't let me go."

She faced me, her eyes shining, and kissed my forehead. "You are ready. My lovely Vasilisa. My princess."

I stepped to the tent door and froze. My throat tightened, and my underarms dampened. "Mama, I love Staver. Then why—?"

Mama laid her hand over mine. "Every bride feels nervous. It is the shivering forerunner of joy."

An honor guard of twenty soldiers in the tsar's blue led me to a canopy at the far side of the camp, the side farthest from the Scythian army. Dyeda's manor sat in the distance. His orchards and gardens were once beautiful, and I'd dreamed of our marriage in them. But they held too many memories of death, even if an army didn't stand between us. Instead, the forest in dark pine greens and fire-bright foliage provided the decorations.

I walked, holding Mama's arm, between two rows of camp stools filled by my Baba, Irina, and others from Dyeda's estate. Staver and Dyeda stood at the end. My honor guard joined the other soldiers around the tsar's seat. I stopped before him and bowed. He pressed his hands against the arm supports of his camp chair and stood, then bowed to me.

Why is he bowing to me? He is the tsar.

The air filled with the sound of shuffling as everyone else quickly stood and bowed.

I gripped Mama's arm tighter. I wasn't anyone to bow to. I was just Vasilisa. A common serving girl who was lucky enough to have Staver fill my life.

The tsar straightened from his bow. "Lady Vasilisa, I give my gift before you marry. You are now Princess Vasilisa and have an annual income of ten thousand rubles, plus your choice of my lands, even my finest orchards along the Balka."

My lips parted in protest. I didn't need all that.

He held up his hand and continued. "I have stamped my seal to the new law that commoners and nobility may marry. None other shall bear the pains that you two have."

I bowed my head to hide the tears that threatened. "Thank you, Little Father."

The tsar lifted my chin and kissed my forehead. "Now go. He waits."

I turned from him and looked to the canopy made of timber lashed together, topped with pine boughs and trailing red vines. Staver stood under it, tall in a brushed military tunic with a sleeveless overcoat.

"Vasilisa." He held out his hand and took mine. A shiver of joy ran through my body.

Dyeda stood before us. His voice, still weak from his illness, whispered over our ears—as if his words were for us alone. "Staver Orlov, do you promise to love, cherish, and honor Vasilisa, through joy and trials? And let nothing else, be it person, ambition, or desire, come between you?

Staver turned to look at me, his eyes tender and earnest. "Yes. For as long as I have a spirit on earth or in heaven."

Dyeda spoke again, though I only saw Staver. "Vasilisa Volkova, do you promise to love, cherish, and honor Staver, through joy and trials? And let nothing else, be it person, ambition, or desire, come between you?"

Nothing, not war, jealousy of others, longing for the forest, nothing. We'd let none of these come between us. We'd fight for our love. "Yes. For as long as I have a spirit on earth or in heaven." The promise wrapped me in peace.

"Then by the authority given me by the tsar," Dyeda's voice flowed over us, "I bind you husband and wife. May God bless you."

Staver slipped an iron ring on my finger; it was the only metal the blacksmith had. A diamond glittered in the black depths. Then he sang. It wasn't one of his songs, but an old wedding hymn in a language forgotten by all but priests and scholars. His voice flowed over me—rich, full, longing.

I rested my head against his chest. The vibrations of his voice soaked through me until the last note trembled to a stop, and I only felt his heart beating against my cheek.

War seemed to retreat into the dark corner of night while I danced with Staver in the gentle light of torches set around the wedding grounds. The tsar left after the ceremony, called away to meetings to seek peace. He took Dyeda with him. The next day we'd travel north, far from the battle, and perhaps make peace with Staver's parents. An impossible task, but Staver had already accomplished impossible things. For now, I lost myself in Staver's touch and motion, as he led me through several dances to the piped notes of the army fifer, who only knew military tunes.

The music stopped.

Staver spun me into his arms, kissing the top of my head, then turned to the piper.

A messenger stood beside the piper, his face solemn. He bowed then held out a folded and sealed paper.

To Princess Vasilisa and her consort Staver:

The peace treaty is approaching agreement. The Khan demands a manor in Ruska to act as a trading house between our two lands. He demands Duke Nicholas's palace and lands.

I bit the inside of my cheek. Dyeda's home and lands.

Staver held me closer as he continued to read, his voice soft with sorrow.

I have offered other lands for the trading house, but he will not. Though he is our prisoner, he knows we want him ruling rather than the Scythian general, and holds out against our threats and pleas. Duke Nicholas has agreed to move to other lands, farther from the border and less dangerous. He told me that these lands hold a special place for you. Please forgive me. I would offer you any of my lands, but for peace, I plead with you to let these go.

A double-headed eagle, the seal of the tsar, marked the bottom of the page.

I bit my cheek harder and an iron taste coated my tongue. I wanted to claim these lands and live with Staver, close to my first home and my papa's grave. And now we'd have to leave my papa.

No. We wouldn't! I turned to face Staver. Torchlight flickered off his face. "Staver, we are taking my father's bones with us."

His eyes grew wide with surprise, then settled into seriousness. "We'll bring him with us when we leave. And we'll bring saplings from your birch grove so we can create a new home for him in the north."

I nestled in his arms, his warmth helping hold back my tears and shock. "We should send a message to the tsar, so peace may come." Then I remembered what night it was. The thought sent a thrill down my arms and blush to my face. I said, with a fair helping of stubbornness, "I don't care who the next messenger is. He can wait till morning."

THE NEXT MESSENGER *didn't wait.*

The wolf howled plaintively outside our tent. He'd never before left the woods to get me. I slipped from Staver's sleeping embrace and shivered at the loss of his warmth. Did the wolf have to come on my wedding night? I'd chosen Staver.

He howled again, and his voice pulled me to the door of our tent. He caught hold of the shoulder of my underdress and tugged.

I pulled back. "Even in my dreams, I'm staying with Staver."

He pulled harder, and the material ripped.

I slapped his nose. "I'm staying with Staver."

He let go and whined, his eyes wide with pleading.

"I know." I rubbed him between his ears. "I don't like the Scythians either, or that they are taking our home. I'll come one last time, but it won't be in a dream. I'll gather my papa's bones."

The wolf looked into my face a long time, then turned and melted into the forest.

I swallowed a sob against the ache of his absence.

23

—————

PEACE WAS PAID by giving the Khan Dyeda's estate and all the treasures in it, plus all the land south of it. The peace treaty said the land wasn't either Scythian or Ruskan, but rather a neutral ground between the two for trading. Yet the Khan held control. And even with the stipulation that a Ruskan must be caretaker, the Khan would decide which Ruskan.

Both armies withdrew, the Khan withdrawing first with his armies a day's march to the south, and then the tsar with his armies a day's march to the north. The Khan left behind four hundred men to "protect" the neutral ground. Every Ruskan had to leave the estate, and any found on the lands would forfeit their freedom to the Scythians. Worse, if any Ruskan soldiers were found, the Scythians would consider the peace broken and attack Ruska again. It was a hard-bought peace.

We camped with the tsar's armies north of Dyeda's estate. Staver looked up from packing a saddlebag as I stomped into our tent. He raised his eyebrows in a silent question.

I hit my fist against the tent post, and the canvas rippled around us. "The Khan didn't even give us a day. Dyeda had to leave his daughter's grave and I my papa's. The tsar wants to send soldiers with me when I go gather their bones. But it may restart the war if the Scythians see them, so I refused him." I gripped the tent post. "Staver, I'm going anyway. Papa's will be easier, but I'm sure I can get to Dyeda's daughter's grave. It's in a wild corner of the estate because she loved nature. I can do it unseen."

Staver's jaw tightened as I spoke. He looked down at the saddlebag and back to me. "I can't stop you, so I'm coming with you. We'll face this danger together."

That was what I feared he'd say. But I'd promised to love, cherish, and honor Staver, through joy and trials, and that meant I had to trust him enough to let him come beside me into danger. Besides, I tried to assure myself, he knew how to move quietly—enough to not startle an otter. We'd not be noticed. I smiled at the thought and the memory. The last time we went into an adventure together was when we listened to the shrike's evening song. Since then we'd been divided too often. It would be good to have him at my side, as long as we weren't caught.

"IT'S WORTH THE PEACE," I muttered as I mounted the horse. The ground was too far away while seated on the hulking beast.

Staver reached over to me and patted my clenched fists. "You told me in your letters you disliked horses. I believe you now." He wore peasant clothing, as did I. If we were caught, we'd lose our freedom but we'd not start a war.

We rode through the forest, Staver to my right and Mama to my left. Mama would come with us through the forest to Papa's grave and then return to the tsar's army without ever crossing into Dyeda's lands. Then Staver and I would go to Dyeda's daughter's grave and return through the forest. Her grave was almost in the forest. No one would be watching that side. We had nothing to fear. We wouldn't be caught.

We walked a delicate balance.

Our horses rustled through and crushed the autumn leaves, spicing the air with scents as rich as summer blooms. Would any other forest smell as good? Would any other land feel like home? I glanced at Staver. Any land would be home while he was there.

We passed under trees, through meadows, and over streams; and finally dismounted to climb the hill to my birch grove. Blackened fire circles and the stench of the latrines were all that remained of our camp with the refugees from Dyeda's estate. Papa's grave, with the words "remembered always", sat in one corner. The memory birches rustled their papery leaves. Memories, both of my papa and then of Staver, poured over me. *Papa tossing me in the air. Staver teaching me to dance.*

"Thank you," I murmured to the still quiet around me.

THE AFTERNOON SLIPPED by like rain through an oak canopy. One minute at a time it dripped away, until not even the sun could hold it back. Memories grew stronger with the darkness. Fog like images of a tall black-haired man clothed in wolf fur crept at the corners of my vision, rich and wild scents, the brush of breath across my cheek. The memories had never been this strong before. Was Papa's spirit here, bidding our home farewell, just as we were?

I touched the freshly turned soil and then the stone that had marked his grave. "It's all right, Papa. I'm taking your bones to a new resting place. I love you."

Staver laid his hand over mine. "We should rest. We must leave at first light."

I curled up next to him. Burlap-wrapped birch saplings stood in a row, ready to go with us. The birch trees towered above us in the flickering firelight.

It wasn't right that the Khan would take my birch home. It wasn't right that Papa's rest had to be disturbed. It wasn't right that some Scythian would soon lord over the rooms where Dyeda and Baba had loved me despite myself. "It's not right!" I cried into the night air.

THE BLACK WOLF stood before me. His shoulder was as tall as mine. *Come*, he growled in my mind. Then he bounded off.

I loped after him through a glowing grove of birch. Stars hung from the branches and swayed among the yellow autumn leaves. The grove stretched on as far as a forest. I fell behind, panting. He'd never before pushed me this hard.

The wolf turned. *Come, quickly.*

I held my aching side as I loped after.

We reached a pool, and I dropped at its edge, gulping down water.

The wolf stepped into the water and walked deeper until just his head showed, then he ducked under where the moon lit a path. The water trembled, and a man stood from its depths. Tall, black hair, black eyes, and a strong, wild face that called forward all my first memory joys.

I only have a short time, little one. His voice, the same as the wolf's, growled through my mind.

"Papa!" I pushed my way through the restraining water. "You can speak to me. How?"

He shook himself so that water scattered from his long hair and fur coverings. *Our people do not speak as the humans. You were too young when I died, and I could not teach you. But I've watched you each time you've come to the memory birches. And I've felt your struggles even when you've lived far distant.*

I reached his side. "Why haven't you spoken to me before?"

He frowned and laid a hand on my cheek. *I wanted to, my little one, but only with the turning of my bones could I be free to speak in the mortal realm, and when I have spoken, I must pass beyond this world into another. I have much to teach you in this hour.*

I laid my hand over his and held his warmth against my face. An hour to be with my papa, to hear his voice, to learn. I looked up into his long face and sad eyes. "Teach me."

Hand me the amulet.

I pulled out the wolf amulet from my blouse and handed it to him.

He pulled the loop over his head. *What creature would you have me become?*

"Creature?"

Images washed through my mind. A wild cat, snake, bear, rabbit...

I blinked with surprise. "Rabbit?"

He closed his eyes, and the amulet glowed. He shrank while his clothes merged with his skin. A moment later a black, lop eared rabbit paddled toward me. The outline of a golden wolf marked his fur where the amulet had hung. He nudged my leg with his nose. *The amulet allows us to change form.*

"Us? I thought it just healed."

It can do that for all, even humans. Only our kind may change shape.

"I'm half human."

The black rabbit grew back into Papa. *You are fully my daughter.* He handed the amulet back to me. *Place this against your skin, over your heart.*

"Won't it make me fall asleep?"

Only if you are injured. Think of a creature. Create it in your mind until you feel you are it.

I slipped the amulet under my dress, against my skin. It lay warm over my heart. I pictured a shrike, its small body swooping in the air and its mouth open in a fierce call. I reached out my arms into its wings; the wind pushed against my fingertips. My legs curled up into my feathered chest. The amulet no longer hung from my neck, but its warmth glowed within me.

A hand scooped under me, lifting me to air. I gasped and blinked away the water. Papa's face was oddly colored, and my other eye saw the forest—all the leaves shimmered with colors where it once was pale green. I shook my head to clear the double image. Papa's face and the forest spun around me. Where one image ended the other began. My stomach churned, and I closed my eyes. This was no dream. It was too vivid, too real. I was truly with my papa, and I could change form!

A shrike. Papa's pride rumbled over me. *I've never changed into a bird. You are powerful.*

I tried to speak. A whistle emerged from my throat.

Speak with your mind.

I leaned my thoughts towards him. *Like this?*

He stumbled back a step in the water. *Yes, but softer.*

I softened my thought words. *Do I need a full moon and this pool to change? Is that why you led me here?*

No, little one. This pool and moonlight help when you first are learning. But all you need is the moisture of your skin and even a sliver of the moon in the sky, though it will be harder. You'll learn to feel when the moon rises and sets, even when you cannot see it. We will try again on land. He carried me from the pool and set me on a low branch. *Change form again.*

I thought of the otter and my body lengthened into sleek firm muscles. My vision moved back into one image, though the coloring was still strange. I scampered down the tree trunk to the ground.

Again, he instructed.

I changed from one animal to another: deer, bear, squirrel. Each brought a different kind of movement and senses.

Again.

I thought of Papa's wolf form. As I shifted, the scents of the forest sharpened into individual herbs and trees. The rustling of the leaves and the lapping of the water shouted for attention.

But Papa still stood taller over me than he should have if I was a wolf. I glanced down at my paws. Everything was in blues, yellows, and greens. But my paw didn't look like a wolf's paw. *What am I?*

Papa laughed and ran his fingers through my fur, scratching behind my shoulder blades. I yipped in delight. *You are your true other form, my little fox.*

New scents wove their way through the forest. Rich, moist, a touch of blackberry and a zing of iron.

Papa stiffened. *My time is short. They come for me.*

I shifted back to my human form, and the amulet hung again from my neck. *Who comes? Why must you go?*

He placed his hands on my shoulders and looked into my eyes. *You must learn one more thing. Most call our kind monsters. But not all of us are. If you ever learn the name humans call us, know that you are a being of goodness. Now go.*

I threw my arms around his neck and kissed his cheek. *I love you!*

He held me close in his powerful arms. *I will search the paths of eternity to find you again. Even if my penance is a thousand years. Now, go!*

Two figures entered the clearing. One was a white-haired, white-clad man. Golden eagle wings spread from his shoulders to his feet. He held a staff twined with thorny blackberry vines.

The other figure was a man from shoulders down, but bear-headed. A rivulet of red ran down the side of his spear.

Even in my human form, the iron tang of blood and the sweetness of blackberry pushed towards me. "Who are you? And where are you taking my papa?"

The bear-headed man growled and lowered his spear.

Papa stepped in front of me. *Go!*

No. Not until I know where you are going, so I can find you again.

The eagle-winged man stretched out his staff and touched my forehead with it.

A rush of images tumbled over me. Chasing Papa around a pine. Mama carrying me away from the forest. Years of serving and suffering mocking. Staver appeared again and again, each time a little older, and always kind. The war. My legs collapsed under me.

The man touched his staff to Papa's head.

Papa clenched his fists and howled, changing back into the wolf, and then into human form. *I choose to be a man.*

The eagle man planted his staff into the ground, and it stretched upward, the staff and blackberries climbing past the treetops and into the night sky. "Do you choose the trials to gain a human soul?"

Yes.

The bear-headed man growled, and an image surrounded us like a fog. Creatures that were part human, part animal roamed about a lush forest. They played together like the otters, raced over the long-flowered meadows, and hunted fleet animals. Emotions of thrill, pleasure, competition, and contentment pushed against me stronger than the images. But the land lacked love, peace, and joy.

Papa laid his hand on my shoulder. *I choose the trials. I will gain a human soul.*

The eagle man pointed to the staff. "Then climb before the

path vanishes. Others will guide you along the next trial if you reach the top."

Papa grasped the thorny vine-wrapped staff and pulled himself upward. Blood welled between his fingers. He climbed above the trees and disappeared into the night sky.

The eagle man rose on the air and turned to me, his wings beating wind against my face. "Your time is not yet. Go."

I raced back through the star-strung trees. I had so much to tell Staver.

24

———

THE FAIRY-STAR-LIT WORLD faded into a cave, and at the end stood our firelit camp. I stumbled out of the cave into the shelter of my watching birches.

I shook Staver awake. "Staver, my papa came. He showed me how to use the wolf amulet. It was wonderful!"

He rubbed his eyes. "Give me a moment to wake up and then start again at the beginning."

I bounced on my toes as he rolled his shoulders, yawned, and slapped his cheeks, then turned to me. "So, what happened?"

I plopped to the ground beside him. "My papa came. He took me to a moonlit pool and taught me to use the wolf amulet to change forms."

Staver stiffened.

It must have been a shock for him, just as it was for me. "I turned into a shrike! And then an otter! You should have seen me. I tried many forms. My senses changed with each. But then I learned my true fair-folk form. I turned into a fox. It makes sense, with my fox-red hair. Isn't it wonderful? Maybe you can change forms too. You are part fair folk—Dyeda told me. I'll teach you. Oh, Staver, this is the second-most wonderful night of my life." I grinned at him. "My first being our marriage."

Staver still sat in stiffened silence.

"Staver?" I stroked his hand, and he flinched. "What's wrong?"

He took a shaky breath. "It was just a dream. It didn't happen. You can't change form."

This was the first time he'd ever said I couldn't do something. "I can. I'll show you." The moon was still in the sky. I looked up at it, and its glow washed over me, seeping into my skin, causing me to tingle with energy. I grabbed my water pouch and poured water on my hands then thought of the fox.

The world shifted, and Staver grew large beside me. His shocked features lay in blues, yellows and greens. His scent turned almost rancid with fear. He scrambled backward.

I yipped. Why was he frightened?

He leaned over and hesitantly touched the tip of my ear. "Why, Vasilisa? Why do the heavens mock us?"

Mama leapt from her bedroll and knelt in front of me, her face dark and her scent a sharp tang of fear and anger. "Vasilisa, turn back. You should never change shape again."

I changed back to my human form and knelt facing Staver and Mama. "Why should I not? I don't understand. It's a gift from my papa. He taught me. It's because I'm fair folk."

Mama's voice grew sharper. "Fair folk don't change forms. Only ogres can."

"No! You're wrong!" The world spun. "My papa was one of the fair folk. He came to me last night. He spoke with me. He taught me how to change shape. And then he left to suffer trials to gain—" My words died. He'd said that most called our kind monsters. The mocking from my childhood danced around me. *Ogre-child, demon wild, devil strong.* I pressed my hands into the leaf-strewn ground. "Papa wasn't—I'm not—we're not ogres!"

Staver mumbled something incoherent.

"Hush, child," Mama commanded. "You can't undo the damage you've already done. You must never change shape again. You are half ogre, but you don't have to act on it."

Anger burned like acid in my heart. She said I was an ogre. The beast of nightmares. How could she turn on me?

My voice hardened around my next words. "He was my papa. He loved me. Yet, you tell me he was an ogre," I scoffed. "Why did you marry him if you hate him so much? Why did you keep me? Why didn't you just leave me in the forest when he died?"

Her face creased with pain. "I was trying to protect you. Please listen. I will finally tell you my story."

I pulled away from her and leaned against Staver. He put his arm around my shoulder but didn't pull me close.

She spoke in slow, wincing words. "I was a servant to a Ruskan princess who lived along the Scythian border, on the other side of this forest. Because the princess was too poor in gold, or maybe more because she was jealous of my beauty, I became her tribute to the Khan."

I shuddered. I'd also almost been made the Khan's concubine.

She continued. "I fled into the forest, preferring to die by a wild animal. I almost did. I wandered lost for three days and made myself sick with berries that only caused stomach cramps. Then, as dusk fell on my third day, a giant wolf, black and about as tall as my shoulders, walked into the clearing where I shivered. It sniffed me then bit the hem of my dress and dragged me. I kicked its nose. It growled, snapped at my foot but didn't bite, then grabbed my dress again and dragged me deeper into the thickly treed forest.

"We came to a steep hill, and with the wolf pushing against my shoulders, I climbed up. At the top was a stand of birch trees and a cave. Gnawed bones lay about. I curled up, knowing I would die. But instead the wolf shifted and changed into a man. I screamed then fainted.

"When I woke the man knelt next to me, holding out a chunk of raw meat. A half-skinned deer lay nearby. Day by day he nursed me back to health. You came along two years later."

That was it? That was all her story? "He couldn't be an ogre." My voice came out pleading. "He was good. He saved you. Aren't there any stories of fair folk changing shape?" I turned to Staver. "You've read many books. There have to be stories about fair folk changing form. Tell me one; tell Mama."

He shuddered and whispered. "I don't know any. But you are right, there have to be some. You are fair folk. You can't be an ogre. Your mother is wrong."

His stiffened body said differently. He thought I was an ogre.

What if they were right? What if I was part man-eater? What if I became like the ogress in the story Staver told—the one about the sister and her swan brothers? The thought made my stomach curdle.

"Did he ever eat a person?" I leaned forward, daring Mama to hurt me again.

She shook her head. "Not when I was there."

"But did he?"

She nodded. "I found a man's skull amongst the animal bones in his camp."

I curled into a ball and trembled.

Staver pulled me into his arms. But his touch was rigid, and even my human nose could smell his fear.

I was an ogress.

❧

STAVER FINALLY FELL into a flinching sleep. His hands brushed over me as I slipped from his arms, and I gasped in a sob. I wouldn't cry. I wouldn't wake him and make this harder. He'd made marriage promises to me when he thought I was human and fair folk. The promises didn't bind him to an ogress.

I slipped off my wedding ring, tucked it into a pouch next to my earrings and laid them on the ground next to Staver. Then I leaned over to kiss him—just one last time—but pulled back before our lips touched. No! He wasn't mine anymore.

I turned my head and my thoughts to what I must do. I'd go to Dyeda's daughter's grave and bring her bones back for Dyeda. Then I'd disappear into the forest where I belonged and where I couldn't hurt anyone.

I donned my dress and tucked in my wolf amulet.

Mama caught my hand as I came to the edge of our camp. "I'm sorry for my words earlier. I'd hidden who your father was for so long, and feared you'd find out, that when you shifted shape, I panicked. I let my emotions guide my words."

I pulled away from her. "You said enough. I'm an ogre-child. The mocking boys were right."

Her shoulders slumped. "I said what I shouldn't. Now I'll say what I should. Your father wasn't like the ogres of the stories. He never hurt a person. The skull I found was old, from a time long before I came. He was like a hound—faithful and watchful. He protected us. He treated me with gentleness. He was good, even if he was more animal than man."

To her, my papa was still an animal. A good ogre, but still an ogre. And I was his child. I fought back the tears that had threatened since Mama first told me who I was.

"I'm going. I'll bring Dyeda his daughter's bones, and then I'll leave forever. Tell Staver I'm sorry. Tell him I love him but I won't make his life a tragedy by binding him to an ogress." Tears clouded my vision. "Watch over him for me, please." I turned away and then swung back and threw my arms around Mama. "Thank you." The tears flowed down my cheeks. "Thank you for raising me, despite what I am. I love you."

She clung to me and whispered, "You don't have to go."

"I do. The forest is my only refuge now."

THE MOON LIT my path and pulled me along. I poured water on my hands and shifted into a fox. My clothes merged with my body, changing from grey wool dress to red fur. The wolf amulet disappeared inside of me and sat heavy near my heart. My movement was fluid and the world clear and sharply scented. How could changing forms be wrong when it was so beautiful? I wrapped my aching heart in layers of senses—spicy fallen leaves; cold, biting streams just beginning to frost over; wind rippling through my fur; the squeak of a mouse as a silent owl swooped overhead; pine needles pricking my paws; the moon making stripes of dark and light blues with patches of ghostly yellow. I wrapped sense upon sense until I could hardly feel the torn heart beating in the center.

The senses changed as I ran. Ripe apple scent, frost-nipped and sweet, drifted on the wind. Dyeda's—no, he wasn't my grandfather, I was no fair folk—Duke Nicholas's estate lay ahead. Mingled with the apple came the sour scent of fermented grain. The Scythians were drinking. I smiled, and it stretched my fox maw. It would be easy to get in.

In the orchard's corner, a stone bench carved with a woodland scene sat next to a flower-planted grave. I changed forms to a badger and dug. My paws dug into the soil as though I was dipping them into water, and the soil flew behind me. Within minutes I struck the hard wood of the casket. I scraped at the wood with one paw and gouged a track. Adrik, the huntsman, was right: a badger could dig through anything.

The moon hovered on the horizon as I dug a shallow hole under the stone bench and hid the bones. It was too late to do more today. That evening I'd find fabric and rope to bind them and carry them to the Duke.

At least I could do this for him and his wife—it was a small thing for all their kindness.

And after that?

I pushed the thought away and wrapped myself again in sensing. But as a badger, my main sense was smell. Being in a place of death only brought memories I would rather not have.

I changed back to a fox. The moon slipped from the sky, taking with it a power that had flowed over me since I first shifted. I couldn't shift again until it rose.

The pre-dawn filled with the skittering of the night animals returning to their dens and the autumn leaves rustling on branches. The banked campfires of the Scythian army whispered scents of the previous night's meals—fatty pork, probably from the farms people had been forced to abandon as a result of the treaty, and curdled milk. The sun rose and cast the fruit tree shadows westward toward the wall and me. The last time I'd sneaked onto this land, the Scythians had filled the air with their drunken singing. It was the night I came to get the herbs for Dyeda—Duke Nicholas's—heart. If I'd known my shape-shifting ability then, I'd never have been caught. But then I'd not have been imprisoned with the prince, and the war would still be going. If I still didn't know about shape-shifting, Staver would be beside me as we gathered this last gift from Dyeda's home, and we'd go back together.

A whining yip rose in my throat.

No. I couldn't long for Staver. It would break me to see him again, to see his fear and revulsion, to know by his face that I was a monster.

Horse hooves pounded through the forest, approaching the orchard. They stopped, and then feet crunched through leaves.

I darted under the bench, into the shadows cast by the rising sun.

Someone hopped onto the orchard wall then landed by the freshly turned soil of the grave. "Vasilisa," Staver whispered.

Get out of here, I wanted to warn. But I could only yip. He crouched down and looked under the bench. His face flashed from worry to relief. His fear stank, but it was a different stink than the night before, less rank. He reached out and held an open palm a short distance from me. "Vasilisa."

What do you want me to do? Break? Go away where you are safe. Safe from the Scythians, safe from me. I yipped again. The moon had set. I couldn't change into a human form again until it rose that evening. How would I get Staver to leave?

He stayed crouched by the bench, hand outstretched, well within sight of any walking the orchards. He had to go.

I darted forward and nipped his finger. His blood tasted salty. I'd wounded him! I gagged, vomiting like a dog on the dry autumn grass.

He clutched his bleeding finger. His jaw hardened. His scent changed, a new scent overlapped the fear. Something strong and unyielding.

I cowered, putting one of my paws over my muzzle.

"Vasilisa, you can't make me go until we've talked. I don't understand what is happening. But I know who you are and—"

A bellow cut off his words. Other shouts joined in as four Scythians raced between apple and plum trees. Staver pushed me back under the bench and turned to face them.

I darted between Staver's legs and bit the calf of the foremost

Scythian. He shouted and shook his leg, snapping my head back and forth. I clenched my teeth tighter. Salty blood soaked through his wool pants. The world whipped around with his movements, and then he fell.

Staver sat on top of him and pummeled him. The Scythian struck Staver across the mouth. Blood poured from a split lip.

I let go of the Scythian's leg and bit his hand. He bellowed.

The three other Scythians converged on us. Two grabbed Staver. One yanked me away and threw me against the wall. I smacked, and the world split into flashes of light. The wolf amulet pulsed warmth inside me, and the world came back together as a spear descended. I rolled as the point buried itself in the ground. The world spun with the movement.

"Leave the fox alone," Staver yelled. "I'll not fight. Take me. Just don't hurt her."

One of the Scythians grunted in broken Ruskan, "No fight. You prisoner. Fox already dying."

They dragged him off. I tried to follow, but the world tilted, and I ended on my side. My back right leg hung limp. I screamed. It came from my fox throat as loud as a man's death cry. The Scythians laughed. Staver disappeared around the end of the orchard.

I needed to heal so I could help Staver. I pulled myself into the hole I'd dug and into the empty casket. The stale air from before had freshened enough for me to breathe.

I reached my thoughts out. *Papa, I found out you are an ogre and so am I. I don't know what to think. I'm frightened. But none of that matters right now. Staver is a prisoner because he followed me. I need your amulet to heal me—but not make me sleep for three days. Please help it do just enough so I can help him.*

Silence met my thoughts. My head thumped and my leg lay crooked behind me.

Can you even hear me?

The wolf amulet pulsed warmth within me. My world softened and disappeared.

~

I LIMPED THROUGH A SUMMER MEADOW, my back leg stiff but working, and my head tender. My fox tail swished through the tall stands of grass, and pollen dusted my nose. I sneezed, and two butterflies danced upward from columbine.

A wolf padded up beside me. 'My strong one,' his voice rumbled through my head, 'I have been granted an hour to teach you before I start my next trial. What seek you?'

I looked into his dark eyes, darker than any wolf's eyes. My papa's eyes. 'Must all ogres pass through trials as you are doing, to be accepted into the heavens? Are they all evil from birth?' My question felt wrong in my thoughts. All my memories of Papa were of a good and loving father. Even now his teaching was gentle and patient. But every story of ogres was of evil beings. And Mama said there were human bones in the birch grove. Which kind was he?

He slowed his walk, easing my limping stride. 'Being an ogre is not a mark of evil. No more than being a human is a mark of goodness. Both races have good and evil.'

'Then why...' I sent my thoughts towards him. He flinched, and I softened my thoughts. 'Why do all the tales tell of evil ogres who deceive and eat humans? Why are there none about good ogres?'

'The animal's world is simple, clear. Eat, rest, take pleasure with their mate, protect their young. They don't have a right and wrong, only survival. A human lives in a world with laws even more important than survival. The ogre is a bridge between the animal and the human. Many ogres live at the level of survival, hunting for what will fill their bellies—be it bear or man. I did so for the first part of my life.'

I cringed away from him. He had eaten men. My stomach rebelled, and I retched.

He paused beside me and waited.

I backed away from the foul substance and stared at the wolf that had given me my first memories, ones of joy.

He tilted his head. 'Is the owl evil for hunting mice, or the wolf for capturing a deer? Are you evil for eating pig or cow?'

'Those are animals! Not humans!'

His ears flattened at my shouted thoughts. 'I know that now. I didn't know then. Then one day I heard a voice weaving through the air, using the sounds I'd heard before, but this time they were beautiful instead of cries of hunted terror. A dark-haired woman stood in a clearing, speaking to a small group of listeners. As she spoke, the sounds wove through my mind and became words. I don't know how I could understand her, when I never understood a human before. I think she was a fair folk storyteller, and her magic was to make the stories real to the listeners.'

'A fair folk changed you? You were no longer ogre?'

'I am still an ogre. But yes, in a way she changed me. When I understood the words, the stories captured me. Tales of heroes and honor, of villains and hate, of sacrifice and joy even in loss. I fell into them. They tumbled me about like the push of a waterfall into a river. I emerged on her last word, drenched in sweat. The storyteller turned from her audience and looked into the tree where I crouched. Then she said these words: "I've given the tales. What will you do with them?"'

'What did you do?'

'I never ate a man again.'

A tremor of relief passed from my forehead down to the tip of my tail.

He continued. 'I rescued those lost.' A laugh rippled through his thoughts. 'Though many screamed the whole time I carried them from the forest. Then I met your mother. She was close to death. I couldn't just carry her to the edge of the woods. She'd have died. I carried her to my den and tended her until she regained her strength. In those days a new emotion grew in my chest. I loved her, and when you came, that love doubled.'

'Are you only good because of the fair-folk spell? Can you lead me to the fair folk so they can cast such a spell on me?'

He nudged my shoulder with his nose. 'Remember, there is good and evil in each person. Beauty and vileness battle like two creatures in each of us, and the one we feed is the one that grows stronger. Each ogre who steps beyond animal survival into human thought must decide which one to feed. Some feed the evil within themselves. I heard three tales of such ogres in the day listening to the storyteller. And one of an ogre that fed the good. That is the one I chose to follow.'

My nose twitched. 'There are tales of good ogres?'

He laughed again. 'At least three. The one I heard, the one I lived, and the one that stands in front of me.'

'Me?' The world that had seemed to right itself when Dyeda told me I was fair folk, then turned upside down when I learned I was an ogre, shifted sideways.

I could be both ogre and good.

Papa looked up, and I followed his gaze. The sky was awash with crossing rivers of stars instead of the sun. Combined, they were bright enough to light the meadow in a warm glow. Papa nodded once, and his thoughts sighed. 'My time grows short. I will not see you again until you depart your mortal life, though I will hear you, if you call. And perhaps I can help again. Keep feeding the good within you. Do not let despair eat you.' He breathed on my tender head then my limping leg. The pain and stiffness disappeared. 'Now go. Your mate needs you.'

The meadow folded inward.

I woke in the dark of the wooden casket. Within me, the amulet pulsed warmth and power. A glimmer of soft light came through the hole. I crawled up to the chill night air and shivered with joy. *I can be both ogre and good. I don't have to choose one over the other. I can use my ogre abilities to help free Staver. I'm not just strong, but also good. I will free Staver!*

I am Vasilisa the strong!

I am Vasilisa the good!

25

I scurried along the wall of the grand hall. The brilliant colors of tapestries and goldleafed archways were all shades of grey. Trestle tables sat along the edges of the grand hall, and in the center men danced in rhythm to clapping hands and shouts. A servant pushed along the edge of the room with a tray of sliced meat. I squeaked and scampered under a bench before his leather boots could crush me. Maybe changing into a cat would have been better.

I peered around the leg of the bench at the man lounging at a table raised on a dais. Gleb!

The stomping dance ended. Gleb set down a goblet and stood. "My fellow Scythians." His voice carried through the hall, and a Scythian at his side translated from Ruskan to Scythian. "We celebrate our great Khan's victory."

The men stomped and cheered. The wood floor shook.

I scurried up the backside of a tapestry till I was level with Gleb's head and peered between the loose weave.

Gleb waved his arm in an awkward and affected manner, the fieldhand trying to act like nobility. "It was a victory in which I played no small part. I, Duke Yahontov, was the one to trick the prince from the safety of the tsar's armies. I was the one who brought the Khan great riches in these lands and manor. Look around. See the riches I've gained for our great leader. And many more will come to him because I will rule over this trading house between the trickster Ruskan and the great Khan."

I twitched my whiskers at his bombast. I already knew he'd joined the Scythians, but not that he'd been the one to take the prince and almost destroy Ruska. So the Khan rewarded him by making him caretaker of the trading house between our nations? In one way, it would make it easier to free Staver. Gleb was an ignorant fool. But he was also cruel and had an unpredictable temper.

Gleb drained his goblet and belched. "I want music befitting my station. Bring in the prisoner."

I forced a slow breath against the animal fear that froze me.

Two large Ruskans dragged in Staver. He hobbled between them, hopping forward on one leg, while the other leg hung at an odd angle. His face was a swollen mess of bruises. He moaned with each step and gave a strangled cry as his leg caught on the edge of a carpet spread under the head table. The men dropped Staver onto a chair and one shoved a balalaika into his hands. Staver stared at the stringed instrument, his shoulders slumped.

Gleb sneered. "Sing us a hero's ballad."

Staver lifted his chin, his face a sorrowful defiance. He plucked a few notes, twisted the tuning pegs, then sang of the great warrior Ilya Muromets who killed the Nightingale Robber. His voice caught with pain and made the notes even more powerful. As he sang, he changed the words. No longer was the Nightingale Robber a monstrous ogre, but a strong but cowardly man who betrayed his country to the Scythians.

Gleb's face grew darker with each verse until he threw his

heavy goblet, striking Staver's chest. Staver hunched forward, and the balalaika fell from his hands, jangling.

"Send him back to his cell!" Gleb's pinched brows smoothed, and he smiled. "We'll have our first beheading when the Khan arrives."

I squeaked protest and my mouse heart pattered fast enough that the room began to darken. I forced another deep breath. I'd have to free him. But how? I could slip in as an animal, heal him, and together we'd fight our way out. Images of the piled dead outside the cellar flashed like blinding lightning in my mind. All the first who tried to free the tsar's son had died. Could Staver and I fight all those set to guard him?

I scurried down the tapestry and scampered after Staver. The guards dragged him through the manor house and up flight after flight of stairs until they came to an attic in the onion dome. They shoved him into the drafty space, slammed the door, and locked it. Then they stood to either side, facing the stairway.

One slouched against the wall. "Tough luck that we have to stand watch. I'll wager those guarding the lower stairs get some of the feast."

The other elbowed him. "You'll guard him with full attention. You heard what Duke Yahontov said. This man's lover will come for him, and she's the one who captured the Khan. If she frees him, we'll both be executed, if she doesn't kill us first. I saw her knock out the duke with one blow."

The one that had been slouching straightened and gripped his sword.

I clung to the corner. I could change into a wolf and kill them. But could I do it fast enough that they didn't call for help? And I'd have to kill the other guards too. How many were below? I'd have to carry Staver while I fought, and—I shuddered. The game was set against us.

Staver's muffled moans came through the door. The guards ignored the noise and watched the stairs.

I'd find a way. I had to. I scurried for the door, keeping along one wall. *Please don't notice me.*

One guard jumped back and the other laughed. "Now you're jumping at mice? Just watch for men, or a redheaded woman."

I slipped under the door.

Staver lay on his side where he'd fallen. He hid his face in his hands. Words slipped between moans and fingers. "Vasilisa, my sweet Vasilisa. I will see you soon."

Tears turned the grey-colored world foggy. I chattered a dark laugh as I blinked away the droplets. Even mice cried.

Moonlight filtered through a crack in the onion dome lattice. I scurried into the band of light and shifted back to my human form. The amulet hung from my neck once more. "Staver. I'm here."

He lunged to stand, his leg folded under him, and he fell.

I bit my tongue to keep from yelling his name as I ran to him. I turned him over, laying his head in my lap. Vodka wafted on his breath. Someone must have taken pity on him and given him a drink to ease the pain. "Hush. We must be quiet. I'll free you."

"You're alive." He touched my cheek.

I placed my hand over his and held his touch against my skin. "My Papa's amulet healed me."

He stiffened for a moment then half smiled. "Your father's amulet is a gift. It has preserved your life and mine. Truly you are fair folk, for only they make such things."

I held back my sigh. I was part ogre. He knew that, and someday he'd admit it, but for now, it didn't matter what he thought I was. We had to plan. "I'll use the amulet to heal your leg. Then I'll get the key and free you. We'll have to get past the guards."

Staver winced as he shifted. "The amulet will send me into a deep sleep. The Khan comes in two days to collect the duke's treasures, and when he comes, I'll die."

"But the treaty. He can't come so soon!"

"He can if he only brings ten men. I'll not sleep away my last days. Let me spend them with you." He gripped my hand with his sweaty palm.

If the Khan was coming in two days, we had to escape before then. But his leg was broken, and the amulet would take too long to heal him. We couldn't fight our way free. "We have to bargain with Gleb for your life."

Staver's face blanched. "Don't. He hates me. He hates you even more. He'll never give me up, and if you try, he'll kill you too."

"Then I won't let him know it's me. I'll change form. And I won't let him know that I'm bargaining for your life. Gleb's greedy. He's proud. We can trick him. Tell me everything you know."

A smile crept across Staver's bruised face. "You said the fox was your real form. When we get free, I'll find the tales of fair folk shapeshifters. I'm sure there is one about a beautiful fair-folk fox who is wiser than all the tsar's ministers."

His words tickled a curve into my lips. When we got free, he could look for those tales, while I would find the tales of good ogres, even if I had to find the fair-folk storyteller.

Staver touched my lips. "I love your smile. And your thinking face. I'll tell you everything I know, but it isn't much. They dragged me to Gleb, and he interrogated me privately. When I held my silence about where you were against threats, he used force. After he broke my leg, I almost passed out, but that sweet release from pain didn't come. He gloated over my writhing, then boasted about how he was hiding the duke's treasures before the Khan came and how he'd use those riches to turn part of the trading house into a place of gambling and ill-repute, and become richer than the Khan."

I raised my eyebrows. Gleb had planned for the future? His whole plan was based on chance—chance that the Khan wouldn't discover his duplicity, chance that he didn't fall from favor with the Khan. But the odds were in his favor, if he was careful. I fingered my wolf amulet. So he liked to gamble? A plan took shape.

Staver shifted and winced with a moan. Sweat that had beaded on his forehead from the start now soaked his clothes. I touched his leg. It was hot around the break.

He laid his hand on my arm. "I'll be fine. You're here."

He wasn't fine. My plan would do little if he died of infection before I freed him. "I'll use the amulet to heal the worst of this."

He nodded. "Only for a moment. I can't sleep away the week like I did last time."

The fabric stuck to his skin as I rolled up his pants. He stifled a shout as I pulled the fabric away, revealing an angry red inch-long gash with the white of his shin bone pressed against it. Blood seeped from the reopened wound.

The room grew foggy for a moment. I gripped the wolf amulet tightly and closed my eyes. *Please, Papa, help the amulet heal the infection and straighten the bone but not make him sleep for more than a day.*

A memory pushed forward. A child fell from a full hay wagon, and a sound like a tree splitting ricocheted over the harvested fields, followed by his screaming. Fieldhands pulled his leg straight and bound it between two branches. The child walked with a slight limp for years, but he healed.

"Staver, I'm going to set your bone, so it won't take as much magic to heal you, and you won't sleep as long. This will hurt."

He tried to smile, though it came out a grimace. The grimace turned to muffled curses as I dragged him to the beam that supported the center of the onion dome and leaned his back against it. The vodka must not have been holding off much of the pain.

I needed ties and something to hold his leg straight. Two dusty chests sat along the curved wall. Both held woolen garments folded around lengths of cedar. I pulled out a green riding dress that would have fit me. It was the same one that a young woman wore in a painting in Dyeda's study. This was his daughter's.

"I'm sorry," I whispered both to Dyeda and Staver as I tore strips from the dress and bound Staver to the beam. If only Staver could faint now. If I used the amulet, he'd sleep through the pain, but I dared not before setting his leg, lest it heal the bone and not the infection. And then I'd have to use the amulet longer and he'd sleep longer.

I grabbed his leg.

"Wait," he whispered. "Gag me first, to muffle my shouts." He opened his mouth for me to push in the fabric.

My tears dripped on his hands. He nodded, his jaw stiff and his body braced.

I bit the inside of my cheek and pulled his leg.

A muffled roar rumbled from his chest and then his head slumped forward.

I braced, ready to leap, if the guards entered. But no key turned in the lock. The guards must have been more concerned about approaching enemies than if their prisoner bellowed in pain. Thank the heavens.

Quick, I need to brace the break while he's in the faint. I extended his leg against the tug of his muscles and fit the bone back in place. It was like drawing a bow, needing a steady and strong pull. I struggled to hold the bone in place while securing the cedar bracing with wool strips. Sweat made my fingers slippery before I finished.

Now the amulet. I laid my hand over the infected break then touched the amulet to Staver's chest. The skin knit together as the fever drained. I jerked the amulet away. *Let it be enough, but not too much.* His pant leg fit over the bracing. I removed his gag and bonds, then laid him on a layer of dresses and tunics and covered him with a winter coat. If the guards came in, they wouldn't see his leg brace right away, and even if they did, they'd have to assume he did it himself.

I kissed Staver and changed back into a mouse. *I'll get you free.*

26

———

I STUDIED my appearance in the moonlit pool. Thick black eyebrows rose in surprise on a moon-round face surrounded by short black hair that stuck out like a thistle burr. No one would recognize me even though I hadn't changed my body shape or size. I needed all my abilities and the skill that came with knowing my body. The stolen Scythian tunic hung baggy on me, hiding my curves and the golden wolf mark between my breasts.

Parchment lay on a stump with stones weighing down its corners. I'd changed into a squirrel and stolen the supplies, then used my best script to write an order ending it with a small drawing of a galloping horse. It looked like the Khan's seal on a treaty. I hoped Gleb wouldn't look too closely. Could he even read?

I glanced heavenward. *Papa, you said you could hear me. If there are others who will help me, please tell them my need. There are so many things I don't control. I'm doing everything I can. I need heaven's help.*

Then I squared my shoulders and strode away from the hiding spot where I'd shifted, across a short stretch of forest, and into Dyeda's moonlit garden.

The palace still glowed with lanterns. Strummed music and many voices poured from the open windows, even though it was after midnight.

I worked my way to the front and knocked on the door.

A half-drunk man in Ruskan garb opened it. "Oh, so it's another one of you. Come in, come in, and wipe those muddy boots, or I'll have to mop up these floors again." Smears of mud showed his previous attempts.

I wiped my boots and followed him to the great hall. Gleb still sat at the head of the room. His booming laughter carried over the musicians plucking balalaikas.

I strode across the room, dodging men who splashed their drinks in expressive drunkenness. As I approached the dais, four guards stepped forward and lowered their spears. "Duke Yahontov," I called out, deepening my voice. "The Khan sends his congratulations on your new dukedom in Ruska, and he wishes to share in your joy."

Gleb looked down at me with drink-muddied eyes. Sauce and meat stained his velvet coat. "When he arrives, I'll give him a feast that won't be matched in a hundred years."

I held out the parchment. "He won't be coming."

He grabbed the parchment, unrolled and glanced over it, spending a moment looking at the bottom--would he realize the seal was forged? He grunted and handed it back to me. "I can't read Scythian. You tell me what it says."

A tendril of hope pushed through the darkness. He couldn't read Ruskan either, for that was what I wrote it in. I lifted my chin as I read, "My valued servant, Yahontov. A traitor amongst my generals has risen against me. I'll soon hang his head on a pike. Because I cannot come, you will send a gift: half the treasures of the estate. Do not disappoint me."

Gleb choked and sputtered. "Half. But it's already been robbed clean by those thieving Ruskans after he left." He glanced at the rich tapestries that hung around the great hall walls. "All except for those. Nothing else. I'll send half of the tapestries."

"I doubt he will be satisfied. He gave you this power. He can take it away. But he might accept a wager to decide what to send."

Gleb raised his cup. "A fine idea. What is the contest?"

Inside my long sleeves, my clenched hands relaxed, then tightened again. He'd moved his first chess piece. I studied my options—three pieces I could put into play. I'd need all three. Which one first?

"A test of skill and endurance. I'll dance the hopak against your finest dancer, and whoever lasts the longest without falling wins."

He rested his bearded chin on his hand. "You are just a boy. Surely you'd pick some contest that would provide longer entertainment. But then, I have other entertainment. If you, by some miracle, win, then I'll send the gold-plated dishes from this feast, along with half the tapestries. And if you lose, you'll wash the dishes of this feast."

Winning wouldn't get Staver free. And the dishes would take many hours, probably until morning—was it time I could spare? I bit the inside of my cheek. I couldn't argue with him, not yet. I needed to put him in my debt first. I'd win and then increase the wager. "Agreed."

I grabbed a table to help clear a space to dance.

"No." Gleb motioned me to a chair. "You sit. I don't want you worn out before the contest begins."

Once the tables were gone and the floor mopped of splattered food, men gathered around a space about ten strides by ten. Coins passed from hand to hand. As I entered the square, a man patted me on the back and grunted something in Scythian. It could have been *good luck* or *I'll kill you if you make me lose my money.*

A lean Ruskan entered the square to boisterous cheers of "Mikhail!" He doffed his cap and bowed in four directions before turning to me with a confident grin.

The musicians started a lively tune on their balalaikas.

Mikhail and I started into the first steps of the dance, circling each other with a high cross-step, touching our hands to knees. I spun on one foot and high cross-stepped in the opposite direction. Mikhail mirrored me across the square. These were the easy parts, the warm-up so our muscles didn't cramp.

The tune shifted. I leaped into the air, spreading my straight legs far apart, and touching my fingers to my toes. Mikhail repeated it on the second beat. Then I. Then he. Ten times we leaped up, alternating like the two ends of a child's totter log. He moved into the next dance motion, and I added an eleventh and twelve leap. I grinned. I'd win.

Scattered cheers broke through grumbling. Mikhail turned a spin into an elegant bow. He wasn't breathing hard, but tightness started in my chest. I'd not slept for more than a day. He kicked a single leg high in front of him, so his foot reached above his head and his knee almost met his face.

I followed with my own high forward kicks, double-timing one after another. Six times. Mikhail stopped before I couldn't continue. Why hadn't I spent more time learning these dances? I'd learned because Staver wrote about them, but I never thought his life would depend on them.

Mikhail squatted down and kicked his legs out, holding his body in steady balance.

My legs trembled as I matched him low kick for kick. I stopped first, partly out of need and partly because I wanted to choose the next step. Mikhail smirked as I stood and high cross-kicked in place for six beats. But he also took up the easier step.

When my legs warmed back to standing and my light-headedness cleared, I leaped and rotated sideways, so that for a moment my head was a hand-span from the floor before I came back to my feet. A roar erupted around me. I moved into a quick skipping step.

Mikhail's face tensed. He leapt and rotated. His hair brushed the floor before he landed in a stumbled step, but he didn't fall. Held breaths let out in a whoosh. And the clink of coins passing hands combined with the plucking of balalaikas.

Ah, so, that was not one he liked. How about this one? I flipped backwards. This one was easier than the sideways flip but made my stomach twist as I went into it blindly. I landed and stumbled, catching myself an inch before my knee struck the floor.

Mikhail flipped backwards twice, touching his feet to the ground, once between the two.

It was time. I could do this.

I flipped once, then again.

And slipped.

My knee cracked against the floor. *No! I need to win!*

The music stopped, or maybe it continued but was buried under the voices yelling and screaming, thumping each other on the back, and dropping into their own squat-kicking dance. Men shoved tables to clear more floor space. Benches overturned. Platters crashed to the floor. I picked up one platter and carried it from the chaos, toward the kitchen.

Gleb's bellow followed me. "That's right, boy. Go wash and soak away that pride."

I set the platter down on a pile of others in the kitchen and rubbed my knee. My pride stung more. And fear gnawed my heart like a bone. The Khan would arrive soon. I still had two more pieces to play but too little time to place them.

27

─────────

I SCRUBBED dishes through the night. I had to finish them to play the next piece, but each minute scraped over me with scouring questions.

Did I pick the wrong contest? Why did I agree to the dishwashing part of the wager? I don't have time for this. How is Staver? Is he still in the amulet-induced sleep? Have his guards checked on him, or will they leave him alone and let him slowly starve since they believe the Khan isn't coming anymore? Or will Gleb order his execution earlier? I scrubbed harder at the scorched meat on an iron grill.

Finally, in the hour before dawn, I set the last pan on the slatted table to dry. My body shook with exhaustion. I'd been awake a full day and night. The moon sat low in the west. I'd have less than an hour while I could still shift shape, and then I'd have to wait until the evening. At least the manor was blessedly silent.

I stopped. *Silent? Are they all asleep? Are Staver's guards also in a drunken sleep?* Sparrow hope hopped in my chest. I could free Staver now. I'd get the key. I'd carry him away. No one would know.

I slipped from the kitchens to the main house and up two

flights of stairs, treading lightly as I passed slumped forms that hadn't made it to their rooms before they passed out. I turned the corner and pulled back. Four guards stood in front of the door that opened to the spiral stairs. Sconces lit the hall between me and them. The guards stood, scanning the hall.

Those four, plus the two at the top. I could do it.

I pictured a wolf and shifted—into a fox. I'd do better as a human. I shifted into my disguised form and almost stepped into the hall, but froze. Idiot! If I could shift into that form, why not a more trusted form? I pictured Gleb's face in my mind; his sneering, cruel features, his bulky shoulders, his meaty hands. My body shifted.

I strode out into the lit hallway. Two guards snapped to attention while the other two kept watch.

"I want to see the prisoner!" I ordered, deepening my voice with gruffness.

One reached for the keys at his belt.

This would work! I stepped forward and reached out.

"Stop!" the other guard jerked the first guard back. "It's not the duke! He has no beard!"

I slapped my smooth face.

The four guards converged on me, the two in the front wielding swords and the back two menacing spears.

I ducked around one swordsman and grabbed the shaft of a spear, yanking it from the back guard's hand.

A sword struck my thick padded Scythian tunic. And stopped. *Thank the Scythian armour makers.*

I twisted around, knocking the spear shaft against the heads of three of the guards. Two went down with an *oof*. Where was the fourth?

A clanging alarm came from the corner. The guard struck his sword against a brass bell again, and the sound of clomping boots came from below. How many men did Gleb keep sober? If I tried to take Staver now, they'd kill him. They still might.

I knocked over the last two guards with the spear and raced up the stairs, changing into a mouse as I ran. The spear I carried clattered to the ground.

The two guards at the top stood with ready weapons as I scurried by their feet and under the door.

Staver lay silent where I'd left him. His chest rose and fell in deep, slow breaths. I changed into my own shape, and the Scythian clothes hung baggy. My red braid, streaked with black, hung over my shoulder. The cedar chest was my only weapon. I hefted it and stood ready to clobber whoever came through the door.

Boots thumped up the stairs. "Where is he? Where is the man that ran up the stairs?"

"No one came up the stairs."

"Did he leap out a tower window?"

"I don't know, sir. But no one came to the top."

"Let me see the prisoner."

What if they weren't going to kill him? They would if they saw me.

The key scraped in the lock.

I set the cedar chest down, shifted back to a mouse, and scurried under the cloth that covered Staver's feet. I'd shift back if any man drew a weapon.

Hinges squealed as the door swung open. A man entered holding a lantern. He glanced around, opened both cedar chests, threw out all the clothes that remained in them, then strode to Staver.

My mouse heart fluttered in my chest and the wolf amulet glowed close beside it. I prepared to change form.

He kicked off the coat I'd laid across Staver.

Staver flinched and moaned. The amulet sleep was wearing off.

He'd better not kick again, or I'd bite him.

The man grunted and spun around. "No one's here. I think the guards below must have fallen asleep on duty or gotten drunk and fought each other. Either that, or this place is haunted. I'll take the first. And I'll take my bed. Don't you dare ring that alarm again unless it's an actual attack."

He left, and the key scraped in the lock again.

I scurried under the blanketing clothes to Staver's chest and curled up over his heart. His beat pulsed against me with the warmth and comfort of the wolf amulet. I'd have to go before the moon set.

Sixty of Staver's heartbeats later, I scurried from the room, down the stairs, and back to the kitchen. There, I shifted back to my Scythian messenger form. As I grew from mouse to human, something large pounced, claws dug into my shoulder, and yowled. A tabby cat leaped from my shoulder, spitting and hissing.

I collapsed to the floor laughing at the startled cat as tears trailed my cheeks. Disguising myself as Gleb should have worked. Why didn't I have a beard? Was it because I remained female in each form I shifted to?

It didn't matter now. Even if I could shift to a male form, they'd guard him doubly. I still had to win his freedom in a wager.

The moon set. Its pull and power fled. I sagged against the kitchen wall and let sleep claim me.

A BOOT NUDGED ME.

I leaped to my feet. Noon sun poured through the window. How could I sleep so long?

Laughter burst from a young Ruskan man. "You sure gave us good gambling last night. Duke Yahontov wants to see you."

I stumbled after him.

Gleb looked up as I entered a cozy study with a fire, empty shelves where books once sat, and blanket-softened chairs. I clenched my hands. This room had once been Dyeda's.

Gleb stood, laughing, and slapped me on the back. "Did a night of scrubbing soften that foolish pride?"

I lifted my head. "The Khan still requires half of the treasures, and he'll not believe a few tapestries is all you have."

"You seem a loyal messenger, but you speak and dance like a Ruskan."

I cursed under my breath and Gleb laughed harder.

Thoughts raced as I met his cruel face. I pulled the truth and a lie together. "I am Ruskan, just like you. And I serve the Khan much better than you."

His eyebrows pulled down and together. "I captured the tsar's son for him!"

"Then serve him by sending the tribute. He only asks for half, when he could ask for all. Or would you rather another wager?"

He tilted his head and rubbed his fingers together on his right hand. "You seem to like washing dishes too much. What if this time you muck out the stalls? The old mucker has a bad knee, though after your fall yesterday, yours could be just as bad."

"And if I win, you'll give a proper tribute?" I glanced around the room and let my gaze rest on an alabaster box carved with a scene of a mermaid rising from the sea.

He followed my gaze. "I'd forgotten about this room. I'll send half of the treasures held here. It will be even better than a chest of gold-rimmed china."

I sniffed as I lowered myself into a chair. "He may accept that. But as to the contest: a test of strength and accuracy in archery."

Gleb laughed and looked at me like the bird he'd once plucked live. "Again, an easy contest. I have Scythian archers who learned the bow before they were weaned. They've been shooting longer than you've been alive. You'll have to explain to the Khan how you gambled away his tribute."

"Not the Scythian bow. The Ruskan longbow."

28

───────────

I PRACTICED all afternoon on the green between the manor and the road, swapping between bows until I found one I liked. Meanwhile, Gleb's men scurried about, setting up an archery range on the far side of the green.

Archery had been part of who I was since age eight, but in changing my face, I'd shifted my eyes wider and changed how I saw. Many of my arrows flew awry, to the delight of my constantly changing audience.

A pit opened in my stomach. I should have kept my face shape the same and just changed my hair. I squinted, I tilted my head, but no matter what I did, the arrows continued to fly awry.

Would my wider-set eyes truly throw my aim that much? I picked up my next arrow and studied the fletching. It had a loose feather. The next had a slightly crooked shaft, and another a tilted metal tip. I grimaced. He was sabotaging me before I even started the contest.

"I need a fletching kit!" I yelled.

Those watching me milled around for a moment before a Ruskan man came forward. "What'll you give me for it?"

I clasped his forearm and squeezed in a comradely way.

"You'll get the best archery demonstration you'll ever see in your life."

He raised his eyebrows. "You boast like a fish seller, all promises and only rotten wares." But he got me the supplies.

I finished fletching a tenth sound arrow. It would have to be enough. I drew the bow back, just to my cheek, and released. The arrow flew and stuck off-center of the target—exactly where I wanted it.

Gleb's voice carried over the green. "Certain you don't want to just muck the stalls now?"

I picked up a new bow. "I haven't practiced in a while, but I'm getting the feel back. I'll do well enough."

He walked over next to me, picked up one longbow and leaned on it like a staff. "What if we up the wager? My men all bet you'll miss on the first shot. But for each shot you don't miss, I'll add a setting of dishes with the silverware to the tribute, whether or not you win. The Khan will get tapestries and possibly a few pieces of silver. You can explain why so little."

"What if..." I bent my weight against the bow and released an arrow. It hit close to center on a middle distant target. "You send a servant to the Khan. You have plenty of men who don't seem to do anything for you. Send one of them as tribute. He always needs new men to slave for him. It wouldn't even have to be one of your men. Did you take prisoners when you occupied this palace?"

Gleb glanced at the palace's onion dome and scowled. "None that the Khan would want."

Curse his grudge! He was worse than an ogre. At least ogres could be good. The bow thrummed as my last arrow lodged itself in a tree trunk half again the distance past the last target.

Gleb's scowl deepened.

I unclenched my fist from around the bow and set it down. I'd have to play my second piece in a dangerous move. "If we are upping the wager, then it should go both ways. If I win, then I get to go through the palace and choose the half, the full half of the treasures to take back to the Khan; and if I lose, you keep me as a slave."

He leaned on the bow until it bent. "What will the Khan do about his missing messenger?"

"You send a different man back. I'll last longer serving you. The Khan will have my head if I return with such a pittance of tribute."

Gleb's gaze raked over me from head to toe. "You are strong and agile. I'll find a use for you. Yes. If you hit every target, you get to choose the tribute, up to half of all the treasures in the palace. And if you miss even one, you'll serve the rest of your life as my personal slave."

I'd win. The afternoon sky dimmed into a still-aired evening. I had to win.

I followed Gleb to the other side of the green. Several hundred men lined the two edges of the archery field.

I motioned to the field. "I want to check each target."

"Go ahead."

Ten wooden disks atop staves sat at different distances through the field. I walked the length, inspecting each. These weren't ringed. I either hit them or I didn't. Some were as wide as from my fingertips to my elbow. Others were no more than the spread of one hand. A few slanted backward. I planted them straighter in the ground.

Gleb followed a few steps behind but didn't stop me.

Then I came to the most distant target. It was the largest one, made of thick, stiffened parchment. An arrow would punch straight through it. I touched the edge, and it rocked sideways.

Cruel laughter boomed behind me. "You'll not adjust that one, boy. You must hit both the front and back target, while the front is rocking." Gleb hit the edge of the target with his palm and sent it rocking faster.

I pinched the target between my fingers, stopping it, then walked around the side. A hand span behind the first target sat a second target, about the size of my palm. The front post was hinged about halfway up, and a series of weights hung from it. I touched the front target again, setting it rocking back and forth, coming within an inch of revealing the back one, but never showing it. I stopped the rocking once more. The back sat off-center.

I scowled at Gleb. "This is not what we agreed to."

"You said archery contest. You didn't define more than that."

"Can your archer hit it?"

Gleb thumped me on the back. "There is no other archer. Just you against the targets. You can give up now and go back to the Khan with no tribute, and whatever excuse you can dream up to save your neck. Or you can compete and become my slave."

"Or I could win."

He smirked. "Sooner a bear will fly."

I crouched level with the targets, lining them up. I'd have to hit the front off-center, slightly below and to the left. I touched the best point of entry, and my finger left a damp sweat spot. That would evaporate all too soon, and the front had no rings for me to line up with. If I could just mark the spot, or even the center, I'd have a chance. "If you are so certain, then let me mark the eye of the target."

"You've had your chance to study them. Get back to the shooting line."

Heaven help me. Please.

I stood a foot behind the chalked line. I'd not lose for the simple mistake of stepping on it. Then I lifted my bow and nocked my arrow. The first target was an easy pace, and the air sat still as a cat hunting a mouse. I drew back and shot. My arrow punched through the thin board and hung by its feathers out the other side.

A single cheer rose and then died away in the surrounding silence. Someone was betting for me. And at the odds Gleb set, he'd be a rich man when I was done, if I could do what I had to.

I hit the next six targets, all close to the center. More cheers erupted, and plenty of groans. Gleb just smirked from his chair.

My fingers trembled as I drew for the eighth target. I released and my dish-washing-roughened fingers snagged the bow string a moment. The arrow swerved to the right, striking the target at the edge.

A sharp prickle ran over my arms, down my back, and turned my stomach. I set my bow tip on the ground and closed my eyes.

"Get on with it!" Gleb shouted.

I snatched up my bow.

A warning whispered through me. *Staver will die if you kill Gleb.*

I lowered the bow again to the ground and clenched my fists. *I know.* I reached into my tunic and placed my hand over the wolf mark on my skin. *Please, I need a small healing, just to make my fingers smooth and not shake.*

A jolt of energy shot through my trembling hands. I rubbed my smooth fingertips together. Then a tug like a breeze pulled me eastward. I glanced up. The evening moon rose above the forest to the east. I could change. But to what?

I closed my eyes. An image flashed. A goshawk floated in the sky. A mouse scampered across the green. The hawk dove and caught it. I needed those eyes. Light flashed behind my closed eyelids.

"Do you give up? You are my slave if you do," Gleb mocked.

I opened my eyes. Everything was a different color, like when

I was a shrike. But more so, everything was crisp and clear: the grain of the wooden post below the last target, the metal hinges rotating with the rocking, and the glowing smears along the crinkled parchment circle. Most of the smears were along the edges, and one just below the center and off to the left, where I'd touched it with my sweaty finger.

I could shape shift just my eyes? What else could I do just in part? I clicked my mouth closed from its gape and studied the glowing smears. Thank the heavens that birds could see moisture. My target was marked.

I drew my bow and shot the ninth target, the smallest one. And the arrow bit firmly into the wood.

Then I studied the rocking motion of the tenth. Back and forth, and for a moment the posts lined up and then separated. The trembling returned to my fingers, and sweat stuck my clothes to my back and arms. I rotated my shoulders to free my skin from the clinging cloth. *Please. I need to make this shot.*

I nocked my arrow, drew my bow, and sighted the spot as the posts lined up, holding to that point even as the target rocked sideways. I held my aim half a breath and released. The arrow flew as the target rocked back.

"For Staver," I whispered.

The posts lined up, and my arrow tore through the front target, slightly above and the left of the glowing spot.

Silence.

Had it hit the second target? It was close. It should have hit it.

No cheers or groans.

I'd missed.

My knees gave out beneath me. I'd missed. I needed that shot.

I howled against the practical thoughts, the logic, and the

strategy. It hadn't helped. Staver was still a prisoner, and when the tsar arrived tomorrow, they'd kill him.

A roar outside of me drowned out my own wild sound.

A hand grabbed my arm and pulled me upright. It was one of the Ruskans. "Look." He pointed. A man had removed the first target, and the second target had a hole at its edge.

29

———————

I BLINKED AT ALL the treasure gathered in the great hall. Gleb's men were keeping him to his openly made boast. Now I had something to wager with.

I'd never explored most of the palace. The only rooms that mattered were the ones where I'd spent time with Dyeda and Baba. And now treasure piled around me: a green marble vase half my height, a gem-lined framed picture, a plate with a painting so real that the deer should have leaped from it and left tiny prints across the table, silks, embroidered wools, spotted furs, a geared clock shaped like a peacock, a dark table with inlaid pearl, and piles of other beautiful and curious things.

Gleb stood glowering as I picked through the piles. Each time he cringed, I chose that item. When I pulled aside a three-tiered necklace laden with rubies, he turned purple and thumped his fist against the wall.

I walked past the marble chess set for the fourth time, then turned and opened it. The green and white marble pieces lay in two velvet drawers. I ran my finger over the white tsar's face. It was gentle and wise like the old tsar. Dyeda and I had played many games in my five months with them. But Gleb couldn't know my longing for it and for those times.

I set it on a table and lined up the pieces. "I've never seen a chess set this fine. I'm sure the Khan won't mind if we play a game before I take it to him. Do you play?"

His gaze flickered to the board and back to me, and his eyes narrowed. "Only for high stakes."

"You won the first contest and I the second. Are you certain you want to risk another on a game of strategy?"

He pulled up a chair across from me.

I set the green tsar on the board. "What are the stakes?"

He grabbed the white tsar and thumped it in its place. "When I win, you'll leave and take only a quarter of what you've set aside, of my choosing, and you'll never return."

I tilted my head. "I thought you said you played for high stakes. Last time it was my life in servitude. These stakes are nothing compared to that. What if, assuming you win, the only treasure I take is one servant of my choosing plus the tapestries and dishes you initially promised? But if I win, I take another tenth of the treasure to keep for myself, in addition to the half I take to the Khan." I let my gaze wander over the treasure in a longing study while watching him from the corner of my eye.

A sneer curled across his face. "You'll play the champion of my choosing."

I eyed a pearl-handled sword. "Any you care to set against me."

"Agreed."

He agreed. He agreed! I danced the hopak in my heart.

A short time later a scribe wrote the terms. I signed *Yeva.* Gleb marked it with an X.

His champion sat down across from me. He was a white-haired man with a long mustache and a pipe clamped between his teeth. Smoke wrapped around him and tickled my nose. I sneezed then coughed.

He set his pieces in two precise rows across from mine. Then he moved a pawn two spaces forward from his tsarina, placing him firmly in the control of the center of the board, while freeing one bishop and his tsarina.

I jumped my knight over my pawns, so it sat diagonal and separated by a square from his pawn.

He moved another pawn next to his first.

I sheltered my knight with a pawn. It was one of the basic starts to many games I had played. Yet this game would be unlike any I'd played before.

Fifteen moves into the game, pieces clustered in the middle of the board, and neither of us had captured any. He played carefully, and his strategy, though clear to follow, was solid. I took one of his pawns for the first capture. He didn't rise to the bait but continued to move his pieces into place. He cut off my places of retreat and then picked off my pieces as I picked off his.

I only had two possible paths left. I took one path, forcing him from his plan. He adjusted and closed in again. He'd checkmate me in two moves if I let him, and six moves if I didn't.

I chose the longer game. Gleb had to believe I'd given it my best.

My opponent made the next move and opened himself for check. He groaned after he let go of his piece. Why did he have to make a mistake? He was so close.

I put him in check. And he freed himself. We were balanced. I could checkmate him in three moves. He'd checkmate me in two, if he saw the path. I moved a piece to allow him that way.

He moved correctly.

I cursed to cover my flood of relief.

He put me in check. And then checkmate.

"Game," he stated and tipped over my tsar.

Gleb broke into an impressive high-kicking dance.

He'd gained my tsar, and I'd gained my Staver.

GLEB'S MEN lined the four walls of the great hall; Scythians, Ruskans, warriors, servants, scribes, musicians. Some ducked their heads as I walked past, others stared at the opposite wall, now hung sparsely with tapestries.

I stopped in front of a slightly built man. He grasped his right hand in his left and fingered chords against it. I bit my lip to hold back the stinging in my eyes at the familiar movement. "The Khan needs a new musician. He had the last one trampled for his poor playing."

The man hid his hands behind his back. "I'm a scribe. He won't want me."

I snorted my disbelief. "I want all the musicians to line up and each play me a simple song so I may decide on their quality."

A scuffle ensued as men bolted for the door. Gleb's soldiers captured them and dragged them to the center of the room. Other men came forward on their own.

The first musician, the one I'd faced, played a stumbling song on his balalaika, the strings screeching as his fingers slid from chord to chord.

I yanked the balalaika from him. "You're right. You're no musician. Get back to your scribe work."

He scrambled off, his face as pale as his white tunic.

One by one, they played for me. Some were proficient and one even played with confidence.

One by one, I found fault. "Poor tone—shoddy playing—bad posture—ugly face; the Khan wants to enjoy his music without being sickened by the player." I turned to Gleb. "Surely you have better musicians than these."

He scowled in thought. "How long do musicians last in the Khan's court?"

"About as long as a fly."

His eyebrows came down at sharp angles, and a cruel smile spread across his face. "Then I have one I don't mind sending. He may last longer than most; he's better than any that played for you."

"Then why isn't he here?" I shouted.

"He's a prisoner."

"Then get him, chained if you think it necessary. If he is any better than the other musicians, I'll make do. And I'll leave this cursed place to never see your face again."

Gleb laughed. "Get the prisoner Staver. His demon lover has abandoned him, and I'll capture her some other way."

A man hustled from the room.

Gleb's words pierced. The echoes of childhood mocking—demon wild, ogre child. I shook off the voices. I *was* an ogre child. Because of that, I'd saved the tsar's son and stopped a war. I couldn't have done that without my ogre strength. Because of my ogre ability to shape-shift, I'd soon free Staver.

The rattle of chains mixed with thumping boots. Two guards marched into the great hall. Staver limped between them, the cedar bracing peeking out from below the hem of his pants. He winced with each step. His head bent forward, his hair hanging in tangles, his clothes rent and stained, his hands shackled.

I tensed to run, to shove the guards aside, to hold him. Instead, I placed my hands on my hips and waited with what I hoped was a sneer. "He doesn't look like much. Are you certain that he can play?"

Gleb shrugged. "I've heard he can put songbirds to shame."

The guards with Staver came to a stop before me.

Staver lifted his head and looked into my face. The bruising from the first night had turned dark. His left eye was blackened, and his right cheek puffed with purple bruising. His skin around it was pale. But his gaze was defiant. "I'll escape from wherever you take me. I have promises to keep." His beautiful voice came out in a rasp.

Staver, it's me. I'm here. You're almost free. I swallowed the word before they could reach my lips and turned to Gleb. "He's in no condition to play. Unchain his wrists. Get him a seat, some water and food."

Gleb repeated my order.

Staver sank into a chair and rubbed his wrists. He gulped the water from a clay mug.

"Get him more," I ordered when he'd finished the first.

He coughed and gulped down the second mugful. Then he poured the last bit of it into his hands and dampened his face, wiping grime from it. He ate a couple bites of bread, set it aside, and returned his defiant stare to me.

I grabbed a balalaika from the collection that the other musicians had left and handed it to him. "The Khan needs a new musician. I'll sing you a Ruskan song that the Khan favors. If you are good enough to hear it and play it back well, then I'll take you."

I sang.

> Timber grows tall.
> Birds nest in its branches,
> Squirrels in its trunk,
> Rabbits burrow under its roots.
> Home.

My voice caught and cracked on the words.

Staver gripped the balalaika. His eyes widened and he opened his mouth.

I held up my hand. "Don't interrupt me. I can't sing well, but I know the worth of a musician. Let me finish." I continued to the next verse.

> Timber falls to ax,
> Sawn and shaped into
> Walls and roof.
> Live in its safety.
> Home.

Staver fingered chords along the neck of the balalaika, his wide eyes fixed on my face. I started changing the words.

> I am of the forest.
> You are of the house.
> Can we find a home together?

My voice cracked and broke off. I clenched my hands inside my long Scythian sleeves. I had to make it through the song, enough for them to believe Staver heard it and repeated it. I grabbed water and gulped it then continued, changing the verse again, stumbling over the in-the-moment words.

> Your music captured me.
> Your kindness caught my soul.
> Your thoughts—good and sweet.
> Your courage. Your love.

His head dropped forward, and his shoulders shook.

> My heart found new place,

Not of house, not of forest.
And wherever we dwell,
I am your home, and you are mine.

Staver kept his head bent over the balalaika and plucked a few notes, turned the tuning pegs, and plucked a few more. Then his fingers flowed over the strings, playing our song. Passion and love filled the room in the vibration of strings.

My eyes stung, and my throat tightened into a held sob.

When he finished, a few men wiped their noses, and one coughed.

I turned to Gleb. My voice came out husky. "You were right. He puts the songbirds to shame. When he has his voice back, he will please the Khan. At least for a time."

30

THE MORNING SUN cut through the autumn briskness but not my internal chill. The Khan would arrive for his treasures today— all his treasures, not just the ones I'd wagered for from Gleb. If the Khan arrived before we left, or we met each other on the road, he'd discover my whole deceit and kill us.

Even with my brusqueness to be gone, Gleb pondered over which tapestries and dishes to send.

I clenched my hands inside my long sleeves to keep from pestering. If I seemed unconcerned, maybe he'd let us go sooner.

The sun rose an hour into the sky.

Gleb finally nodded over the pile to send and ordered his men to load two wagons with rolled tapestries, china nestled in boxes, and small chests of silver spoons and knives. I tucked a box in the corner of one wagon. If any asked, it held a balalaika for Staver to use when he performed for the Khan. It really held the bones to take back to Dyeda.

Staver sat chained to the wagon seat, and I held the key. He shivered, hunched over, but the few times he caught my eyes, his face brightened and the corners of his mouth twitched. I avoided his look. If Gleb saw Staver's joy, he'd grow suspicious.

We had to leave. Soon. Now.

The sun rose another hour.

Gleb clapped me on the back. "Hope the Khan doesn't punish you too much for gambling away his tribute."

I shot back my silent curse. *When the Khan gets here, you'll never have the chance to gamble again. But if you will just let us leave, I'll pray that he has mercy on you.*

The sun sat in the middle of the sky when I scooted next to Staver on the wagon seat, and one of Gleb's men clucked at the horse to pull the wagon from the yard. Another wagon followed; and six other men, bearing swords and bows, rode around us. They were to protect the Khan's treasure as we took it back to him.

The palace grew smaller behind us and then disappeared as we turned from the lane onto the road going south. Where on the road was the Khan? Did he leave early in the morning? Was he riding a fast horse or traveling at the speed of heavy wagons ready to bear his treasures back to his palace?

Staver and I hadn't a moment where I dared speak with him. And even with him right next to me, the wagoner was just as close on the other side. I'd have to move my last piece without warning him. I hadn't known I'd need this piece. I had hoped that once I won Staver's freedom, we could just leave.

I laid my hand over the wolf marking on my chest. *Please Papa, I'm in a shifted form so I don't have the amulet to lay on Staver and send him into a deep healing sleep. Can its power work through my hand to Staver?*

After a long moment, the wolf amulet's power pulsed once inside me. This had to work. We couldn't stay longer with the wagons and guards. I reached over and touched Staver's hand. The amulet power pulsed three times within me, coursing down my arm and through my hand.

Staver's hand went rigid and he tumbled forward, almost falling from the wagon.

I caught his shoulders. "Stop!" I shouted.

The wagoner pulled back on the reins and the creaking of the wagon stopped. "What happened?" He grunted.

"You gave me a dying musician," I shot back. I touched Staver's neck. A deep slow beat pulsed. I cursed, using the blacksmith's strongest words. "He's dead. I'll not take a carcass to the Khan."

The wagoner drew away from us. "Just keeled over and died, did he?"

I scowled as I unlocked Staver's chains and hauled his limp form on my back. "I'll be back once I've left the body far from our path. We need not draw more wolves to the road. They've probably already grown vicious on the fallen from the war, and I have to travel these paths."

One of the mounted guards stopped beside the wagon. "Do you need help?"

"Just throw his balalaika out of the wagon. It's the leather-bound box behind where the prisoner sat. Don't need anything to hint to the Khan that we were bringing him a musician slave for his court. I'll leave it with the body."

I slid from the wagon, dragging Staver's limp form with me, bound him to my back with a bit of rope around his waist and wrists, then picked up the box and trudged into the forest. The guards offered no more help. Praise the heavens for their fear of Staver's sudden death and their selfishness.

The autumn oaks beckoned us to safety with their outstretched limbs. The pines stood as tall sentinels. The sounds of the guards' voices and horses dampened then died away. The sunlight danced across drifting leaves. Staver's breath fell soft and damp across my neck. He was alive, and we were free.

~

THE KHAN'S hounds howled as they caught our scent again. I flinched. I needed to lose them before I headed to my birch grove, but no matter how many times I shifted human scents, Staver's feet dragged behind me and left his own scent trail.

A distant neigh sent another shudder through my body. They were getting closer. I shook with the weariness of a two-day chase. Staver grew heavier. Even when we'd hidden up in a towering pine, I'd slept little. I'd hidden the box with Dyeda's daughter's bones in a rotten log on the first day when the hounds' first baying echoed through the forest. It seemed a huge sacrifice then, but had I made it too late?

The neigh came more clearly, along with a hound's baying.

A horse? Could I shift to that form and carry Staver? If only he'd wake, it would be much easier. But he remained in a deep sleep.

I loosened the rope that bound him to my back, making a huge loop. Then I knelt on the ground with him draped across my back. The moonlight poured through branches as the amulet's power pulsed in readiness within me.

A horse. I am a horse. I tried to feel long powerful legs stretch out from a barrel-chested body. Instead, fear rose up my throat with my many memories of clinging to the shifting, sliding back of a tall beast.

The hound baying echoed.

I pushed the memories away and pulled over top a song Staver sang when we were children.

> When the first wind blew
> over the foaming sea,
> the horse leapt forth,
> formed from waves,

> with a storm's speed
> and all the grace
> of springtime.

I let my body stretch and grow into the song. When the rope grew snug about my chest, I stopped shifting. My legs quivered beneath me. I lunged forward, stretched into a gallop and flew over the land. Staver slid slightly with each movement but did not fall. The air rushed by me faster than it ever had when I was another animal.

I neighed in thrilled joy, and fed the rest of my exuberance into the run. The baying faded. The nighttime trees stood in higher contrast than they had to my human eyes. The horse was amazing! As long as I *was* it and not on it.

But the horse also had an exhaustion point. I finally stumbled to a sweaty, foaming heap in the middle of a stand of evergreens. The pine's sharp scent would hopefully mask ours.

Staver moaned on my back. "Vasilisa."

I nickered a quiet answer. I couldn't change to a human form until the moon rose again.

He reached around and untied the rope that bound me to him, then lay beside me. "Thank you," he whispered, and we both fell asleep.

I DIDN'T HEAR the hounds again. I traveled another day as a horse along many different trails, snatching up grass and gulping water at streams, adjusting my form and my scent at each new false trail. On the third day I headed for my first home.

Staver woke for moments, then slipped back away into silence.

The moon glimmered in a half fullness as we entered the

rabbit downs before my birch grove. I folded my legs beneath me and shifted back to my true human form. The amulet hung from my neck. Staver tumbled off my back and lay with face caked with dirt but healed of bruising. His eyes fluttered open, and he reached over to touch my face. "Is this still a dream?"

"No," I whispered. "We are safe."

He smiled. "And we are together. I'm with my strong, fair-folk Vasilisa."

My heart twisted at his words. "Staver. I'm not fair folk. My father was an ogre." He started to speak, but I rushed on. "Because of it I could rescue you. My papa's blood gives me talents. Not goodness or badness. From now on, I will always claim that side of me as well as the gifts I gained from my human mother. And I'll do my best to be good. It will be no harder or easier for me than any full human. You don't have to fear me."

He pressed his hands around mine and looked intently into my face. "I understand who your father was. I'll never fear you, no matter your parentage."

I bit my cheek to hold back tears. He recognized my heritage and didn't fear me.

The sound of a scrambling descent came from the cliff that led to my birch grove home. Mama stumbled through the dark to us. "You've returned. Thank the heavens." She threw her arms around me and held tight.

She'd waited for us. I had two who knew who I was—no, there were three.

I knew who I was.

I pulled from my mama's embrace and knelt next to Staver. "I love you. I always will. I want to go through this life and the eternities with you. Will you walk that path with me? Even knowing all that I am? I will no longer be ashamed of my heritage, nor hide it from you. And if we have children, I will teach them so they are not ashamed of it, either. I am Vasilisa the strong, the shape-shifter."

His eyes glimmered in the moonlight. "You are Vasilisa the good. I love all that you are, each and every powerful and beautiful part. You are my Vasilisa, and that's all that matters to me."

I leaned over to kiss him. I was forest born, ogre's child, beloved of Staver and heaven wild.

THE BARD

The bard fastened her cloak around her shoulders. "The fire is low. Dawn will wake soon. Go home and find the rest you can before work starts."

"Please tell us who you are," said a youth. "My grandfather said he remembers your tales from when he was a boy. But you must not be much older than I am."

She pulled the hood over her head and face. "I've been gathering stories from before the time your grandfather's grandmother ran barefoot through the meadow. I watched her, and even then I was old. At the end of winter, I'll tell my name and my own tale. But until then, I leave you with another promise. Return on the next rest-day and I'll take you to Nihon, The Land of the Rising Sun, where foxes dance and a mask can transform a person."

~

READ FLIGHT: A Vasilisa Novelette to see more of Vasilisa and Staver.

. . .

IF YOU LIKED *VASILISA*, please leave a favorable review, even if it is just a sentence. And please, share with a friend. I created the book, but the story lives through readers like you.

254

KEEP READING for *Food for Thought* and *End Notes*.

BOOKS BY M.L. FARB

THE KING TRIALS
The King's Trial (also an audiobook)
The King's Shadow

HEARTH AND BARD TALES
Vasilisa
Fourth Sister
Heartless Hette

HEARTH AND BARD SHORT STORIES
Flight: A Vasilisa Novelette
Birth: A Fourth Sister Novelette
Gift: A Heartless Hette Novelette

FREE SHORT STORY
East of Apollo's Palace

FAMILY AND HUMOR
When I Was a Pie: and Other Slices of Family Life

FOOD FOR THOUGHT

VASILISA INHERITED many things from her father. In addition to strength and ability to shape-shift, Vasilisa had an innate loyalty. How did this loyalty impact her choices and actions?

VASILISA FEARED ogres throughout the story. How would you feel if you found out you were something you feared? What would you do?

FOR EVERY NEGATIVE TRAIT, there is often a companion positive trait. For example, a stubborn person can also be determined in their goals. Think of a trait you see as a weakness in yourself. What is a companion positive to it?

STAVER GAVE up his inheritance and served in the army to marry Vasilisa within the bounds of the law. How did his honor to both the tsar and Vasilisa shape his story?

· · ·

Vasilisa's father said, "Being an ogre is not a mark of evil. No more than being a human is a mark of goodness. Both races have good and evil." As a society, we often label others and limit our view on who they are or who they can become. What are some ways in which we can look past the labels and see others as individuals?

Vasilisa's father also said, "Beauty and vileness battle like two creatures in each of us, and the one we feed is the one that grows stronger." What are some ways in which you can feed the good inside of you?

Listening to stories "of heroes and honor, of villains and hate, of sacrifice and joy even in loss" expanded Vasilisa's father's perspective, and he changed his whole life. What stories have changed your life, and how have they done it?

END NOTES

STORY **REFERENCES**

The idea for this book came from a children's picture book *Serpent Slayer: And Other Stories of Strong Women* by Katrin Tchana (with gorgeous artwork by Trina Schart Hyman). A woman dresses as a man to rescue her husband, and to do so she passes three tests of strength, skill, and strategy. The picture book took on tall-tale quality as the woman injured her opponents in wrestling and shattered a tree by shooting it with an arrow. How did she become so strong? I wrote *Vasilisa* to answer that question.

Before lightning struck Vasilisa, Staver was telling her a story of *The Fool of the World and the Flying Ship*, a Russian fairy tale. You can find it in Arthur Ransome's *Old Peter's Russian Tales.* (I highly recommend the whole book of tales)

Staver told a story about a girl and her seven swan brothers. This came from *The Six Swans,* a German fairy tale collected by the Brothers Grimm.

When Vasilisa's papa finished teaching her, he was given a choice—to follow the path to the afterlife of his people, or go through trials to gain a human soul and a place in the afterlife where his wife and child would go. This concept references ideas from the original *Little Mermaid* by Hans Christian Andersen.

Name Meanings

Vasilisa Volkova. Vasilisa is Greek in origin and is a title, like queen or empress. Lisa means fox in Russian. Volkova is Russian for 'daughter of a wolf'. She is queen fox, daughter of a wolf.

Staver Orlov. I couldn't find the Russian meaning of Staver, but that was his name from the original Russian tale, and I kept it. I gave him the surname of Orlov, which means eagle.

Dyeda and Baba are Russian forms of Grandpa and Grandma.

Matushka is the Russian formal form of mother.

Balalaika is a triangular stringed instrument. It can be played like the guitar or the larger stringed instruments, like the bass.

Hopak is a form of acrobatic Russian dancing. The name *hopak* is derived from the verb hopaty (Ukrainian: гопати) which means "to jump" (https://en.wikipedia.org/wiki/Hopak)

Nedelja is the Slavic word for Sunday. It means "the day without work".

Khan is capitalized because it is a family name like Smith or Johnson. Tsar is only capitalized when in direct address.

Thundersnow: Vasilisa was struck by lightning in the middle of a snowstorm. Lightning combined with a snowstorm is rare, but it happens. https://www.thoughtco.com/how-thundersnow-works-4159345

THE THREE TESTS:

Hopak: The Hopak is an acrobatic dance, usually danced by men. It requires immense athletic strength, agility, and balance. Some of the original ones were impromptu: "These celebratory hopaky were performed only by male participants, as they took place in an all-male environment. The performers were young, boisterous mercenaries, and not professional dancers; as such, the dance steps performed were predominantly improvisational, reflecting the performers' sense of manliness, heroism, speed and strength. The steps exhibited included many acrobatic jumps (Ukrainian: стрибки, translit. strybky). Often fights from the battlefield would be re-enacted in pantomime, with real swords, lances or other weaponry, as the performer lashed out at invisible enemies. These dances were not tied down to specific rhythms, and the dancers could change tempo at any point." - https://en.wikipedia.org/wiki/Hopak

Archery: A longbow is five to six feet in length. A longbow's draw weight can be between 90 lbs for a teen, or up to almost 200 lbs for a full warrior. That would be like lifting a 200-lb weight with your arm, shoulder, and back, then holding it steady so the shot goes where you want it. A woman could shoot a teen's bow, but at least in Vasilisa's day, no women drew the heavy warrior longbow.

Some sources say that the bowman pushed against the bow as much as pulled back against the string. "The Englishman did not keep his left hand steady, and draw his bow with his right; but keeping his right at rest upon the nerve, he pressed the whole weight of his body into the horns of his bow. Hence probably arose the phrase "bending the bow," and the French of "drawing" one.— W. Gilpin." - https://en.wikipedia.org/wiki/English_longbow#Draw_weights

Chess: "Chess was probably introduced in Russia in the 9th century AD through the Caspian-Volga trade route. At the time, there was a Volga trade route to Baghdad." - https://www.chess.com/article/view/russian-chess-history

"In the Middle Ages and during the Renaissance, chess was a part of noble culture; it was used to teach war strategy and was dubbed the 'King's Game'." - https://en.wikipedia.org/wiki/Chess

ANIMAL SENSES

If someone shifted into animal form, they'd also shift to that animal's senses. I found birds especially interesting. Here are some fun facts for your enjoyment:

The following about eagles was essential in the archery contest scene. Vasilisa could see the sweat mark because of the ability to see ultraviolet light.

"Eagles have the ability to see colors more vividly than humans can. They can even see ultraviolet light and pick out more shades of one color. Their ability to even see the UV light allows them to see the bodily traces left by their prey. Mice's and other small prey's urine is visible to the eagles in the ultraviolet range, making them easy targets even a few hundred feet above the ground.

"Visual acuity is the eye's ability to separate details of an object without any blur. The normal or a 'good' vision for a human is 20/20. Eagles, however, have retinas with cones and have a much deeper fovea—a cone-rich structure in the back of the eye. These give them a visual acuity of an impressive 20/5, or 20/4 which allows them to hunt even the tiny prey from hundreds of feet up in the air."

https://www.insightvisioncenter.com/human-vision-vs-eagle-vision/

"Birds that are the objects of predators often have a wide field of view and their eyes are placed on the sides of their heads rather than the front. Ducks actually can see all the way around 360 degrees. While the forward-looking overlap of both of their eyes is small, they actually overlap a little in the rear as well. Like a lot of birds, ducks cock their heads sideways to look at you closely. The reason is that their best visual acuity is a small yellow spot called the fovea that contains the most sensitive cells of an eye. Most birds turn their heads because their eyes are not mobile in the eye socket." https://web.calpoly.edu/~rfield/BirdsEye.htm

Birds can see all the colors we see, plus ultraviolet. This page shows photos of what birds probably see with that combination (plus some of what other animals see): http://morgana249.

blogspot.com/2014/07/10-examples-of-how-animals-see-
images.html

ACKNOWLEDGEMENTS

I'd like to say thank you, or as I learned in Russia—spasiba, to so many who made this story possible.

Thank you to Paulina and your family for hosting me for half a year in St. Petersburg, Russia. I'll never forget entering adulthood surrounded by a city and culture older than my home nation. And I'll always remember the kindness and goodness of the people.

Thank you Jesse, for inspiring me with a day-to-day true love story. Words can't capture what you've given me, or how I feel for you.

Thank you to my children. You are my first stories, and my best. Thank you, especially to Alan, for claiming Staver as your hero.

Thank you to my amazing critique partner, Tori Gollihugh. Yet again you've cheered me on with each rough first-draft chapter and provided valuable feedback.

Thank you to my alpha and beta readers Beth Norris Anderson, Shelly Ruble, and Morgan Muir for your insightful critique and suggestions. You were there for the growing pains of taking a sweet fairy tale through the awkward, ugly-duckling phase and into a beautiful novel with a life of its own.

Thank you to my editor, Annie Douglass Lima. I truly appreciate your fine tune edits and polishing.

Thank you Lara Carter for creating the beautiful cover. It is magical.

And most of all, thank you to my Heavenly Father. Thank you for your many tender mercies, joys and blessings.

ABOUT THE AUTHOR

Ever since I climbed up to the rafters of our barn at age four, I've lived high adventure: scuba diving, mud football with my brothers, rappelling, and even riding a retired racehorse at full gallop—bareback. I love the thrill and joy.

Stories give me a similar thrill and joy. I love living through the eyes and heart of a hero who faces his internal demons and the heroine who fights her way free instead of waiting to be saved.

I create adventures, fantasy, fairy tale retellings, and poetry. I live a joyful adventure with my husband and six children. I am a Christian and I love my Savior.

You can contact me at:
mlfarb.author@gmail.com
mlfarbauthor.com
twitter.com/farbml
facebook.com/mlfarbauthor

www.ingramcontent.com/pod-product-compliance
Lightning Source LLC
Chambersburg PA
CBHW050833190726
48286CB00007B/2073